Undeniable Bachelor

Bachelor Tower Series

Book Three

RUTH CARDELLO

Author Contact

website: RuthCardello.com

email: RuthCardello@gmail.com

Facebook: Author Ruth Cardello

Twitter: RuthieCardello

Goodreads

goodreads.com/author/show/4820876.Ruth_Cardello

Bookbub

bookbub.com/authors/ruth-cardello

Sign up for my newsletter to hear about upcoming releases and sales:

forms.aweber.com/form/58/1378607658.htm

Copyright

Dedication

To the greatest husband any woman could ask for!!!!!
And all the bachelors who will not be denied.
(My husband may have written this dedication. I love him
enough to let it ride.)

CHAPTER ONE

Savannah

Boston.
It's even bigger than I imagined.

THE JOKE, *THAT'S what she said*, flashes through my mind and I fight a smirk. It's childish. I'm sure no one in the business section of this city would laugh at something so juvenile. I shrug. They don't know what they're missing. I'm considered one of the most hilarious people in my hometown of Coppertop, Maine. There isn't much competition with a population of twelve hundred and sixty-seven. Actually, Clara Bell had her baby. Twelve hundred and sixty-eight.

I shouldn't brag, but Annie's Seaside Shack voted me Most Likely to Cause Someone to Laugh So Hard They'll Choke to Death on a Lobster Roll—two years in a row. The category was created just for me after I whispered a crude joke to the captain of my high school football team and nearly sent him to the hospital. Thankfully, I'm also good with the Heimlich maneuver. So, not only hilarious, but heroic as well. That's what the plaque on the wall of Annie's restaurant says. Yeah, in my hometown, I'm kind of a big deal.

Everyone knows my name, but very few know me. The real me.

It's for their own good. I started hiding the truth because it was too much for anyone to handle, even me. I've pretended to be something for so long that, since my situation has changed, if I could go back to simply being me, I wouldn't know how.

I put my life on hold because I had to.

I laughed because there are only so many nights a person can cry before they just give up. Before your eyes stay red and blotchy and people start to notice.

I'm a fighter, like my father was. I'm proud to be like him.

Some might not think that's a good thing, but it has gotten me this far. Look at me now. I didn't let fear stop me from buying a one-way bus ticket to Boston. And here I am—me, in one of the most sophisticated cities in the world. No one's kicked me out yet.

I may not look like I belong, but I will. I'll fight until I do.

People hustle down the concrete sidewalks of the city and dodge traffic as they move with intention. I can only imagine where they are going and what exciting lives they're leading. The sun is beginning to dip behind the tall buildings. Two men dressed in similarly styled suits meet and begin to walk together. Their matching conservative hairstyles make them difficult to tell apart from the back, but there is a bounce to their steps. They know who they are.

What they want.

Are they work associates?

Best friends?

Lovers?

Anything is possible in the city. Here people don't live by small-town rules. They break free from the oppression of what everyone thinks they know about them. Boston is where my transformation needs to take place because no one here knows my history.

I can be anyone. The endless possibilities make me tingle.

One bus ticket and the money my grandmother left me will change everything. And everything needs to be changed about me.

More people pass as if I'm invisible, and I don't mind. I love them simply because they exist as proof that life can be so much more than I've known.

A cluster of well-dressed women huddle as if deciding where they'll go next. Blonde, brunette, tall, short, all different but they all have a similar style. Each looks as if they might have just left a job at some high-powered office. Are they about to rush home then off to some exclusive nightclub?

They're confident.

Sexy.

I bet they even smell good.

Men probably fall at their feet—in a city, they could choose a new man each week. I've seen the television shows. Laughing. Comparing notes. Horror stories and happy endings. Girl talk. I wish I could move closer to catch a part of their conversation. One throws her head back and laughs. Her blonde curls fall over her shoulder like a commercial for shampoo. The only way my hair falls is if the elastic band snaps while I'm at work.

The group breaks off. Two pass me. One pauses, gives me a long look. I take the moment to appreciate the perfection of her makeup. She has blue eyes like mine. Will my eyes look the same when done up that way? Smokey eye shadow with a perfect sweep of eyeliner. Will highlights give my dark blonde hair the same glow?

She frowns, digs into her oversized designer purse, and holds out a five-dollar bill to me.

I automatically accept it even though I don't know why she's offering it. But the newness of this experience has me obedient. Like a puppy told to sit. Is this my treat?

She turns to her friend, "I know I shouldn't, but I'm softhearted." She flashes a smile at me. "Buy yourself a coffee, hon. Or a brush."

My mouth drops open, full-on cartoon style, and stays there as they walk away.

I look at my oversized wool coat, stained jeans, and once-white tennis shoes. *She thinks I'm homeless.* The familiar scent of fish and boat exhaust hits me like I'm smelling it for the first time. I want to chase after the woman and explain that I smell like a hard day's work at a fishery. I could have bought a new coat, but I wanted one from here. A trendy peacoat from a boutique.

I don't need your money.

I even have an apartment rented with a view of the Charles River. I haven't seen it yet, but I know it's an area where the right people gather.

Another woman approaches. Tall, with short dark hair. Her ebony skin is smooth. I bet her makeup is perfect, but it's hidden behind sunglasses that bling with diamonds on the side. I pocket my hands and the money I'm embarrassed I accepted. She pops wireless earbuds in, and I catch a flash of my reflection in her glasses as she glances my way.

My hand closes on my own pair of sunglasses in my pocket. I'd hide behind them, but they're held together with a strip of black electrical tape. I wasn't about to buy new ones in Coppertop. I'll have hundreds to pick from in Boston.

Everything about me will soon be new.

I'm overhauling every aspect of my life.

So, don't pity me, lady. Don't hand me your spare change. This won't be me for long. Very soon, Savannah Barre, is going to walk down this street with her head held high. And I'll be wearing those red-soled shoes or whatever style is in this fall.

I'll have stories to tell and they won't be lies. We might even become friends, and you'll smile as you ask me about my latest exciting date. I'll look away and say I don't kiss and tell, but you'll push me for details.

I'll keep it simple because when life is good you don't have to elaborate. And we'll laugh the way women do when they know they can conquer the world.

I move cautiously over a wobbly metal grate in the sidewalk. My dirty, threadbare tennis shoes won't get stuck in it, but I'll have to be careful once I start wearing high heels. The sun fully sets behind the skyscrapers and I pull my woolen coat tighter around me.

As far as first days go, today was full of unwelcome surprises. A less determined person might have taken them as a sign that I should turn around and go home.

Not me. I have too much of my father in me. Maybe a dangerous amount, but I can't change that. I wouldn't even if I could. He always said, "When a door closes you bust open a window and shimmy your ass right through." A lot of doors closed on me today. Slammed right in my face. It's time to shimmy.

I'd rather die a fighter than live as a coward. That's what he did.

My hand closes around the five-dollar bill in my pocket. If I'd had it a few minutes ago I wouldn't have had to walk the rest of the way to Jana Monroe's office. I could have maybe taken a cab. I'm already here, though. So close to the woman who will change my life.

Jana Monroe's agency is on the fifteenth floor of the highest building I've ever been in. I'm late. By over two hours. But the city doesn't sleep. Unlike where I'm from. In Coppertop the shops all close at sundown and nothing but the bars stay open too long after the early-bird special. I can practically picture Jana behind her large desk, burning the midnight oil. I'll tell her the predicament I've gotten myself into, and she'll know just how to work it out. She's got the answers. I'm banking on it.

I slip through the glass doors of the building as another group of women exit, more interested in their plans than in me. The lobby is deserted. It's eerily quiet but I take that as a gift—one less person who has to see the old me.

I'm not alone for long though. The door opens behind me while I'm still taking in the details of the lobby. I break into motion toward the elevator, trying unsuccessfully to look like I belong. I can't afford to be stopped here, not when I'm so close. Without looking over my shoulder I press the elevator call several times. I can't help it. I'm excited.

This is it.

I'm finally here.

Is this how a snake feels when it's about to shed its old skin?

I can't wait another moment to shrug off the old me and start over.

A man comes to stand beside me. I can sense his height, but I don't look at him. He doesn't matter. I'm about to hit the reset button on my life. Who cares about the man next to me?

He shifts away from me. I don't blame him. Inside the building he can probably smell my coat as well. What he doesn't get is that I'm not ashamed of who I am or what I'm wearing. Working at the fishery paid my grandmother's mortgage. Working at the bar paid her medical bills. Just because I want to leave it behind doesn't mean I wouldn't do it all the same if I had to.

The elevator chugs slowly toward us and the doors creak open. It's a tiny thing, barely room for a few people, and I take a moment to appreciate the antique brass. It reminds me of a clock my father gave me. But I sold it along with everything else to ensure my grandmother had the best care until the very end. Things are just things. Life isn't supposed to be easy. Of course I wish I still had it, but she had what she needed, and I have the comfort of knowing I did all I could.

The elevator has an authenticity I'm drawn to. Classic. Cultured. It gives me hope that Jana will understand that I'm not looking to shine like a tacky new penny. I want the kind of sophistication that blends in—that looks like it belongs. Seamless.

Like a child tempted by the cookie jar, I can't help it, I have to see if the man beside me looks as good as his shoes imply he does. They're real leather. Polished. Huge, but not overly trendy. They belong to a man of importance, someone who buys the best without looking at the price tag.

My gaze slowly roams up his navy pants leg. The material is crisp. Tailored. Just above his knees, things begin to get interesting. Muscled thighs. And a package big enough to bring a sigh to my lips. I should stop there. There's no way his face could live up to the promise he makes waist down.

It's a hop, skip, and jump over his black leather belt to the flat perfection of his abs beneath his buttoned shirt. A little paunch wouldn't have killed the fantasy, but the more I see of his body, the less I care what's above his neck. There's a reason romance novels often leave the head off. The image I have in my mind will absolutely beat whatever the reality of his face is, and that's okay.

Who am I to judge at this point? I know exactly how I look.

All I'm doing is indulging in a harmless motivational fantasy. He's my—vision board.

The thought makes me smile, and my eyes slide higher.

If my nails weren't chewed to the quick and I didn't think he'd call security, I'd ask if I could touch his pecs. I mean, holy baloney and mustard sandwich—I bet he makes them dance to impress his conquests. I wouldn't need him to even speak. Nope, I'd just curl up against that heavenly chest and ask him to flex his biceps for me . . . one at a time . . .

We wouldn't have to have sex. I'm pretty sure I could orgasm just from dry humping a body like that. Or I'd at least like to try and find out.

His red tie is a pop of color I'm positive means he has a wild side.

No need to go higher, but I do. I'm tempting fate, inching closer to disappointment, but I can't help myself.

Damn. I'm shocked to find a square chin. So strong. So right. I want to run my hand over the light scruff on it. In my fantasy, he's normally notoriously clean cut, but working late tonight on something so important he doesn't have time to shave.

Like his tie, it gives him an edginess that makes me wish I had a camera with me. Jana, I want that. Do you have one like him for me?

His olive complexion is the perfect match for his thick head of hair and near black eyes.

Whatever he washes his face with must cost more than

my car because his skin is flawless. Do people in the city not get zits?

Not that my skin is bad. I learned to wash my hands with dish soap after touching fish. Also works with stopping poison ivy from spreading. I bet he doesn't know that handy tip.

My breath catches in my throat. Mr. Boston is talking to me and his voice is deep and cultured. I could listen to it all day long. Hot whispers in my ear would be perfect.

I should probably be embarrassed to be staring, but I'm not. When someone is as beautiful as this man is—it's perfectly normal to take a moment to appreciate them. Museums put chairs in front of certain pieces of art for the same reason I'm standing here drooling up at him.

He says something else, in a less than pleased tone.

"What?" I breathe out the word as I blink hard at him.

"Are you lost?"

"No."

His brows furrow and his concern makes my cheeks hot. "You didn't hit a button. What floor are you going to?"

I sputter out a laugh. "Oh, I didn't?" Turning to the lit panel I press fifteen, but it doesn't light up. I press it again—nothing.

"We've passed it." He gestures with his chin up to the old-style indicator above the door that shows we're just crossing over the sixteenth floor.

I try to think of something clever to say. Something that doesn't make me sound like a small-town girl wearing a coat that smells like smoke and fish. "I guess sometimes you have to go up before you go down."

I don't know why my eyes fall to his crotch. Probably because my natural state is awkward as hell. Part of the reason I'm here is I've never put anything exciting in my mouth.

I raise my eyes to his again and flash him a smile that doesn't win him over. I don't look away, although I bet he expects me to. I'm tempted to reassure him that I'm okay with whatever he's thinking because it's nothing I'm not already aware of.

If you see me after I'm done with this journey, you won't even recognize me. My chin rises. So take a good look. Judge all you want. My transformation has nothing to do with you.

The second smile I flash is an expression of the giddy excitement bubbling within me simply because I'm here. Fucking here.

He frowns down at me, looking confused.

In my fantasy, it's because he's fighting a primal attraction to me. Imagine if, after all the money women spend on perfume, the secret to landing such a man is fish oil, smoke, and twenty-four hours without a shower. I wiggle my unplucked eyebrows up and down, sure they are also a selling point.

I probably shouldn't enjoy this as much as I am, I wouldn't be able to if I thought this would always be me. Hell, if he keeps looking at me that way, I might have to flash him a little hairy leg. I normally shave, but I'm expecting I'll have a wax appointment, and I read it's good to let it grow out a little. If I'm brave enough I might go hairless in the nether regions as well. Is it painful? Itchy as it grows in?

Jana told me I can ask her anything. No question is too private or too trivial. She's like having a sister, but one I have to pay to speak to. Most of my friends back home are men. I imagine the shocked looks they would have given me if I had ever broached the subject of waxing with them. I doubt they are aware I even have a vagina let alone that I want to cover it with hot wax and paper and have some lovely woman yank the hair off me.

My smile deepens. That topic might have gotten me a third plaque at Annie's Seaside Shack.

Mr. Boston frowns again then looks away.

I want to tell him to lighten up. How bad could his life be? He's gorgeous and looks like he's gainfully employed. My present state lends me a certain freedom. Nothing I could do would impress the man, so I actually could say what I'm thinking. It's an intriguing thought that flies out of my head when the elevator comes to a grinding, rattling stop.

The lights flicker, and then go out completely.

"That's not good." My shaky voice is small and unfamiliar to me. Did I mention I don't like small dark places? I haven't spent enough time in elevators to have feelings one way or another about them, but I suddenly understand everyone who has ever said they hate them. Fear tightens my chest, making it difficult to breathe.

I refuse to die this way.

Die.

I reach out and clutch a suited forearm in the darkness, wishing fate had delivered a different companion for this experience. Something tells me Mr. Boston doesn't know how to fix an elevator. He also doesn't seem the kind to hand over a paper bag for me to breathe deeply into.

"It's an old building. I'm sure it's nothing." That's his best shot at comforting me.

"Nothing." I release his arm because he's not panicking so I tell myself I shouldn't be.

He illuminates the front wall of the elevator with the light from his phone. "And there is always an emergency call button."

I swallow hard, clasping my now sweaty hands together. "Of course."

He hits the button once, then again, and swears.

I take a deep breath. He has a phone. We're good.

I bet this stuff happens all the time in the city. More people probably die crossing the streets than plummeting down elevator shafts. People in the city embrace danger. I've seen them barely look up from their phones while walking. I'll be that way soon, I'm sure. Something like this won't even faze me.

My stomach twists painfully. Plummeting is my least favorite word.

Mr. Boston swears again. "I've got no service in here. How about you?"

I pat my pocket like it might have miraculously reappeared. "No phone."

"Of course," he replied, his sarcasm grating on me.

"I have a phone, just not with me."

"It doesn't matter." He holds his up higher as though it

might suddenly get service.

What he means is *I* don't matter, and unlike a few minutes earlier, this time I'm offended. Not because he's not attracted to me, but because I do matter. My life might not look like much from the outside, but I sure as hell don't want it to end like this. "It does matter, actually. Someone snatched my purse when I got off the bus."

"I'm sorry to hear that," he says in an indifferent tone.

What did I expect? I built Mr. Boston up in my imagination, but the truth is more likely he's afraid being stuck in an elevator with me will make him late for a manicure. He has no idea what it means to sacrifice. To put your life on hold for something greater than your own wants and desires.

In the dim light of his phone, he leans against the wall and sighs.

I glare at him in the darkness.

The silence drags on until it's uncomfortable. Shouldn't he be trying to make me feel more at ease? Even Jody, my old shift manager at the fishery, would have tried to make me laugh to keep my mind off our impending doom—and no one has ever accused him of being a nice person.

I've never been afraid to do for myself, so I say, "My name is Savannah Barre."

He takes so long to answer that for a moment I think he won't. "Brice."

I press on. "Do you work here?"

"Not exactly."

Another long awkward silence.

I clear my throat. Work with me, buddy. You could have

been stuck with a crier. "I didn't expect the building to be so empty."

"Holiday weekend. Security works through it, though. They might be doing their rounds. I don't imagine we'll be stuck in here for long."

Holiday? I vaguely remember Jana saying that after meeting quickly I'd have a few days to settle in before we did anything official. If I hadn't lost my purse, I would have already met her and would probably be in my apartment, soaking in a bubble bath, sipping from a glass of champagne, planning my first shopping spree. All of her contact information, though, was on my phone . . . in my purse . . . along with my credit cards and cash. I shake my head. Nothing good comes from beating oneself up over things that can't be changed. Jana didn't sound like someone who sprinted out of her office early. She'd be there. All I need is a computer and a phone. Nothing that had happened was irreparable. I just have to live long enough to fix it. To fill the silence, I remark, "You're here late."

"I do a lot of international business."

I won't be changing his name to Mr. Personality anytime soon. Still, talking is better than thinking about how long it might take security to notice that the elevator is stuck. Or what we'd have to resort to as far as relieving ourselves if that didn't happen for a long time. Oh, shit, now I have to pee. "I've never been to Boston before. I'm from Maine."

"Welcome to Boston," he says in a dry tone.

That's it. I've had enough. "You don't have to be a dick."

"Excuse me?"

"I didn't break the elevator. And in case you're wondering, I don't want to be here any more than you do, but I also don't want to freak out and piss myself, and talking calms me down. So, can you pretend you have a personality? If that's not too much trouble."

Even in the dim lighting his gaze is intense. "Please don't piss yourself." He says it as if he's serious, but there's a light in his eyes that suggests he might not be.

I relax a little. Sometimes all people need is a little nudge to be nice.

"Look at you—almost making a joke."

He gives me a look that might mean he didn't appreciate mine, but I'm in survival mode so I'll worry about his feelings later. Or I won't.

"What are you doing in the building?" he asks as if it's his building and I've snuck in. It's far more of an accusation than a question.

I'm tempted to tell him I came in to get out of the cold. Like the woman on the street who gave me cash, he's probably thinking I have nothing. I feel self-righteous for every person who has actually been in that situation. Who is he to look down his perfectly sculpted nose at anyone? "I have an appointment." I do my best to mimic his haughty tone.

He rubs a hand over his forehead. "An appointment? With whom?"

Oh, he's one of those *whom* people. I roll my eyes. There's no way someone like him would understand what I'm doing in Boston. My reasons wouldn't make any sense to him "All that matters is that I'm late for it, and I wasn't able to call to tell her I would be. I chased the guy who took my purse then didn't know where I was. Who designed the street layout in Boston? A toddler with a crayon? And why does everyone give directions by mentioning landmarks that used to be here? Just tell me left or right. Is that too much to ask? And the police station was a nightmare. It took forever to make the police report. I should have canceled my credits cards while I was there but I had a feeling if I stayed there much longer they might not let me leave."

His nod of agreement is a little insulting. I was joking—kind of. A person can't actually get arrested for being robbed and looking like I do—can they?

"Your purse was stolen?" he asks as if I hadn't already said it. He's clearly not hanging on my every word.

"Yes, it was stolen."

"You shouldn't have chased the thief. He might have hurt you."

"One of us would have been in pain, anyway. He's lucky I didn't catch him." I mock a karate chop and make a hi-ya noise.

Mr. Boston pinches the bridge of his nose. Oh, hang on, he almost smiles. I know that look. I didn't get my funniest person plaque for nothing. He's finally getting my jokes.

"Thankfully, I had a few dollars on me. I took a cab part of the way, and then walked the rest. I'm here, though, so the worst of it is over. As long as the person I'm meeting is still in her office, I'm golden."

"Who is this person you're meeting?"

"You almost sound like you care."

"The alternative is not conversing, and you've already warned me about the possible consequence to that. We don't need a puddle."

I smile. He's actually pretty funny. I forgive him for not being an electrician or something useful. "Her name is Jana Monroe. Since she knew I was coming, I'm ninety-nine percent . . . okay, seventy-five percent sure she wouldn't leave until she heard from me. She knows I've never been to Boston before."

"Why does it sound like you don't really know this woman?" The way his eyebrow is arching tells me he's, at a minimum, intrigued.

"I do know her. We swapped several emails and we talked on the phone just last week. I'm positive she'll be here." I nod, trying to convince myself. "No one wants to lose a client, right?"

"A client?"

Don't even go there, buddy. You don't know me. I'm a capable woman who just happens to be without some of her resources right now.

The elevator rattles and the lights flicker. I swallow a scream. Breathe.

"We're okay. They're probably working on it." The light on his phone goes out. "Fuck. My battery's dead."

It's dark.

I'm quietly hyperventilating.

I reach out, grab his arm again, and joke, "Looks like you're no better prepared than I am."

"Evidently," he said dryly, but he puts his hand over

mine. It's warm and strong, and I don't care if he's only being kind to me because he doesn't want me to soil myself; I'm grateful he's here.

"Thank you," I say sincerely. "I would let go of you, but my hand literally won't let me."

"It's fine. I'm actually impressed. I figured you'd be screaming by now."

"Oh, I am—on the inside."

The elevator rumbles, lifts, then falls a few feet. My fingers dig deeper into his arm. Holy shit. This is definitely how I'm going to die.

The elevator drops again. We both stumble a little then brace ourselves. I'm done with this. I don't care what the man beside me thinks, I take the universe head-on and demand, "Stop it right now. I refuse to die a virgin. Do you hear me? Refuse."

Of course the lights choose that moment to come back on. I'm clinging to the arm of Adonis and his eyebrows are up near his hairline, shocked by my proclamation. I release his arm.

He flattens his tie and looks away as if I hadn't said anything.

"Uh"—I catch my breath—"I meant I don't want to die this version of myself." My cheeks blaze with embarrassment. That statement isn't actually a lie either, but he's onto me. "It needed to be said. This day has been a nightmare. First the bus broke down. Then my bag was stolen. Now an elevator is trying to kill me. Do you think I don't see what the universe is doing? It's testing me. That's why you're here.

You're the biggest test of all. You think I don't know what you think of me? But what you and the universe don't get is that I don't cower. I know it's not going to be easy and people will judge me every step of the way, but I'm here, and I'm not the type to turn and run when things get tough. Bring it on. I'm not going anywhere."

The elevator roars back to life and starts climbing toward the top floor.

"That doesn't mean I'm not getting off this thing when it stops. I'm determined, but I'm not stupid." I step toward the door, ready to leap when it opens.

"Looks like it's going to my floor. Thirty."

"Then I'll take the stairs down from there," I mumble. Of course we're going to his floor. Things probably always turn out perfectly for this guy.

"You're going to walk down fifteen flights?"

"I sure as hell am not riding back down in this." The doors open and I step out.

"Because you refuse to die . . . *this version of yourself.*"

What does it matter what he knows or thinks? This is where we part ways. "Exactly. Now excuse me, I have a meeting to make."

"With a woman who may no longer be there?"

I square my shoulders and glare up at him. "Thank you for all of your help and positive energy." This time I'm the one who is sarcastic. "You should consider a career in social work. Or as a motivational speaker. You're a great comfort."

He doesn't look happy, but he didn't look happy before the elevator fiasco, so I'm leaving him as I found him. "Do you know anyone else in the city?"

"You."

He makes a grumbling sound deep in his chest, and I lose patience. I don't need him. Without another word I charge toward the stairwell.

He doesn't call after me, but I don't expect him to. Some books are exactly what their covers project.

As I swing the stair door open, I see something shimmering on the top step. It's a small diamond earring. Simple. Beautiful. I pick it up and place it on the sill of the window. Someone will be missing it.

I take a few steps down, then turn and see the earring shining on the sill. Whoever lost that earring is probably also having a horrible day. Bad things happen to good people. The trick is to not let it beat you.

I could give up now and ask Jana to help me get back home, but I won't. Universe, you like signs? Well, let that be one for you. I just gave some person a better chance of finding what they lost. I believe in second chances and happy endings. I smile at the term *happy ending*. Hopefully my humor evolves too.

CHAPTER TWO

Brice

I HAVEN'T GOTTEN a fucking thing done since I stepped into my office. I have calls to make. Emails to answer. My computer is on. My email is open. Every time I try to read one of my messages my mind returns to the woman whose scent lingers on the arm of my jacket—and not in a pleasant way.

I breathe in a hint of—rotten fish? It's a guess. It's not a smell I'm familiar with. I'll be tipping the dry cleaner extra for this suit.

Stopped elevators and women are normally a good mix. There's nothing like hitting the stop button, feeling a woman's hands tearing at my clothes, hearing her beg for more as she straddles me, then driving into her until the elevator sways with us. The danger of being caught. The scandal for a man in my position only heightens the passion.

It's not something I've done in Boston because unlike in my country, every corner of the United States is under some kind of surveillance. The land of the free? I'd say it's more the land of the recorded.

But I'm not here to judge; I'm here to work.

Although I never thought I would, I'm finally grateful for my father's decision to keep our family out of the global press. My mother's obsession with American culture is also proving to be an asset. My lack of accent is due to her belief that the only good tutor is one who attended Harvard. The less anyone knows about who I am, the longer I'll have the advantage.

I rub my temples and attempt to read another email, but an image of the woman from the elevator distracts me. *Savannah from Maine.* I know nothing about the state beyond it being remote, and apparently having an unappealing smell. And maybe women who are prone to insanity.

If her clothing was anything to go by, she didn't have two pennies to rub together. I groan as I picture her chasing a thief down. Her life wasn't worth . . . what could she possibly even have had in her purse?

I should have given her a few bills to get her by. That would have been the right thing to do. But she ran off. Too proud to heed my warnings.

Did she even know anyone in the building or was that just a story to come inside to warm up? The mystery was killing my concentration.

And if she really is so bad off, why did she look so damn happy?

"I refuse to die a virgin . . ." Her declaration echoes in my head, unsettling and exciting at the same time. As a rule, I don't fuck virgins, and although some men might see her state of desperation as an opportunity, I'm not that man.

So why can't I stop thinking about her?

Guilt?

I wish it were that simple.

First, that fucking smile haunts me. It was genuine and made me curious about what had her so happy.

There were a few times I was lost in those blue eyes of hers. So bold. So determined. No woman has ever looked at me the way she did—as if I weren't quite living up to her expectation of me. Probably because most women in my country know my background. Savannah saw me as just a man in an elevator who wasn't really impressing her.

God, I sound full of myself, but I can't deny that, along with responsibility, being a royal comes with certain perks. I'm used to women being grateful because I show up.

"You don't have to be a dick." I smile as I remember her reprimand. Brave. What brought such a spunky woman to her current state?

No one has ever spoken to me the way she did.

And I have to admit I liked it.

To her, I was simply another man.

I shake my head. I don't want the distraction of her, but I'm doing a terrible job of managing that.

Who is Jana Monroe and what kind of promises did she use to lure Savannah to the city? How does she expect Savannah to pay for those services? I don't like any of the possibilities that come to mind.

Not a single damn one of them.

At the risk of sounding old-fashioned, I am tempted to look up this Jana Monroe's number and warn her that Savannah is under my protection.

But I don't because she's not.

American women don't even like to have doors opened for them; going all caveman might cause this Monroe woman to look into who I am. Brice Hastings has been able to live at the Bachelor Tower and hammer out solid deals with tech industry moguls who underestimate his finances, but there is no such bargaining power for Prince Bricelion Octavias Hastina of Calvadria.

My phone rings and I attempt to shake off the memory of the woman who had grabbed my attention just as surely as she'd grabbed my arm.

She is not my problem.

She didn't ask for my help.

Jana Monroe is probably a social worker who is setting up employment and lodging for her.

"Hello?" I sound as annoyed as I am.

"It's time to come home, Brice."

"Not yet, Mathias." I sigh, wishing I could tell him why I'm in Boston.

My brother, first in line for the crown, is not used to being told no—but it's not the first time I've defied him and it won't be the last. He thinks the state of our country is his responsibility alone and that his happiness is a necessary sacrifice. I'm about to show him I'm more than an insurance plan. A backup prince. Not because I want the glory, but because Mathias has always looked out for me—it's time for him to see I have his back as well.

"Should I be concerned?" His voice is low and troubled.

"Not at all. I told you I wanted to make some changes

now that I'm twenty-five. You'd be impressed, I'm in a suit every day. Being at the Bachelor Tower inspires me. People think New York is the only place big business happens, but they're wrong. You should see the people who live in the Tower. They'd make the top of any *Forbes* list."

"Come home, Brice. Your duty is here. All you're accomplishing there is putting undue worry on Mother and Father. They think you've joined a cult or something."

"Is that what you think?"

"I'm concerned, but only because you're being secretive and went without the Royal Guards. Are you hiding with a married lover? If you're in some kind of trouble, you need only tell me."

"And you'll fix it for me. Yes, I know. I'm not in any trouble, but I'm also not ready to tell you what I'm doing. Have a little faith in me, Brother."

Mathias's silence says more than any response would have. I know I've put him in a difficult position, but it's for his own good. He'll catch the brunt of my parents' worry, but I know he can handle them.

He was groomed to rule Calvadria, and that often required him to be the perfect son. He was the one who needed to be perceived as strong, honorable, faithful to our customs.

I'm not willing to bow that easily—not even before centuries of tradition. Not all sacrifice is necessary. Not all traditions should be maintained. I understand, though, how something needs to replace them, and that's why I'm in Boston.

"I do have faith in you." He corrected himself, "I'm trying."

This would all be easier if I were willing to lie to my brother. Instead, he will need to accept that I am doing something without his permission and not even a royal decree to come home will change my course.

One day he'll thank me.

"I'm not in any trouble." That's the best comfort I can offer him.

Trouble. The word instantly brings a certain woman vividly back into my thoughts. Shit.

"Perhaps I should come to Boston."

"No. No one here knows who I am. I need to keep it that way. People don't recognize me here. They may not recognize you either, but I don't want to take the chance."

"Should you be engaged in an activity you cannot perform as yourself?"

This time I let my silence speak for me.

"Bricelion, nothing would stop me from being there if you need me."

He only uses my given name when he's in full paternal mode. "I know, but I ask you for nothing more than time to figure this out on my own."

He sighs. "Since you're not answering his calls, what would you have me tell Father?"

I'd like him to relay the message that respect is earned rather than demanded. I keep that thought to myself. "Remind him that stubbornness runs in our family."

"That is undeniable. Regardless of your personal endeav-

or, you do understand your presence is required at the announcement of my engagement."

"That's months away."

"You've already been away that long. There are some duties that cannot be avoided. Not by me and not by you. Assure me this will not be an issue."

"It will not." I promise because if my plan works no announcement will happen and my brother will be free to marry a woman of his choice instead of one handpicked for him. "Could we talk of something else?"

"Are you enjoying the change of menu?" By the hint of humor in his voice I know he's not asking about the local cuisine.

"That's not why I'm here."

"When has that ever stopped you?"

"Is it so hard to believe even I might grow up?"

"What's her name?"

"There is no woman."

"Names then. Women?"

"Let's just say I have yet to be tempted. I don't understand the women here. Some less than others."

"Ah, so there is one who's at least perplexing you."

"It's not at all the way you imagine. I was temporarily trapped in an elevator with the oddest woman."

"Trapped?"

"The elevator got stuck between floors."

"And?"

Considering my brother is currently struggling to understand me, it wouldn't hurt to let him in on a matter of little consequence. "She's a woman of limited means. New to the city. Her purse was stolen. No money. Possibly, no one watching out for her."

"Where is she now?" The concerned tone in my brother's voice brings me across all the miles that separate us. For as long as I can remember he's taken the lead. He's the hero charging in on the white horse. I've never taken that role because I've never had to.

Until now, he never needed me to.

No one did.

"She had an appointment elsewhere in the building."

"So, she does know someone."

"She said she did."

I know what my brother would do. He would be downstairs already. Actually, he never would have left her side. Not even if she told him she was fine. It would have been his duty to deliver her to a safe situation. Or at least have someone escort her in his place.

Only in his absence, do I understand him better.

I don't like the unanswered questions. Did Savannah meet up with someone? Was she still in the building?

I had dismissed her as not my problem, and I don't like what that reveals about me. I have never been the one anyone turned to for help. My father is a strong leader. My brother, his very capable heir. I was kept out of the public eye, educated, prepared but not tested, my value nothing more than my ability to replace my brother in the event it is required.

Nothing I do matters as long as it doesn't make the

news.

Savannah is a woman in need.

And I'm sitting in my office—every bit the dick she accused me of being.

I surge to my feet and quickly hang up with my brother after assuring him once again that I'm fine.

I take the elevator with confidence. It would not dare disappoint me twice. I will meet this woman Jana Monroe, confirm that Savannah will be safe in her care, and only then will I return to my work.

If Savannah is in need of more, I will arrange transportation for her back to her family. Surely she has some.

As soon as the elevator doors open on the fifteenth floor I feel a rush of adrenaline. The offices are all dark. The glass door leading to them is locked. Is this what Savannah found when she came? I check my watch. Not that much time has passed. I have resources that could galvanize at my command. I take out my phone to call Charles, the Royal Guard who has watched over me since childhood. He thinks I don't know he has been shadowing me since day one in Boston, but although his loyalty to me is beyond reproach, blending in has never been his strong suit.

I trust him, though. He bore witness to every cookie I stole as a child, every woman I snuck into the royal palace, every hangover I tried to pass off as the flu.

In some ways, he knows me better than my family—and never betrays that confidence. Ever present, ever watchful. He would have seen Savannah leave. Might even know where she went.

As I step into the elevator my phone loses signal. The call is better made from my office anyway, where I'll be free to command the entire Royal Guard if need be. Their allegiance is technically to my father, but I'm the one they share a drink with, invite into their homes, the one who has covered for them when they've needed to sneak their own guests out of the palace. There is a certain brotherhood among those who are deemed less essential to the survival of the royal family—the less elite Royal Guards, the second in line for the crown. We're all dispensable and we know it.

But we watch out for each other.

I groan as I imagine Savannah on the street. Cold. No money. No phone. Lost.

To me, Boston is a tiger I will tame. But to an innocent like Savannah, the city holds dangers she wouldn't know to protect herself from.

The elevator dings at my floor and I find myself moving quicker than normal.

I shouldn't have let her walk away alone. I should have made sure someone was there to meet her. It's a mistake I intend to right.

I come to a skidding halt at the sight of Savannah sitting behind my desk. Her woolen jacket is slung over the back of my chair.

The word beautiful comes to mind despite how rough she is around the edges. Her dark blonde hair is in wild disarray. She's smaller than she appeared in her oversized coat, a fact accentuated by the high back of my desk chair. Her thin shoulders are slumped forward, and she's tapping her forehead nervously with one hand.

I want to tell her everything will be okay, but I'm held silent by a confusing mix of relief and attraction. How is this possible?

Unaware I'm there, she sits back and swipes her hands angrily across her cheeks. Tears.

Our eyes meet, and my heart thuds in my chest.

Crazy.

I step closer and am assailed by a smell that should instantly kill the sizzle in the air, but my cock is convinced there's nothing wrong with her a little soap wouldn't cure. Especially once she loses that damn coat.

My leather chair will never be the same, and I have the uncomfortable feeling my life might not be either.

CHAPTER THREE

Savannah

I CAN'T CATCH a break, can I?

I should have known Jana Monroe wouldn't wait two hours for me. Not today. I could have committed her phone number to memory, but who does that anymore?

I'm beginning to question my role in my stretch of bad luck. If I hadn't decided to come as the real me, I could have headed to the lobby and asked security for her number—but considering how I look and the way my day is going they probably would have called the police.

Coming back to the thirtieth floor was hard enough after my grand exit, but discovering even *Mr. I don't care what happens to you* was gone took some of the wind out of my sails. Maybe he isn't coming back. Maybe I really am alone.

The least he could have done was forget to password protect his computer. If he had, I could have gotten Jana's contact info from my emails, called her from the landline phone on his desk, and been gone.

Then here he is as if summoned up to humiliate me more. "All I want is for one thing to go right today. Is that too much to ask?" I demand as if I have every right to be in his chair.

He doesn't say anything. It's borderline infuriating. He has this strange look on his face that I can't decipher. I hope it doesn't mean he's about to call security. I should probably explain I'm not trying to steal any oh-so-important information off his computer. "I don't have any of the contact information I need committed to memory. If you let me check my email, I'll get out of your hair."

He steps closer, not taking his eyes off me. If I didn't know better, I'd think there was a spark between us. My body is certainly revving, but I'm realistic enough to keep a clear head. I'm alone in an office with a man who doesn't look happy to see me.

It might be time to be nicer to him.

"I'm sorry. I know I shouldn't be in here, but I didn't know what else to do. I hoped I could simply ask you if I could borrow your computer for a minute, but you weren't here."

Okay, the last part comes out like an accusation he doesn't deserve, but I'm barely holding it together. I'm tired, hungry, and if I'm honest—a little scared.

"I went downstairs to check on you."

My breath catches in my throat. I must have heard him wrong. "That's where you were?"

He folds his arms over his chest and looks down at me like I'm the one acting out of character. Dude, you just said something that sounded like you cared—why do you still look annoyed? Unless you went to check on me because you thought I didn't belong in the building and now I'm in your office.

I don't want to go to jail.

I stand up and grab my coat. "Listen, I get that you don't know me, but I'm the type who would return a wallet I found—with the money still in it. All I need is Jana's phone number."

"Sit down."

I sit and instantly curse myself for it. He speaks with authority—like someone who expects people to jump when he commands it. I'm not into that. Standing now would be ridiculous, but I shoot him a glare anyway that attempts to say, I'm sitting but not because you told me to.

I shrug my coat back on because I really have no idea what is going on behind those intense black eyes. I'm not intimidated by him, but when he looks at me like that, I get all fluttery on the inside. Sex scenes from my favorite novels fly through my head, and he replaces every book boyfriend I've ever mentally given myself to. I wish he spoke more, so I'd have less time to picture us naked rolling around on the couch on the other side of his office.

Someday soon, I will find out if couch sex lives up to the hype, but not today and not with this man.

I smile in an attempt to reassure him I'm not as crazy as I seem. Harmless.

He doesn't smile back, but he does come to stand beside me. I let myself indulge in an X-rated version of how this plays out. In my fantasy, he leans in, sweeps my hair back from my ear, and growls something suggestive.

Desk sex. That has also always sounded incredible to me.

I imagine him commanding me to stand, strip and . . .

He types in his password, closes out his email, then steps back.

I let out a shaky breath. Yeah, that's the other way this could go . . . "Thank you," I say and inwardly give myself a smack. Part of why I came to Boston was to have sex, but not with an unvetted stranger. I don't want what I could have found on Tinder, Grinder, Hookup Tonight or any similar app. Stand down, overeager vagina—you've waited this long. I didn't fill out a ten-page questionnaire with Jana to throw my first time away on just any man.

I glance at Brice. He has put an appropriate distance between us. Part of me is tempted to ask him for advice on which search engine to use—just to draw him back to my side.

No.

Sorry, Mr. Boston, I don't have time for this. I need to focus on contacting Jana.

Oh, my God, I have imaginarily dated, fucked, and now broken up with a man who is probably still trying to figure out how to get me out of his office.

I turn quickly back to the computer screen. Jana. I open my mail, scan our messages for—bingo—her number. Normally, I would text her, but since I don't have my phone and I can't imagine asking to use Brice's . . . I write the number on a piece of paper and reach for his landline.

Then pause.

I should ask first. "Do you mind if I . . .?"

"Of course."

Jana didn't answer because that would have been too easy. I apologize about missing our meeting, say I've gotten myself into a bit of a tough spot by being mugged straight off the bus, and ask her to call me at this number . . . hoping it shows up on her ID.

I hang up and sit there frozen for a moment. Brice heard me. Is he okay with me waiting for her call?

He takes a seat in the chair in front of the desk. "You should also call your credit card company. Cancel the cards and order new ones."

"Yeah, I'll do that." I start using his computer again without asking this time. The formality is melting away as my situation gets more complicated.

I sign in to my credit card company and put a halt on my cards. I can't order new ones until I have an address. Shit. When I close out of the site, up pops an article about *what to do if your things are stolen while you are traveling.* The Internet is handy, but downright scary some times in its ability to know what you need.

I scan it quickly. "I need to take the police report to the bank tomorrow. Possibly get some cash out. Maybe even some temporary checks so I can pay for the apartment I'm leasing for the month." I nod to keep myself focused. This will work. I can make this work.

"And tonight?"

His question makes the lump in my throat double in size. Nothing on here tells you what to do if you're stranded until the bank opens.

"I'll call a friend back home."

"Allow me to lend you enough to carry you through until you can access your own money."

I scoff. "I can't take your money. You're right, though. I could borrow some. My boss back home could wire me some. This will work out." If I say it enough times, I wonder if maybe it'll become true.

"You sound certain, but you were also sure the woman downstairs was going to wait for you."

It's a pinprick to my already rattled nerves. A jab that he's not wrong about. "The bar is open, and I've known Jimmy my whole life. He'll send some money, and I'll get it right back to him."

Brice gestures to the phone as if he's challenging me to prove him wrong. Jerk. If I hadn't already broken up with him in my imagination, it would definitely be over now.

Thank God I know the number of the bar by heart. I dial, and bite at my lip.

"Hello?" Murray shouts into the phone so I have to pull it away from my ear. He's been tending bar there for forty-one years. My Ghost of Christmas Future if I don't make some big changes.

We threw a party for Murray last year. What does forty years at the same place get a person? A lopsided homemade cake. Some balloons and a card signed by all the regular customers who don't have anywhere else to spend their nights. If they're happy, I'm happy for them, but I feel like I was meant to do something more.

My mother had the unfortunate fate of dying during childbirth. Never having held me. Never getting that rush of joy. I never let myself get down about not having a mom, because my dad was so amazing. For the first ten years of my life he was everything I needed. But when I lost him too, it left me with little to hold on to. The guys at the bar became my family.

I love Murray. But I don't want to be him.

"Murray, it's Savannah. I need to talk to Jimmy." I try to keep my voice level. Any sign that I'm panicking, and I know exactly how they'll react. Which is to overreact. I also don't want Brice assuming he might be right. I don't want to have to kiss that smug smile off his face. *Smack—not kiss. Smack.*

"Hey Savannah. How's the big city?" Murray clears his throat. I convinced him to stop smoking a few years ago, but he still has that rasp to his voice.

"It's great. I'm having a blast. Meeting the nicest people." I glare at Brice and then roll my eyes so he knows I'm not referring to him. "Let me talk to Jimmy."

"He's setting up karaoke right now. You know that. He can't talk. He's the only one who knows how to get those speakers working." Murray's voice is quickly drowned out by music. "Your favorite song is about to start. No one sings "Achy Breaky Heart" like Old Man Koy. Want me to hold the phone up so you can hear him?"

"No, Murray. Don't." It's already too late. The phone is held in the air, and I'll have to wait out the song. I don't look over at Brice. He wouldn't understand any of this. I doubt he's ever stepped foot in a bar like ours or even considered doing karaoke. When the screechy song ends,

Murray says, "He's getting better."

"He's not."

Murray chuckles, and it breaks into a cough. He still looks tough on the outside, and probably hasn't even seen a doctor, but I worry about him.

"Have Jimmy call me back at this number. Did it come up on caller ID?"

"Uh," Murray pulls the phone away from his ear again, and I worry he's about to forget what we're doing. "Yeah I got it. He'll call you."

"Thanks Murray. The sooner the better." I consider for a second that maybe I should tell him it's urgent. I open my mouth and fish for the right words, but he hangs up before I think of what to say. It's for the best. I don't want them worrying.

When the line disconnects I feel my chest burn with frustration. I know exactly how busy the bar is on karaoke night. The whole town comes out. I've been just as quick to get people off the line, but right now I want to ring Murray's neck.

My eyes slowly rise to meet Brice's gaze. "He's going to call me back."

"After the next song?"

"It's a busy night there. I wouldn't expect you to under-stand. You don't look like the type to hang in a bar."

He looks intrigued. "What type am I?"

"Stiff." The word sends my eyes to the bulge in his pants. *I bet it's impressive even at half-mast.*

Oh, shit. I'm doing it again. I stand and raise my eyes to his. In my imagination he winks and we have a moment.

In reality, he looks as uncomfortable as I feel. "You must have work to do. Don't let me stop you. I'll just sit over there and wait for Jimmy to call back." I cross the room to a chair in the corner of his office. The leather is full grain and firm. I run my hand over it, letting myself enjoy the luxury of it. It's so comfortable and the rich mocha color matches the room perfectly. The whole office belongs in a magazine.

Just as he does.

I could rock the cover of Maine Ice Fishing Guide. My backpack, weathered by years of cramming it full of school books and later novels I'd borrow from the library, looks like a heap of trash in this perfectly decorated room. Right now, it's literally all I have so I hug it to me. There's only a change of clothes and a few toiletries in it. I hadn't anticipated needing much since this limbo wasn't supposed to last longer than the bus ride. I feel something in the front pocket of my bag. A tiny piece of joy.

Brice can have his fancy office with the supple leather. I have something better.

The foil wrapper is cold on my fingertips as I slip it out of my bag and feel a rush of calm. A bit of home. I'm nosier than I mean to be, but suddenly I'm starving. The adrenaline of this adventure is wearing off and reality is setting in. The rustling of the foil draws his eye.

"What are you doing?" Brice frowns as he stares at the wrapper in my hand.

I wave it at him, but his expression doesn't change. He's seated at his desk, and I wonder if it's his job that keeps that sour look on his face.

"I'm eating a Pop-Tart."

Nothing. No response at all. Not even a nod.

"Strawberry filling. Frosting. Tiny colorful sprinkles."

He looks confused. Or annoyed. "Are you hungry? I can order something up. There's sushi. Italian. Whatever you want."

"I'm fine." My smile doesn't seem to convince him. "You've had Pop-Tarts before, right?"

"No." He shakes his head and leans back in his chair. The way he tosses his pen to the desk I can tell he's decided working while I'm here is futile. "That's not food."

"You know what?" I take a big bite, chew it, and let the familiar sweet taste ground me even further to my resolve. I am going to make this work and this little snack is just the bit of cheer I needed. "You're right. It's not food. It's a piece of heaven. Here, it's a two-pack. You can have my other one."

"No." He waves me off like I'm a stray cat trying to offer him the garden snake I'd just hunted. I expect him to return to working on whatever it is he does, but he just sits there looking at me.

"Don't be a foodie snob. You have to try this. Consider it my way of saying thank you for letting me use your phone and computer." I'm walking the second Pop-Tart to his desk, expecting his face to soften. It doesn't. "Come on, it's like ninety-nine percent sugar. What's not to love about that?"

"This is crazy. You need money for a hotel room. Plus a

cab. Real food." He reaches to his back pocket and pulls out his wallet. His jaw is set and determined.

"No! I'm not taking your money."

He sighs. "You have no idea if your friend will call back, and I'm clearly not going to get any work done until you go. Anything I give you is a business investment at this point. I'll write it off."

"I know this situation isn't ideal, but I promise I'll leave as soon as Jimmy calls. Sugar always makes me feel better. Maybe you should try it." I lay the Pop-Tart on his desk.

He looks down at the pastry like I'm trying to talk him into huffing some illegal substance for a high.

The phone rings and I jump. "That's Jimmy," I say with confidence.

"Or since it's my work line, it could actually be for me." He lifts the phone off the cradle.

"Yes, you've the right number, hang on." Brice passes me the phone.

I try to look like I'm not also shocked that my luck is turning around. "Jimmy?"

"Hey, girlie. You didn't tell us you knew someone out there. Is that what you didn't want to say? That this is about a man?"

"It's not like that, TRUST ME. He's nobody."

"Then what is it like? Murray said you sounded upset. Don't tell me you already went and got yourself in a bind. What do you need?"

The accusation, as correct as it is, fills me with defensive pride. Even without knowing what brought me to Boston, they expect me to fail. They care about me, and that's what makes their low opinion of me sting more. They're wrong, though. I won't fail. I shoot back, "No I'm not in a bind. I'm perfectly fine. Enjoying the city."

I see Brice's head snap up, but I turn my back a little to avoid the look that is full of very fair questions.

"So why are you calling me? Home sick?" I am a little. Jimmy's voice is a comfort. After my transformation, I'll make time to go back and visit. Right now I have more immediate concerns. Still, there has to be a solution that doesn't involve taking a hit to what little pride I have left.

"You know I hate missing karaoke night."

"It's not the same without you." I can picture him, white rag slung over his shoulder. Salt-and-pepper hair at his temples. He's definitely chewing a toothpick. His over-crowded smile is genuine and beautiful in its own way.

"I was just calling to remind you that the kegs are getting dropped off tomorrow. I won't be there to meet them so someone has to come in early." I fidget with a loose string on my shirt and avoid eye contact with Brice. I can feel him looking at me. I can't imagine what he's thinking.

"Sure. I remembered."

"You didn't."

"Totally forgot," Jimmy admits with a hardy laugh. "All the regulars are asking about you. They're worried you're not coming back."

"Tell them I say hello. And don't forget you told Mitchell he could have next Wednesday off. You'll need to cover his shift."

"See I don't know how I'd get by without you. I'd like to tell everyone around here they're wrong. Of course you're coming back. But you've been so secretive about this thing in Boston. Now you've got this guy answering the phone. Where's your cell phone?"

"Battery died on it. I'll charge it tonight. You've got nothing to be worried about. I'll check in again in case you forget about the electric bill you need to pay by the end of next week."

"You could just be back by the end of next week. That would be easier."

"It's good talking to you, Jimmy. Sing a song for me tonight, will you?"

He clears his throat and begins a painful rendition of some old love song. It's so loud I pull the phone away from my ear and hand it back to Brice to hang up.

Brice looks like he's trying to figure me out. Good luck with that one. None of this was part of my plan.

Brice hangs the phone up and cuts the loud song short. "You didn't ask him to wire you money."

"I don't need him to. I'll be fine." I shrug, wishing I'd kept the other Pop-Tart.

"You don't think he would have sent it to you?"

"Of course he would. If I'd asked him to, he would have driven to Boston to pick me up." Jimmy isn't the problem. I am.

"Then why didn't you ask him to?"

That's a tough one. I could lie, but I'm getting tired. A little honesty is easier. "Because I'm here for a reason."

"In my office?"

I can't tell if he's joking or being an ass, but really, does it matter? More for my benefit than his, I say, "In Boston. I left Maine because I had to. If I run back, even figuratively, I'm no longer moving forward. Today has been rough, but nothing that's worthwhile is easy, is it? Trust me. I'll be fine."

"You will be fine," he asserts. "You'll take the money I'm offering for a hotel and cab." He opens his wallet. It's a decree not an offer.

Nice try.

"I'd rather sleep in the street." I prop a hand up on my hip and tip my chin up proudly.

"People say that only when they know there is no risk they will have to."

"You don't know me. What do I need besides a warm coat?" I pull my coat closed.

"Not happening. So sit your ass back down or take the money. Your choice."

"No to both kind offers." I bite the words out angrily.

"You're infuriatingly stubborn. Why do you have to make this difficult?"

"Me? I'm difficult?"

"Yes." He stands, his sexy chest and dominating height stealing my breath for a second. "I need to get back to work and you need a place to sleep."

"Why do you care?"

"I don't." He cracks his knuckles, and I imagine it's a tick that only comes out when he's thoroughly annoyed.

"But I also don't want to be the last person you talked to before they find you dead and floating in the harbor. I don't have time to be investigated for murder."

"You're a real charmer." I shrug, and like that, it seems to annoy him. There's tightness in his jaw that has me once again imagining how differently this could be going. If this were a movie, this would be where he angrily sweeps me into his arms and kisses me in that love-hate kind of way. All this anger? Sexual tension.

And the scowl on his face? Foreplay.

Oh, crap, did he say something while I was picturing him naked again?

"Then where will you sleep tonight?"

I look at him for a long moment before answering. There's definitely something going on between us. An angry tension with something else mixed in. Desire? Anticipation? Every time I think this is all one-sided, I see a fire in his eyes that not even a virgin could read wrong.

I probably should leave. The old me would.

Instead I head back to where I left my bag. "This chair is pretty comfortable. It reclines. Nice." On the outside I might look the same, but I'm already becoming more confident. Boston has thrown its worst at me. A weaker person would turn tail and run home.

Look at me, Boston. Still here.

Take that.

"What are you smiling about?" His face twists in confusion. I get it. To him my situation looks desperate.

I settle back into the chair without answering his question. He doesn't see how making it this far is a triumph in itself. Unfriendly as he appears, the truth is he'd played a role in this small victory. "Thank you for not throwing me out."

With a shake of his head he returns to his desk. Does he normally work straight through to the morning? Will he ask me to leave when he finishes his work?

I don't know, but what I do know is I'm not going back to Maine.

So, bring it on, Boston. You don't scare me.

CHAPTER FOUR

Brice

SAVANNAH IS TESTING my nerves as she settles into the chair in the corner of my office as if it's a hotel suite. I can tell her to get out, but I can't let her go again until I know she's safe. I don't allow myself to acknowledge that part of me would be left wondering if I'd see her again. Her sexy body and sparkling eyes would fade to a memory.

"You won't hear a peep out of me." She throws her hands up as though that gesture is some kind of binding contract. I highly doubt that's a promise she can keep.

"I have calls to make." I look for the number to dial and vow to keep my eyes off her.

A promise I quickly break. With a rapid and easy motion, she sweeps her hair into a ponytail. Seeing more of her features, I'm struck by her beauty. Her dainty heart-shaped face and high cheekbones are fully exposed, and I lose my train of thought for a moment. I could kiss my way down that jawline. Every time she changes anything even remotely, it's like a slow burn. An unveiling of her beauty in parts rather than an *in your face* overdone woman who tries too hard.

She runs her fingers over her lips as though she's zipping them shut and turns a pretend key to lock them. Her eyes flutter with hopefulness, and I answer with only a sigh.

When I don't protest any further, she knows I'm granting permission. Her hands clap together as she already falls short on her promise. *Noise.*

She can't be quiet. I barely know her, but I am already certain of this. Quiet is not her thing. She will make many peeps.

"Thank you! I swear by tomorrow you can forget all about me and this terrible night."

I doubt it. The thought skitters across my mind before I can stop it. Savannah doesn't seem easy to forget, and that's half the problem. All the more reason I need her gone.

"Plus," she continues excitedly, "staying here means I can also meet with Jana Monroe early tomorrow and get down to work." She meets my gaze. "Oh right, I forgot." She zips her lips again.

I nearly ask what kind of work she and this Jana woman will be doing. A prickly heat crawls up my back as I imagine the endless trouble she could get herself into. Luckily before I break and inquire, she pulls out a tattered novel with a bright pink bookmark in it. It's clearly a romance of some kind. I can tell by the loopy scrawling print and the muscular man on the cover. Something my sister would read and we'd ruthlessly tease her about. There is hardly any real romance in the world. Anyone practical knows that. By now, I know Savannah is far from practical.

I try to catch the title and mentally slap myself. I don't

care what she's reading. I don't care why she's meeting with Jana. I can't care right now. I won't.

She lets out a happy sigh as she reads. One minute I swear she's trying to seduce me and the next I think she wouldn't have the first clue how to. She's completely enthralled in the story, and I watch as she slides her feet out of her sneakers and pulls her legs up onto the chair with her, curling in comfortably. She stares with unwavering focus at the words in her thick book. Smiling a little when she gets to various parts. Frowning at others.

Fuck. It's mesmerizing, like watching huge snowflakes fall lazily toward the ground. Hypnotic, but I break the trance.

I pick up my phone and dial in to the investor call. I'm terribly late but it's not an interactive call, just a dump of information I need from the CEO and board of a company I'm interested in. I press the phone between my shoulder and my ear and lean forward as I jot notes about the latest quarterly results and forecast for the rest of the year. I force myself to stop looking at the smooth skin of her ankle as her jeans pull up.

Stop wanting to fuck her.

Just stop.

The word virgin keeps playing in my head. How is she still a virgin? No matter how small her hometown is, there had to be men lined up to be with her. She's obviously a handful, but her allure outweighs her nuttiness. Not to me, but surely for someone else by now.

When I think of all the ways I could bring her to ecstasy,

it makes me hard. I adjust in my chair and try to push the thought away.

I nearly shout, *stop licking your sexy lips as you read. Stop twisting that curl of hair around your finger.*

Savannah is the embodiment of everything I'm trying to avoid. Distraction. Indulgence. Thinking about parting her legs and devouring her means I'm not thinking about work. I imagine how tight she is. What she might think if I tugged that hair she was curling around her finger.

Tough. Witty. Happy when all signs point to the fact that she shouldn't be. That kind of woman takes up too much bandwidth in a man's life. A sexy, vapid, selfish woman is much less time consuming.

When I made the decision to come to Boston and invest my inheritance to help my brother, I knew I couldn't let anything stop me. Not my family. Not any outside factors. It's why I chose to live in Bachelor Tower. A place of business. Casual pleasure. Focus. No women. No relationships. It will take a disciplined and multifaceted strategy of investment to give Mathias the opportunity he deserves to have a real life. There is no room for error.

I don't worry about sneaky businessmen with bad intentions. A challenging negotiation doesn't bother me in the least. But this woman, curled up in my chair, yawning and getting emotional about fictional characters in a book, is a threat I can't allow.

She laughs and then covers her mouth for a second. "Sorry," she mouths silently. Luckily, since I was sure she'd be incapable of being quiet, I have the call on mute. Plus, I've hardly been listening. I don't know if the company has set quarterly records or is on the verge of bankruptcy.

"It's just a call I'm dialed in to. On mute. Investor update. A quarterly thing. I'm not really listening." I don't know why I'm telling her but before my sentence is finished she's sitting up straighter and leaning in. My words an invitation in her mind.

"Oh good. How tall are you?"

"Six foot three."

"And your eyes are dark brown? Would you say chocolate brown or coffee?"

"I'd say brown because I don't refer to myself with food-based adjectives."

"Where are you from?" She has the book pressed to her chest as she leans toward me.

"Why?" There's an edge to my voice, and I can tell by her expression she hears it. There is great power in my anonymity here. I am a wealthy man who plans to invest, but people don't need to know anything besides that.

"Oh no reason. It doesn't matter." She waves her book at me and clears her throat, the first time since she yelled she was a virgin that she looks even mildly uncomfortable. Is she blushing? As I get another glance at the cover I wonder if she's creating some kind of fantasy of us. Am I the man she's picturing in that story? I'm half hard again as I think about clearing my desk with the swipe of my arm and licking my way up her body. Romance book style. Quivering bosoms and forceful kisses.

"What are you reading?" I narrow my eyes as she holds up the cover for me to see.

"It's so good." Savannah melts back against the chair as though the book has a physical effect on her.

I want to have a physical effect on her.

"There is this king, and he has two lovers. One is an older woman he visits often in the middle of the night. Since he was just a teen she's been his lover and showed him all the various ways of pleasuring someone. She's a real cougar." Savannah flips to a passage in the book and begins to read it to me.

> "He clutched her waist tightly and dragged her to him. Her body crushed against his. A gasp burst from her lips as he tipped her chin back, demanding everything of her supple lips. Within the span of a breath she clung to him as tightly as he did her. Their passion bursting like sparks between them."

"Descriptive." I take note of how her face doesn't blush pink now. Her voice doesn't falter. She reads the words as if she's written them herself. As though she's lived them. But I get the feeling she has not.

"Then his second lover is his half-sister. You know how royals are." She waggles her brows at me, and I strain to keep my face level. The world looks at a royal family through a bizarre lens. It's not easy being on the other end of it. "There were always these rules about having royal blood stay in the family, and it made for some really messed up situations. But in this story it works perfectly. This girl is young and inexperienced. Ripe for all the skills he's learned. For most of the book they don't know about his time spent with the other.

And in the end it becomes clear neither woman is right for him. It's tragic."

"He doesn't end up with either of them?"

Her face lights at my question. She's as surprised as I am that I asked, "He has nothing in common with either woman. They have nothing to talk about. Nothing to experience together. It's all lust and sneaking around. He's starting to realize the woman who works in the kitchen can match wits with him and make him laugh. And there is something much more appealing to him about that. But their love can never be."

"Seriously? You really fall for all this stuff?"

"She's a commoner. He's royalty. Star-crossed lovers."

I can't ignore the irony of our conversation. Savannah leans back and sighs at the drama. The deliciousness of it. When her back arches her breasts perk up, and I rake my eyes across their perfection. She could be the kitchen worker. The cougar. I wouldn't care. I'd make her purr with pleasure.

"And that's a good book to you?"

"You probably read nonfiction business junk all day, right?"

"As opposed to fictional fantasies about sex? I don't get the appeal. Why not just have great sex?"

"When I want to escape, these are my getaway cars. Absolutely. It's a fantasy. A place to go when circumstances keep me from being anywhere else. But now my life is different. I can go anywhere. And I intend to. But I'm taking my books with me."

My mind flashes to what Savannah may be running from. I feel an impulse to crush anyone or anything that might be out to hurt her.

"What do you do when you want a break?" She tilts her head and looks at me with intensity.

I fuck a woman until she quivers in my arms. I always find that a nice escape.

"Maybe you should give one of these books a try. I'm happy to lend it to you. You could learn something maybe."

I chuckle and flatten my tie against my chest. "I could teach that author a thing or two, and she'd have a hell of a lot more to write about when I was done with her. One night and she'd have enough lessons for ten more books."

"I doubt that."

"Really?"

"Really." Her assertion makes me lean in across my desk.

I take the challenge seriously. "Trust me, there is nothing someone behind a keyboard could come up with that compares to what I could do. The next book wouldn't be suitable for sale. They'd ban it. They'd have to burn it to save the women of the world who clutch their pearls at such scandalous things. The author would never be the same."

Savannah snorts out a laugh. She is a mystery to me.

"I'm telling you the author wouldn't be interested."

I puff up my chest and smile wide enough for the dimple in my cheek to show. Something I'm certain I haven't done since meeting her. "And I'm telling you—"

"The author is Thomas Watterson. I think his wife would prefer he thwart your advances."

I snap my lips shut and mentally score a point for her. She got me.

"So you want to borrow it? Next time you're feeling

stressed?" Her smile is one of victory.

"I never need a break. I'm doing exactly what I want to do. Stress is all part of the fun."

"You're telling me that's your happy face?" She feigns concern. "I'd hate to see you angry."

"If you keep talking you just might."

She smirks. Unafraid. Silly. Completely at peace with sleeping in a chair in a stranger's office and reading a book that sounds outlandish all while eating some weird sugary pastry that looks like it's made for a ten-year-old. And yet I'm the one who can't stop watching her.

The longer she's here, the deeper the mystery of Savannah grows. A rabbit hole I am determined not to fall down.

"I'll go back to my book." Settling into the chair, she pulls the book over her face, but I can see her eyes still peeking over. Fixed on me.

"Reading?" I shake my head and our eyes stay locked.

She nods. Still clearly not reading. "Just getting to the best part." Her brows rise, and I know she's smiling again. At my expense. "It's getting spicy now. The hunk is really something in this one. Sullen but sexy. The scowl really works for him." She's still peeking at me, and I've got a raging hard-on now. It would take almost nothing to come. A brush of her body on mine, the clutching of my hands on her small hips.

Two people on the phone call I've forgotten about begin barking loudly at each other and it pulls me back to what I'm supposed to be doing. Thank goodness for a mute button.

I hear her giggle again, but I don't look up. I don't even glance at her. Because I'll run the risk of never looking away.

CHAPTER FIVE

Brice

I LOCK DOWN everything in my office. Papers all put away. I don't know if Savannah is a snoop or if she could even make sense of these boring documents, but I don't want to find out the hard way I should have hidden them.

She's been asleep for three hours. Out cold. Still curled up in the oversized chair. She fell asleep reading and dropped the book unceremoniously onto the floor next to her. I stand and look her over. She's petite but strong. Her skin looks like the expensive silk the designers in one of our oceanfront homes selected for the window treatments. I'm compelled to run a finger over her exposed neck. But of course, I don't.

The office is cool so I reach for her coat to cover her. I suddenly remember the smell and wonder if it's worth the risk of getting more of that stink on me. Instead I slip out of my suit jacket and lay it over her. Savannah stirs with a tiny sigh and I hold my breath. She coos herself back to sleep and I slip out.

I make a phone call I had hoped I wouldn't have to.

"Hello. Sir?"

"Bring the car around." I'm curt but I have my reasons.

"Uh, sir what do you mean?"

"Well Charles, you've been following me around Boston for the last month. You can drop the charade. Just have a car out front. You'll need to give someone a ride."

"I don't know what you're talk—"

"Charles. Seriously. I've spotted you at least ten times. I know my father would not be able to sleep a wink if he thought I was parading around Boston without at least one bodyguard. Have the car out front. You'll be driving a young woman to the bank when she's ready."

"A woman?"

"Yes Charles, pretty hair, boobs, long eyelashes. A woman. You are familiar with them?"

"Very." Charles laughs. "I just didn't realize you had company."

"Trust me, it's not at all like that. You'll understand when you see her. Or smell her. She just crashed into my life a few hours ago, and I'll feel better knowing she's safely out of it."

"Is she some kind of threat?" His voice is sharp and I consider the question. She couldn't kill me but she could derail my plans.

"No. She's harmless. Just a handful. Never stops talking. Has an answer for everything. The answers just don't make any damn sense. We were stuck in the elevator together when the power went out."

"I see. Well, I'll make sure she gets to her destination."

"Actually, I'll need a bit more than that." I look back into my office before I step onto the elevator and lower my voice. "I need you to keep her busy for a while. I want time to look into something. Who she's here to meet. Something isn't right, and I know the second she finishes at the bank she'll be back in this building getting into who knows what."

"Because you're trying to get rid of her?" His sarcasm does not go unnoticed.

"I'd like to make sure she's not going to turn up at my office when whatever scheme she's into falls apart. Something isn't right."

"It sounds like she's lucky you were in the elevator. I'll keep her busy. For how long?"

"I can't imagine it'll take me long to track down the information I'm looking for. I'll send you a text when the time is right."

"Yes, sir."

"Be discreet. She doesn't need to know anything about me. She knows me as Brice and nothing more. I'm just a businessman. I can only imagine the questions she's going to hit you with tomorrow."

"I'm trained in seven of the most effective kinds of interrogation. I have endured some of the world's most intense torture techniques. She won't get a thing out of me." Charles, always dutiful.

"I don't doubt your skill. I'm not sure there's any training in the world to prepare you for Savannah."

"She's up there with you now? Maybe I need to come assess the situation." I can hear him chuckling.

"Laugh all you want. You're the one who's going to be trying to get the smell of fish and gasoline out of your car for a week."

"I've had worse, driving royals around after parties. But no parties for you? You're heading back across the street. That's an odd place you're staying. It took me a while to sort out what exactly was going on there. It's sort of a . . ."

"A sausage factory. Dudes everywhere. I know. It was intentional."

"Something else you want to tell me then? Know that I'll love you no matter what. I'm very open-minded."

"Did my father pay you extra to start your stand-up comedy career too? No. I'm here for a reason. I'm limiting my distractions. Or I was. Until Savannah."

"Stuck in an elevator. Sounds serendipitous."

"Much closer to involuntary imprisonment. I was close to prying the doors open with my bare hands and climbing up the elevator shaft. It didn't make for a good night of work. I just need to know Savannah gets where she's supposed to this morning."

"Because she's a pain. Never stops talking? Stubborn?"

"Exactly."

"Yeah." He laughs again. "Exactly what I remember thinking about my wife when we met."

CHAPTER SIX

Savannah

I WAKE WITH a start. *Did I just snore myself awake? Did anyone hear me?*

Every morning I can remember I've woken up in one house. I never did sleepovers or vacation homes. So before my eyes open, my heart knows something is very different. There's a warm, amazing smelling suit coat covering me like a blanket. I'm turned awkwardly in the chair, but I've nodded off in plenty of chairs in my day. You get used to it when you're someone's primary caretaker.

I look around the unfamiliar space of Brice's office as I blink away the sleep. Everything about last night floods back to me. My stolen purse. The meeting I missed. The elevator getting stuck. Brice. His pecs. The size of his very capable looking hands. The dimple he flashed the one time he smiled.

Brice isn't behind his desk and the ache I feel is impossible to ignore. Last night was a disaster. He was intolerable. Yet I had hoped he'd still be here. I did quite enough to disrupt his night. He probably crept out of here on tiptoes just to get away.

Checking my watch, I'm disappointed it's only seven thirty. Jana didn't return my call as far as I know, and I don't remember what her office hours are. The bank opens in half an hour.

I pull on my beat-up sneakers and try to make myself look moderately decent. If that woman hadn't given me five dollars yesterday, she sure as hell would if she caught sight of me today. When I stand to leave a small note falls off me. It's a slip of paper folded in half that must have been on top of my coat.

There is a black town car downstairs that will take you to the bank. He will not let you leave otherwise so just take the ride. Eat something that doesn't come wrapped in tin foil. Brice.

There is something about the way he orders me around that is equal parts infuriating and sexy. If he'd bent me over his desk last night I've have folded quicker than a stack of sweaters at the mall.

My nipples perk up at the thought of it. He's not even in the room and my body is responding to him.

I consider my options. A nice warm town car would make the morning easier. The bank is important, but not nearly as important as letting Jana know I'm still interested in her services.

I take out her phone number that I scratched down last night and dial from Brice's desk phone. He's not here to ask permission this time. But I still feel sheepish.

"Hello?"

"Jana," I say with far too much enthusiasm. "It's Savannah Barre."

"My no-show?" Her voice is cool and formal but not in a snooty way. She's sure of herself and I love that.

"I'm so sorry. I will fill you in on all the crazy details when we meet. My purse was stolen and I was stranded. I'm in the building though if you can meet with me now."

"I won't be in until ten, but I can make a little time for you then." She sounds concerned, as though I'm stringing her along. Cautious, like a woman made wise by years in the city.

"I will be there. Again I am so sorry about last night. Once you hear the story you'll totally understand. It was crazy. I'm going to the bank now so I can get everything squared away. But I'll be to you by ten."

"Do you have a way to get there? You said you were stranded."

"Apparently"—I snicker thinking of Brice and the car he's ordered for me—"this man I met last night while we were trapped in the elevator has a car service downstairs waiting for me."

"What?" More concern. I can't blame her. "What man?"

"Yeah, it was a comedy of errors last night. You know the elevator in your building tried to kill me. They should get that thing fixed."

"I'd be more worried about the man whose car you're about to get into than the elevator. Statistics are much more staggering for that scenario than death in an elevator." There's a mild hint of humor in her voice, but it's still guarded. The gatekeeping process for even having contact with Jana is nearly cult-like in its secrecy. I jumped through every hoop. Followed every direction. All the way up until I missed my appointment yesterday. Her services are a closely guarded secret, and now I'm a mystery to her again. A risk.

"No, Brice is great; I'm sure whoever is driving the car is from a reputable company. And really the story is quite funny. When I see you at ten you'll be doubled over laughing." A lump grows in my throat as I consider the possibility she might change her mind about working with me.

"Just be here at ten and we'll regroup." A wave of relief washes over me.

"See you then."

I hang up the phone and do a little end zone victory dance, even though I'm still miles from anything that resembles a touchdown. I slip my coat on and toss my bag over my shoulder. Jana's concern for me isn't completely misguided. I could be walking into a dangerous situation.

There's a fancy pen on the desk. It's steel and sturdy. It has a presence of its own, if that's possible for a writing utensil. Not surprising considering its owner. Of course his pen would be substantial.

I'm not a thief. That *should* be the end of that sentence. No but. BUT, let's just say this driver is someone to be concerned about. This pen would make a great tool to stab an eye out.

Maybe a good jab to the junk?

I pick it up and convince myself I'll return it after I meet with Jana later this morning. Or if things go badly, Brice can retrieve it from the eye socket of his driver.

I take the thirty flights of stairs down. Still determined not to tempt fate with the elevator. Bad idea.

As I reach the curb I'm winded, almost doubled over as I try to catch my breath. My side is cramped. I look like I'm dying.

"Miss Savannah?" A large man with a shaved head and bulbous nose stands a foot from me. His suit, his tie, and chauffeur hat are all a crisp black. The white shirt beneath is starched as rigid as the man's back. "Are you all right?"

"I took the stairs," I gasp out, clutching at his arm to steady myself. He tenses under my grip but not out of discomfort. It's his attempt to be as sturdy as possible for me. "I might rather die in the elevator than die of a heart attack right now."

"No chance of that, ma'am. You're under my care. I don't allow people to die. It's bad for business."

"Under your care?" I take another gulp of air and eye him.

He is unbothered by my scrutiny. "My name is Charles. I've been hired to take you where you need to go this morning. There is cold sparkling or flat spring water in the car. Please help yourself."

"And you'll be driving me where I want to go?"

"Yes."

"Which is?" My test is rudimentary but it's all I have. He might slip and say *to an abandoned warehouse on the edge of town* and then I'll know to stab him with Brice's pen.

"The bank. Then perhaps to get something to eat. Or a

place to stay?"

"The bank, yes. My apartment is on the other side of town. I won't be able to make it there this time of the morning and still make my meeting. Maybe I can find somewhere around here to change and shower," I say in an oddly regal way for no apparent reason other than I'm awkward as hell.

"We'll work that all out. Shall we go then?" He gestures toward the car politely. He gets suddenly all ceremonial and formal. It suits him. Unlike me who just did a half curtsy like an idiot.

To his credit Charles offers me a small obedient kind of smile as he gestures again for me to head for the car. I don't. I'm not ready.

"Are you going to murder me?"

"Excuse me?" His chin folds in on itself as he looks down at me. I take a little pride in the fact that I've rattled him. He seems unflappable, yet I have flapped him. I make a note to myself not to ever say that out loud to anyone.

"I appreciate the ride but I don't know you, and I'm just wondering if you have a penchant for murder?"

"I do not." He looks around as though he's worried someone passing by might hear. I'm besmirching his reputation out here in the street. When I continue standing there like a weirdo, he reaches for his wallet. I put my hand in my pocket and grip the pen tightly. Eye-jabbing style.

He pulls out some photographs with tattered edges. "These are my children. I have two girls. My wife. We have cats. Two of them. Binxy and Tabitha."

"Your cats' names or your kids' names?"

"The cats. I picked those names because my wife wouldn't let me have anything to do with naming our daughters. I have a lot of aunts with tremendously bad names."

He flips through the pictures and oddly enough, it does the trick. Maybe it's the mangy looking yellow cat with one missing ear. Or the toothless grin of his littlest daughter.

I believe him.

"Okay, let's go." I skip forward and watch from the corner of my eyes as his face twists up in exasperation. Getting that reaction from people is my superpower. I don't even have to try.

He folds his wallet and tucks it away. I'm at the passenger door getting in as I hear him protest with some kind of grumbling noise.

"What's the matter?"

"I'm to open the door for you, Miss Savannah. Traditionally."

"Oh, Chuck . . . I am the furthest thing from traditional. Don't worry."

He clears his throat, seeming to swallow back his reaction to his new nickname. "And usually passengers prefer the comfort of the back seat."

"Nah, I'm good up front." I want to be in eye-stabbing distance if things get hokey. I've seen one too many shows about cab rides gone wrong. Rigged not to unlock. No thanks. The weird cat with one ear is cute, but I prefer to stay in striking distance with my pen.

He skitters around the front of the car and gets in with a muffled puff of air.

"You work for a service? Which one?" I check the dash for some kind of badge or company name.

"I work for Brice."

"You just drive him around?"

"Among other things. Yes."

"What other things?"

"Buckle up, Miss Savannah. Safety first."

"You're dodging my questions."

"I'm a dutiful employee."

"More like a deer during hunting season. Jumpy." Biting my lip, I narrow my eyes at him.

"Hunting season? Are you aiming for me? Should I be worried?" He chuckles.

"I'm just chatty by nature." I give him a warm smile. "Your boss was a man of few words last night. I'd like to know at least something about the man who ordered me to take this ride. What can you tell me about Brice? There has to be something you can share."

I watch him sort through the answer. "I don't usually do something like this. But you seem like a nice girl. Harmless. I suppose it wouldn't hurt to share something with you. Since you're so interested in him."

"I'm not interested in him. I have no intention of ever seeing him again." I think of his pen in my pocket and wonder if maybe taking it had more to do with having an excuse to give it back. "Trust me, last night was a disaster. I'm just curious. Not interested in him."

Charles nods and lets his face fall serious. "I'd appreciate if you didn't let it get back to him that I told you."

"Of course." I lean forward a bit, like I'm in the frigid waters of Coppertop, bracing for a wave to crest over me.

"He isn't a fan of soft cheeses. Hates them actually. Prefers nice hard long-aged cheddar. He tells people he's allergic, but truly he just doesn't like them."

"Fascinating." I sit back in my seat and watch the city begin to roll by us. "You're a funny man, Chucky. If this driving thing doesn't work out, you should consider stand-up comedy."

"I'll consider it." He reaches for the radio and turns it up. He thinks that's going to keep me from talking to him. Cute.

CHAPTER SEVEN

Brice

IT'S NOT POSSIBLE. In this day and age everyone has a digital footprint. I've spent the last ten years trying to drag my family, and in turn our country, into the future. Success is now dependent on evolution. Yet, Jana Monroe, and whatever she does on the fifteenth floor of this building, seems to have no real website. No public phone number. No mission statement. Nothing.

I consider calling in a favor. It's not hard as royalty. People have indebted themselves to my family for generations, and I get to reap the benefits of that. But it can come with strings attached.

Nothing stays secret from my father. The questions would begin. *Why would I be interested in this woman and her company?* My mother would be calling me within the hour of getting word I was looking into Jana Monroe.

I reach for my pen and realize it's gone. My father's gift to me on my twenty-first birthday. I open the drawer and look beneath my desk. It's gone.

She took it. I'll have Charles pat her down before he drops her off. Or maybe I'll do it myself.

My hands grow hot at the thought of touching her, searching her. I imagine having her back on my desk, legs spread, head tipped back. Begging for my cock. I have to physically shake my head to dislodge the image.

Charles calls, and I right myself quickly.

"Yes?" I'm irritated.

"She's squared away. It went pretty quick. I'm guessing because people wanted to move her along as fast as they could."

"I told you, she's a nightmare."

"I meant because she's so sweet. Charming everyone we've met today. She's at the hotel on South Street taking a shower and changing for her meeting. Shall I drop her off?"

"No. I can't find anything about this woman she's meeting. Just some bogus website front that leads nowhere. It's like a shell company or something. I need more time."

"She has an appointment with Jana at ten. It seems quite important. We've only got about an hour."

"Has she told you anything else? Anything about what the meeting is for?" There's an unfamiliar pitch in my voice that I quickly drop. "Anything about Jana?"

"Just that she can't miss another meeting or she thinks she will not work with her."

"What kind of work?"

"She hasn't said. But she's quite persistent about getting to the meeting."

"And I know you'll find a way to make sure that doesn't happen."

"Sir."

"You won't be able to sleep at night if you think you're dropping her off to some sleazy woman with bad intentions."

"I don't think your diplomatic protections cover me against kidnapping." Charles clears his throat and lowers his voice. "We're walking a fine line here."

"You're a persuasive man. Just get it done. Keep her busy and away from this building."

"You did say you spent time with her right? You must have noticed she's determined."

An understatement. "I don't know what exactly this Jana Monroe woman is offering, but Savannah wants it. And she's no fool. I can't just hold something shiny up and expect her to forget why she came here. Keep her busy." My voice is flat, and he knows well enough not to challenge my order.

"Yes," Charles replies dutifully. "I'll create some issue."

"Fake a heart attack? She seems like the kind of woman who would hop in an ambulance with a perfect stranger just so they weren't alone."

"That's a good kind of woman."

I sidestep the trap he's trying to set for me. "She's gullible."

There's a silence. "Just get it done. Buy me an hour or two."

I hang up and cue up a number that will answer my questions but not stir the pot for my family.

"Simon. It's Brice. It's been a long time. How's the family?"

"Brice, you don't have to bother with the niceties. If a prince calls my line, I drop what I'm doing." Simon is the son of James. James, the son of Louis. And for many generations the Linfield family is the first call my family makes when they need something done off the record. From what I understand there have been dozens of issues over the years the Linfields had solved for us. None happened without my father knowing.

"What can I do for you?" His voice was gritty but patient, likely out of duty.

"I need to know more about a company. It's operating in the building I'm renting a floor on in Boston."

"Do you think it's a security threat?"

Shit. I recognize the concerned tone and quickly dismiss it. "Nothing like that. Likely harmless. I did a little recon on my own, and as far as I can tell it's a shell company. What I don't know is what they're trying to hide."

"Hmm." Simon sounds intrigued. "And perhaps they're just there for intel on your family? Could be something nefarious. In the same building? It's close access to you. I'll send some extra men your way today."

"I have one guard here already, and that's one more than I need. These people are no threat to me. They've made no contact at all with me."

Simon lets out an unconvinced hum. "Then why are they on your radar?"

"It's complicated. I came across a woman who plans to deal with Jana Monroe Enterprise. The story she told doesn't sound right. I poked around a bit and found the shell company and the bogus website. That's why my antenna went up."

"What woman?"

"Unimportant."

"No detail is unimportant when it comes to possible security breaches. I'm sure your father would agree." Simon makes some kind of clicking noise with his tongue.

"My father is a busy man with more to worry about than some stranger I barely know and a company I don't plan to do business with. If I thought for a moment this had any serious implications for myself or the family, I would alert you to that. It's nothing more than my curiosity. We won't make this bigger than it needs to be."

"The woman. I'd at least like her name. I want to run her information too. You two *crossing paths* could be a setup. Maybe she's an actress. Associated with this Jana Monroe. Trying an angle to get close to you."

I chuckle at the idea that Savannah's playing me. She has no poker face. Is a complete mess. No one is that good of an actress. "Fine. You won't find anything scandalous or dangerous on her. If she wants to kill me she had her shot last night."

"What's that mean?"

I grunt out a dismissive laugh. "Her name is Savannah Barre. She's from Maine. I'm pretty sure this company has lured her here for some reason. She's their mark. I had some contact with her when we were stuck in the elevator and she didn't have anywhere to go because her purse was stolen. If this Jana Monroe company does mean her some kind of harm, I don't want our name getting mixed up with any of that. I'm calling so you can get me the intel and I can get out ahead of it."

"Good call. But I'd like to do more than just pass you the information."

"That's all I want to happen. Do you understand?"

"So you said, it's Jana Monroe Enterprises? I'm looking at the same thing. Definitely trying to shield their real intention. Their website encryption is quite sophisticated. Where it asks you to sign up for their monthly newsletter, it's actually looking for a password. Not sure how people get the password, but that must unlock more in the site." Simon pauses, and I wonder if he's going to crack this code right while we're on the line.

"I need this information pretty quickly."

"Is the girl with you?"

"No, she's with Charles."

"So you spotted Charles?" Simon chuckles. "I figured it wouldn't be too long before you realized your father wasn't letting you wander the streets of Boston on your own. You're all the talk here. The son who keeps defying his father but won't say why."

"I'm glad I can be of entertainment to you all."

"Are you really going to keep everyone in the dark? You've run off to Boston and buried yourself in some work that doesn't seem to need to be done at all. Your family has everything it needs."

"Have you found anything yet?"

He clears his throat, realizing he's put a toe over the line and better step back quick. "I'm going into the dark web now. If there is some kind of gatekeeper, there's a chance the only way to access it is there."

I let him stew for a long moment in his concern about insulting me. I could let him off the hook, but I'm hoping it might be enough to get him to keep his mouth shut about this entire exchange.

"I'm not seeing much on the dark web. Some chatter amongst some men. Asking questions about what the company really is. If it's an escort agency and how they can get in touch."

"Escorts?"

"No one seems to answer affirmatively. One man said he found a business card from Jana Monroe at his date's house one night, but he didn't pay her for anything. He also said there was no phone number on it either. Which he thought was weird. It gets a little slimy from there. A bunch of bros trying to impress each other."

"But there is no contact site? No way to get in touch with anyone there? That's impossible. How do you run a business of any kind without a digital presence?"

"Word of mouth? If it's elite or illegal, staying off of the web would certainly help the longevity of a company. Less liability of someone getting caught."

"There's nothing else?"

"I'll dig around a little more and let you know what I come up with. I'm sure there is something we can shake loose."

"She's supposed to be meeting with them this morning."

"You may need to stall her then." I can hear his cocky grin. "Maybe take her to breakfast."

The line disconnects, and I'm left wondering why this woman would be worth the drama I've just created. Then I think of her lips. Her delicate hands. Her innocent smile. There's no way in hell Jana Monroe and her weird secret company can stay private on my watch.

CHAPTER EIGHT

Savannah

THE HOTEL ROOM looks straight out of a fancy city-themed HBO show. The kind of bed the main character would flop into, arms wide, smile wider. The tiny soaps and fancy shampoo are little symbols of sophistication. Everyone knows tiny versions of things are always fancy. Except penises. I hear those go by the *bigger is better* standard.

I pocket every free sample thing from the bathroom and slather on a little extra-fancy lotion. I need a hell of a lot of man-made fragrance to get the fish smell out of my hair.

I'm getting swankier by the minute. I've rented a hotel room for the morning.

Who does that?

Apparently, I do. I didn't think I had time, but Charles assured me he could get me to my appointment with Jana. The idea of cleaning myself up was too big a temptation to deny.

A hot shower. Clean clothes I bought in the shop down-stairs. Although I originally thought Jana should see the Coppertop version of me, I decided a pair of slacks and a blouse might give my lagging confidence the boost it needs.

The flats I chose aren't flashy, but they're a step up from my tennis shoes. The smell of gas and fish is gone—she'll be grateful for that alone. I toss my coat into the lobby's trash can and feel bad that they'll probably spend the morning trying to figure out where that smell is coming from.

Charles is still waiting for me outside, and part of me is shocked. He's been obediently carting me around the city all morning. I have cash from the bank. A new phone. A new set of fresh clothes and now I'm ready for my meeting. He's probably counting the minutes until he can drop me there and never see me again.

"Are you hungry?" Charles asks as I settle into the front seat next to him. An action he still seems uncomfortable about. At least, for his sake, I smell better.

"I'm hungry, but I have to get to this meeting. Jana is expecting me in twenty minutes."

"Yes ma'am." Charles puts the car in gear and pulls away from the curb. I'm so close to turning this whole nightmare of a trip around.

Just as my heart flutters with excitement, there's a weird jolt in the car and then a pop that turns to a hiss. Smoke rises from the hood, and Charles quickly turns the car off.

"Better get out, ma'am. For your own safety."

I hop out of the car, but by the smell of it, I already know the issue. "It's coolant. You blew a radiator hose. You might be able to work it back on if it's not totally destroyed, but the car has to cool down first."

"I'll have it fixed in a jiffy," Charles promises as he takes off his coat and rolls up his sleeves.

"I've got to get to Jana's. I'll catch a cab." I crane my neck to see if any are heading that way.

"I'd feel better if I could drive you. This has happened before. It'll take just a minute to fix."

My mouth opens to protest, but Charles is already snapping the hood open, fumbling with the latch to keep it up. "This does stay up on its own, right?"

"Are you sure you know what you're doing?"

"Ouch." He jumps back from the splattering coolant. "Yes," he chokes out as he waves the smoke away. "Radiator hose."

"And the radiator is?" I lean in and wait for him to identify it. Instead he points to the battery.

"Charles, you'll need a mechanic. The hose slipped off. They can put it back on with an O clamp and then top off the coolant. It won't take long. Just make a call."

"Wait! This has happened before." He snaps his fingers as though he's just remembered something as he moves toward the glove box. "Is it this kind of clamp?"

"Yes," I say, checking my watch. Fifteen minutes to get to Jana's. I could call her and tell her the situation, but she already thinks I'm a flake. Getting connected with Jana was beyond challenging. Blowing my shot would crush all my plans. As Charles fiddles around with the hot hose, I know he'll be a mess if I leave. Probably burn himself.

"Stand back." I push him to the side and take the hose and clamp and his handkerchief from his pocket to use like a rag. I've worked on boats and small engines a lot of my life, and my lack of manicure makes it apparent. So much for smelling better. "Do you have any bottles of water?"

"Yes."

"Pour some water in, then put the cap back on tightly. The hose looks like it's in good shape, it just slipped off. Flat water . . . not sparkling."

"Yes, it's happened before. That's why I have those clamp things in the glove box."

"You need to get it properly serviced and tightened so it doesn't keep happening."

Charles shuffles to get the water from the back of the car and does as I've instructed. He's moving quickly, but it won't be quick enough for me to make my appointment on time. My hair is back to being a frizzy mess, and now I smell like antifreeze. Tears start to well in my eyes. How on earth does this stuff keep happening? I fix one thing and then something else falls to shit.

"Are you all right?" Charles asks as I close the hood and realize my cheeks are wet with tears.

"I'm going to be late now."

"I'm very sorry."

"I've blown my shot."

"Shot for what?" Charles looks at me paternally. "I'm sure whatever it is you'll work it out. This Jana woman must be understanding. Look at all you had to go through yesterday and today."

"She doesn't need to be understanding. And she won't be. I'm one of hundreds of women who want a chance at her services. Life-changing services. And now some other girl will probably take my slot."

"What kind of service is this?" His jolly looking face turns serious.

I sigh and wipe my cheeks dry. "It doesn't matter. Can you please just take me there, and I'll try to salvage this? Maybe she'll take pity on me. I'm certainly pitiful."

"Can't you find another company?"

"Not like Jana Monroe. Not for what I want to do."

He wipes his hands and stares at me curiously for a long moment. I'm not making sense. But I'm not going to sit here and tell him what I'm in the city to do. I haven't told a soul. I've signed a nondisclosure with Jana, stating I would keep her services and practices confidential. Now I'll never get the opportunity to figure out what was so special about her and what she does.

"Can we please just go?"

"Yes, ma'am." Without thinking he opens the front door and waits for me to get in. "I'll sit in the back this time," I say with a sniffle.

I call Jana's secretary, who informs me she is already in with another client. I ask if I could wait. She tells me she's booked for the rest of the day.

Can I reschedule?

She'll call me.

Is that the same as a no? I hate that I don't know.

Charles looks at me with genuine apology as he moves to open the back door for me.

When his phone rings I see his eyes dart to me in the rearview mirror before answering quietly. I'm sure it's Brice wondering why his driver is still out parading me around instead of back on the clock for him.

"Yes. I understand." Charles closes the petition window between the front and back seat and it swallows up his voice, leaving me in silence. In thought. What would I be doing right now if I were back in Maine? Freezing my ass off at work. Then sitting alone in my grandmother's house, missing her. Isn't failing here better than barely surviving up there?

The question lingers with me as the city, its shimmering skyscrapers and herds of people, blow by. A bad day in Boston is still better than my best days in Maine.

That's what I am telling myself anyway.

CHAPTER NINE

Brice

SAVANNAH LOOKS FIERCE, standing in my office door. Another interruption. Another break in my day. I'm angry with myself for arranging it. My eyes trace the curve of her breasts under the clean clothes she's put on. She's conservatively dressed, but I'm committing every inch of her to memory as if this were a much more intimate moment.

This is not me.

I've never been distracted by a woman. If I want her, I have her. No chase. No games. I fuck her until my name is the only word she can remember. Out of my system. Move on.

My intentions are always clear. But this? The way I'm picturing Savannah riding my cock as her perky tits bounce up and down but not planning to do anything about it? That's a problem.

I move to the front of my desk and sit back against it. She comes to stand in front of me with sad looking eyes and pouty lips. Fuck.

"I missed another meeting with Jana. Can you believe that? I won't be buying any lottery tickets any time soon. My luck has not turned."

Her eyes are rimmed red, and I remind myself it was for her own safety. She may be disappointed, but she's alive.

You're welcome.

"It's probably a good thing. You've put a lot of faith in a stranger who likely doesn't deserve it."

I'm late for a lunch meeting, but I don't stand and put my coat on. Nothing has been worse for my schedule than Savannah in my office. Yet I don't kick her out. I want to make sure she's safe. I'd really like her mouth wrapped around my cock. Neither will happen if she leaves.

"What's that mean?" She sucks in her lip and narrows her eyes at me. "My private life is not open for debate especially not when you walk around like you're some mysterious agent for the government. Is Charles your driver? Bodyguard? Who are you?"

I fold my arms across my chest. The truth wouldn't help either of us at this point. I snap back to the topic I brought her here to discuss. "What do you really know about this Jana Monroe? Nothing, correct? You have no idea what you might be getting mixed up in."

"Mixed up in? I don't know what you think is happening, but I know exactly what I'm doing."

"Forgive me if I don't believe that from someone who had their purse stolen within an hour of being in the city."

Low blow. But true.

"Every time I think maybe you're not a pompous know-it-all asshole, you find a way to remind me first impressions are usually right."

"Typical American."

"Excuse me?"

"In the age of the Internet, how do you remain naïve to how the world works?"

"Why do you say American like it's an insult? Where are you from that's so much better? And if it's so great why are you here and not there?"

Our conversation was derailing. "My apologies. You're correct; every country has merit of its own. I'm merely suggesting you proceed with caution when it pertains to someone you don't know personally." I shake my head and think of the little bit of information Simon provided. "Do you know what can happen to women who come into the city and meet strangers? Whatever she promised you will come at a cost. Nothing is free."

"You think I'm penniless, don't you? And an idiot?"

I open my mouth to argue, but she's at least partially correct. I don't think she's dumb, but I'd bet my sister's crown collection she's broke.

She props a hand up on her sexy hip. "There is a cost to Jana's services, and I'm happy to pay it. You have misjudged me, and that's the only typical thing about this situation. Everything else is weird as shit."

"What exactly are Jana's *services*? She has virtually no information on her website. The nature of her business is not anywhere on her lease or on any public documents I could find."

She takes a step back and gives me a long look. I've shown my hand. Something I never do. Another example of how Savannah is an earthquake to my plans.

"You checked into her?"

"I need to know who else is working in the building. Some shoddy secret organization hanging around is bad for my business. If the FBI bursts in we all look bad." I set my jaw and dare her to challenge my answer.

She doesn't.

Instead she eyes me as though she's onto me. "You don't have to worry about me. I've been taking care of myself for a long time."

I find it surprisingly hard to breathe for a moment. I want to sweep her out of there, across the street to my place. The ride up to my apartment. Throbbing with the anticipation. The previous tenant had a practical sex den setup. Would Savannah like the swing? Playful restraint? If what she said in the elevator was true, she has no idea what she likes. What makes her wet? What makes her blur the lines of pleasure and pain? I could spend days mapping out those points.

Down boy. This is about taking care of her, not taking her . . .

"Before I forget." She pulls my pen from her pocket and tosses it over to me.

My reflexes are quick. I snatch it out of the air and inspect it to make sure she hasn't done anything to it. "You stole my pen?"

She huffs at me. "Borrowed."

I crease my brow in disbelief. "You had some important letter to hand write and needed an expensive pen to do it?"

"No." Her chest puffs, pressing her breasts upward seductively. Does she know she's turning me on? "I was going to jab Chucky-boy in the eye if he was actually a creep instead of a hired driver. Turns out he's just a lovely guy who didn't need to be eye stabbed."

I choke back a laugh. "How lucky for him. Please tell me you called him Chucky-boy to his face."

"He seems to like the nicknames. I came up with quite a few."

"I'm sure."

"I'm going to Jana's office now. I'm late, and Jana has no reason to give me another chance, but I'm willing to wait until she does."

I haven't known her long, but I already recognize that nothing I say will change her mind. My phone rings. It's Simon with an update about Jana Monroe Enterprise.

I hold up a finger. Demanding with my eyes that she stays put. This could be the information that finally wakes her up.

"Speak. What do you have?"

"Nothing. I dug in deep to the dark web and there is nothing of concern with Jana Monroe Enterprise. No criminal history. No alerts to the Better Business Bureau. Whatever they do, it's not tripping any alarms anywhere. I'll put some other queries out, but as of now I have nothing concrete to raise concern. I'm trying to find out more about the woman herself."

"Not what I hoped to hear." I can see impatience growing in Savannah's eyes. She's itching to go, and I have nothing to change that. Well, nothing I'd feel right about unleashing on an innocent. "Keep me posted."

After ending the call, I rake my eyes over Savannah. Devouring every inch of her, I notice there's a fresh grease stain on her shirt and a slight unruliness to her hair. I think back to Charles and his short update.

She fixed the car. Why am I not surprised?

I can picture her leaning over the hood, brushing her hair out of her eyes with the back of her sexy little hand. She's this odd mix of fierce and fragile. Capable but delicate. Innocent yet daring.

She motions toward the open door behind her. "I'm sure this is goodbye. Thank you for all of your help."

"Be careful with this Monroe woman. I'd hate to hear you went missing."

"Because you'd have to come looking for me?" That same damn smile is back. She's getting a kick out of this.

I lean back, gripping the desk on either side of me. "You made quite the impression on Charles. He'd insist we do something."

"Right. Tell Chuckles I said thank you."

"You are one frustrating woman."

"Eat a Pop-Tart, Brice. Chill out a little bit. You're as stiff as your over-starched shirt."

The word *stiff* slips from her mouth and is far sexier than she probably intended.

She has no idea how stiff I am.

"Bye, Brice." She turns on her heel and sweeps her hair off her shoulder as she walks away. The sway of her ass in her slacks is hypnotic. Her hips were made for grabbing. Holding. Gripping tightly.

The scent she leaves behind is an odd mix of floral soap and some kind of car fluid. I walk out to the hallway in time to watch her enter the elevator. The same one she swore she'd never ride in again. She didn't let fear stop her.

What the hell is she doing in Boston?

And is her bravado about to get her into a situation she can't handle?

CHAPTER TEN

Savannah

"SO THAT'S WHY I'm late and smell like antifreeze." I can feel my chest growing tighter like a vice squeezing my ribs. Jana looks wholly unimpressed with my story. But what's not clear is if she believes me.

I sat for two hours in the office of her secretary, waiting for a chance to explain why I missed another appointment, so I had plenty of time to hone my summary as well as my apology. Did it work?

"You're an interesting woman." Jana leans across her glass-topped desk. It's intimidating in its New Age design. Much like her. It's the focal point of the room. It looks almost dangerous with its stark modern style and sharp edges. The entire office is in contrast to Brice's. His has warm leathers and inviting dark woods. This room looks sterile. New. Powerful in its own way. But not welcoming. I'd never be able to sleep on any of these chairs.

Jana's silky strawberry-blonde hair is in tight curls resting on her shoulders. They look obedient as if they wouldn't dare move out of place without her permission. Her dress is well-made gray wool with gold buttons down the front. A chunky gold necklace wraps around her neck, a matching bracelet on her wrist.

There is a flawlessness to her face. Not necessarily her features but what she's done to enhance them. Makeup applied with precision. Perfectly symmetrical eyeliner. A matte lipstick that matches her skin tone perfectly. If I were let loose in a makeup store with a blank check, I still couldn't come out with a decent palette for myself. Applying it is a whole other challenge. No one is ever around to show me these things. My grandmother was a simple woman who wore her very long gray hair in a bun. No makeup. No fuss. The money we had was never spent on frivolous things.

"I guess being an interesting woman is a good thing?" I edge out the words as if I'm creeping to my car on an icy day.

"You came to me in a unique way. I usually take referrals from former clients, and then I reach out to the person they suggest only if I think we'll be a good match. If I decide it's not a match, those people never know a thing about me or what I do. For you it was different. I didn't have a chance to research you at all. Someone gave you my number. I'm still not happy about that."

Although I know she's already aware of the details, I rush to say, "My grandmother was ill. I was caring for her. After she died, her nurse gave me your phone number and told me you were what I needed. I thought it was strange, but I was curious."

"People sign nondisclosures for a reason. Smoke and mirrors to keep my services elite. You made quite an impression on Holly. After hearing from you, I contacted her, and she was adamant I would not regret working with you. And you were"—she searches for the right word—"persistent."

"Once I knew the kind of services you offered, I knew Holly was right; I need this. I'm willing to do whatever it takes to change." I gesture down at my grease-stained clothes.

"It's not about changing little things about yourself," Jana cautions. She folds her perfectly manicured hands and lays them on her desk. "It's about changing the trajectory of your life. It's about owning up to what brought you to the place you are. This process is not a superficial altering of your appearance. It's a mindset. I'm not certain you understand what it entails."

"I'm willing to do whatever it takes to better my life." My voice is urgent, and I know I'm bordering on desperate. That doesn't seem like it would work for Jana. I force myself to chill.

"The story you just told me about last night and this morning is an example of what needs to change. The chaos. The serendipity of meeting some man. You're coming to me for a very specific reason. The choices you've made brought you to this place. Tell me, what do you think you're here for?"

"To lose my virginity," I grin. I know it's more than that, but my humor might be the way to her heart.

Nope.

She shakes her head and closes her eyes for a long beat. "Sex is easy for a woman. You could walk out to the street right now and find someone who would sleep with you. Your virginity is a small part of your metamorphosis. People whisper about what I do. It's more myth than anything. Let's live in reality. You are a twenty-three-year-old virgin. That's perfectly fine if that's what you want. A choice you've made because of some belief you hold. But let's not pretend it's because you haven't had any opportunity to have sex."

"You know I was caring for my grandmother." I fidget uneasily as she seems to look right into my soul.

"Savannah, I don't care how small your town is. I don't care what you were busy doing. There are men there. If you wanted it to happen it would have by now. I read through your entire questionnaire. All of your *very detailed* emails to me. The photos were particularly telling." She winces a bit. "You need to figure out what you really want. Then I can help you."

"I know what I don't want." A desperate wave sweeps at my feet again. "I've given so much of myself over the last five years. I've walked away from opportunities for fun and happiness. I've been on the edge of the diving board for years, my toes hanging over. I need you to shove me off the end."

"No. You need a new pool. A new diving board. You need to learn how to swim. I don't push. I guide. I provide opportunities. You decide what to do with them."

"I can do that."

"That being said, to be effective, there are rules you must adhere to. Trust is important between us. If you truly want to change, you must give yourself over to this process. The chaos and the man you met last night. The people from back home. You need to close the door on those things. I can only help you if you're done hiding."

"Hiding?" The words feel like an accusation. I'm not weak. I'm unwaveringly dependable. Always there when I'm needed. I don't hide.

"Circumstances may have made it difficult for you to take care of yourself and your needs, but it didn't make it impossible. You made choices to block your own joy. It's time to stop that. Situations like last night, the craziness of it all, will not get you where you need to be. Close the door on that. Random circumstances do not create positive outcomes. We will create positive outcomes."

"Last night was crazy, but it all worked out in the end. Brice might be a little full of himself, but he's not a bad guy. He was actually very helpful."

"How many men like that do you have in your life?"

"What do you mean?" I'm defensive again.

"The men who are a little bit of this and little bit of that but overall not bad guys. Men who are not right for you. How many men are like that in your life?"

I nearly tell her that Brice is different. I could fuck him. But I get her point.

I think of all the other men back home I've been friends with my whole life. The guys back at the bar. On the docks. It sums all of them up. "A lot of them I guess."

"And you've never slept with any of them. Never dated them?"

"No." I laugh nervously. "They don't see me like that. I

don't see them like that either. I'm one of the guys to them."

"You surround yourself with these men. Wall yourself in."

"I guess." I squirm a bit. I never saw them that way.

"It's possible to have a male friend, but these men are more than that to you. They're security blankets for you. They stop you from moving on to more intimate relationships. You won't be able to make a meaningful connection with any man if you continue to surround yourself with unsuitable ones."

"I see what you're saying."

"And your jobs," she says, putting a finger up to her chin thoughtfully. "Working on the docks. Working in a bar. Are there no other jobs where you are from?"

"I guess there are some."

"Yet you picked the ones that have you surrounded by men you aren't interested in and keep you smelling in a way that would keep any other prospects away. You could have worked at a school. An office building. These were choices. Again, working hard, even in a really dirty job isn't some disqualifier for finding a healthy experience with a man. I admire what you do. There are strong women who might have jobs that make them smell terrible, but they go home, clean up, and have healthy relationships. Do you follow me?"

"I do." My voice is small and sheepish.

"And being a caregiver. You gave up everything to care for a dying family member. It's honorable. It's courageous. I also know it's draining. Thankless. Easy to lose yourself in it. But people are caregivers and still manage to self-care. To preserve themselves and what they want."

"I didn't do that."

"I know."

"I lost myself in it."

"Savannah, you are wielding these things, these choices, like a sword. You cut down and swipe at any opportunity of finding what you deserve. I'm not a doctor, and I don't need to know what made you think you don't deserve better to recognize the pattern of what you've been doing. It's time to put those weapons down and redefine your life."

I hear her. I believe her. Straight talk is painful but important. It's why I'm here. But for some reason I feel the need to explain one thing. "I'm already changing a little. Brice is not like the men in Coppertop. He's not even my friend. Just a man who was nice enough to help me out. A gorgeous man—so there's that."

She doesn't look impressed. "Put him behind you. Part of this process is finding a certain kind of man for you to have your first experience. The ones you'll meet through me will be vetted. Clean background. Good intentions. Safe. Healthy. I'll find you that man. We'll get you to a place where you won't feel you need to hide any side of yourself. You'll find your passion on the inside first—with confidence. And things will begin to happen. Take a class. Apply for a job you think is out of your reach. You'll have a makeover, but going to the spa is just the beginning. I'll schedule appointments and assign tasks. If you follow my advice, you will look amazing. Feel amazing. And have incredible sex with a good man. Claim your space, your life, and start enjoying it."

How could I turn that down?

"I'm in," I say with a smile. "Thank you for giving me this chance."

"And of course, you tell no one about any of this."

"I understand."

"I hope you do. You'll receive the paperwork via a courier. Where are you staying?"

I tell her the address. "I rented the apartment for the month. I have my ID sorted out and access to my funds. No more chaos."

"Good. Get settled in your new place and expect to hear from me soon. Remember, no distractions. Not if you want this to work."

"No distractions." How hard can that be, considering I don't know anyone in the city? "I promise I'm committed to this process."

Jana stands, which I take as my cue that our meeting is over. She walks me to her office door. "Some people call me a life coach, but I see myself more as a fellow traveler on this walk through life. We only get one shot at this journey. You've kept your life very small, my friend. Claim your space. Breathe in the possibilities."

"I'm ready to."

"Settle into your place and explore the city. If the past comes knocking, don't answer. Old patterns will only get you back to the very place you're trying to escape."

CHAPTER ELEVEN

Brice

"FOLLOW HER," I bark into the phone, knowing I'm going to draw protest from Charles. Most people in his position would never question my orders. But it's why my father sent him. He would die for me, but he also doesn't hold back his opinion when he thinks I'm wrong. He's known me too long.

"I'm under direct orders to protect you."

"Charles, you spent time with Savannah. She's trusting to a dangerous fault. She just left a meeting with Jana Monroe. Who knows where she's sending her? People like Savannah go missing. I refuse to let that happen."

I disconnect the line without giving him a chance to argue. His duty might be to protect me, but Charles would never let an innocent come to harm.

I roll my neck. I'm tired. I'm distracted. My last meeting with Savannah should have been just that—the end of this craziness.

When my phone rings I'm hopeful it's one of my fellow tenants at Bachelor Tower. I've made the necessary connections, all I need to do is stay the course for one of them to pay off.

My mother's voice snaps me to attention. "Who is this woman you have Simon looking into?"

"Hello, Mother." She doesn't sound pleased with me, and I can understand why, but it's still nice to hear her voice. This is the longest I've been away from our country.

"Don't *hello Mother* me. Your father and I are losing patience with your American vacation. You're beginning to worry us."

My mother has a flair for the dramatic. I blame the American soap operas she's obsessed with. "There's nothing to worry about, Mother."

"I'll be the judge of that. Now tell me about this woman."

"She's someone I met in an elevator." That was true.

"Why is Simon working with a private detective regarding her? Who is Jana Monroe?"

The real question was why Simon hadn't kept that tidbit to himself, but I already knew why. His first loyalty would always be to the ruler of our country, and that wasn't me. It never would be. I was okay with my role in the family, but it was frustrating that it was working against me even while I was fighting for its future.

"Safety sometimes requires hyper vigilance. Both were in my building. I thought it was important to know more about them."

"Hyper vigilance," she parrots back as if weighing my claim. "Safety is important. You're far from home. When are you planning to return? Before the announcement of your brother's engagement, I hope."

"Of course." I'm still determined to make that announcement unnecessary.

"I miss you, Bricelion." Her voice breaks with emotion. "I can't sleep; the family is scattered."

I remind myself my trip here is for them. For the future of our family. For my brother. For our country.

"I'll be home soon enough."

"You never call." She sounds wounded, and it inflicts a blow.

I've avoiding speaking to my parents because I don't want to lie to them about what I'm doing. "I'll call more. I've been very busy."

"On what?" she scoffs. "What are you doing in Boston? Charles won't tell us anything, which I say means he's the wrong guard to have sent. Your father says it means the opposite."

For once I agree with my father.

Rare.

I should add this date to a calendar in case it never happens again. He and I could argue about the time the sun came up.

My decision to come to Boston came out of one of our last *talks*. In my country a royal marriage is a political decision. Economic stability was driving the union between Mathias and a princess who also deserved more of a voice in the decision. Arranged marriages are archaic and dangerous because they stop my family from reaching for more modern solutions.

The pillars of our culture need to be supported internally. The future economy is technology based, and I'm determined to bring Calvadria into the twenty-first century. I'm gambling my inheritance that sustainable wealth is better found in a boardroom than in a walk down an aisle with a stranger.

"I'm sorry you're worried." I clear my throat. "I'll call more."

"What's this building you're staying in? The Bachelor Tower? Is it some kind of brothel? I don't like what I've read about it."

The last thing I want to discuss with my mother is a brothel. "It's just a building for successful men who want to discuss business without the distraction of women." As soon as the words are out of my mouth I regret them.

"Oh, I thought you liked women."

I want out of this conversation, but I need to say something to appease her or she'll appear with half the Royal Guard and drag my ass home. "I do. I needed someplace where I could clear my head. Mathias is taking a big step soon, and I felt it was time I do as well. I'm enjoying learning the ins and outs of American business culture."

"You sound like you're growing up, Bricelion," she said, and I winced. As the wilder of her two sons, I'd earned that backhanded compliment.

"Have to go. Busy day. I have plans with my concubines at the brothel. Then a jog through the worst parts of town with my headphones to buy some pills from a guy so I can relax. You know, vacation stuff."

"My heart is too weak for these jokes."

"I doubt that. Although, you might not want to tell Father I said that."

"Trust me, I wasn't planning to. Oh, and call Mathias. He hasn't looked happy since you left."

Yes, I'm sure it's my absence rather than his life sentence of a marriage with a stranger. That couldn't possibly be bringing him down.

"I will."

"You would tell me if you were in Boston for a woman, wouldn't you?"

"Good night, Mother."

Given two possibilities, my mother found it easier to imagine I was in Boston to hook up with someone than believe my claim to be learning about the culture of American business. I was both relieved and a little insulted.

CHAPTER TWELVE

Savannah

M*Y APARTMENT.*

I take a moment to soak in the beauty of the building. I've already been inside and was pleasantly surprised it appears all I'll need to buy is a new wardrobe. Furnished, thankfully, this time means with everything.

Finally, my luck is turning around.

Someone else might dismiss its exterior as plain, but to me it looks perfectly solid and modern . . . just like the life I intend to build for myself.

My apartment. Everyone I know who left Coppertop, Maine always had an apartment of their own. Or a dorm. Or backpacked through Europe in hostels. I had a bedroom in my grandmother's house for most my life. Since my father died. Since no one else wanted me. That's all I had. Jana is right. The space I've chiseled out for myself is much too small. But now I have my apartment. It's a start.

I read a few articles about this side of town. Up and coming. Sophisticated. I couldn't believe the deal I got on the fourth-floor apartment. Furnished. Walking distance to amazing restaurants. Public transportation right around the corner. I'll be living this urban life. Meeting people who live and breathe the city.

"Hi." There's a woman next to me with a bobbed haircut and big sunglasses. She's watching me stare at the building. "Are you looking for someone?"

There's a baby on her hip and a toddler in the stroller she's pushing. She's rocking back and forth in that way mothers do.

"I just moved in."

"Oh nice. We live here too. How many do you have?"

"How many what?" I should probably be prepared to sound like an idiot for a while. This is probably some kind of city lingo I don't know.

"Kids?"

"Uh, none."

"None? I hope you like kids." She lets out a tired laugh then adjusts the heavy baby on her hip. The toddler throws his sippy cup across the pavement and squeals.

I retrieve it and smile as I hand it back. The second he has the cup back, he launches it again.

"I'll take the cup," the woman says, sounding defeated. "He thinks we like to play fetch. The more you give it back to him the farther he throws it."

"Why did you say I should like kids?" I ask, turning my head up curiously.

"This building. It's families. Most of us have young kids. It's what the building is known for."

"I didn't realize."

"It wasn't always like this." She rocks the stroller back

and forth as she sways the baby on her hip. "Then two really amazing schools opened and drew all of us in. Are you new to Boston?"

"Very."

"Here alone? Like single?"

"Yep."

"And you're renting a place here in the building? You poor girl. I hope you weren't planning on bringing a date back here. This building is six floors of birth control. Men get a whiff of sour milk and dirty diapers and they go running for the hills. And if you're smart don't get chatty with anyone's husband. That never works out well. But welcome."

When her child's shrieking hits a new octave, she finally hustles them into the building, leaving me on the curb looking up at the six floors of crushed dreams. My liberating bachelorette pad just turned into an unruly preschool.

Day one and I've already received my first threat, well-meaning as it probably was. I'm tempted to chase after her and tell her I don't need to dip into their stash of men—I've lined up my own. Vetted ones. Isn't that what Jana said?

I wasn't entirely sure what that meant, but hopefully it started with not married.

I take two steps toward the entrance of the building then freeze as one of the windows reflects an outline of someone sitting on a bench across the street. A man.

Is that?

No. It can't be.

"Charles?" I call as I spin quickly and jab a finger

through the air in his direction. "Are you following me?"

He looks down at his phone as if he didn't hear me, but I know he did. I start walking toward him.

He's on his feet, looking both ways as if about to dart across the street to escape me.

"Stop," I call out.

Surprisingly he does.

"Miss Savannah. Small world."

"Yeah, except it's not. Why are you here?"

"Here?"

"Did Brice have you follow me?"

"I can't say."

"Okay, then give me your phone." I put my palm out to him and stand there expectantly. Unwavering.

He plucks his phone from his pocket and pulls up Brice's number before handing it over.

"Charles, what did you find?"

"He found me." Okay, so I didn't exactly think through what to say to a rich man who seems to have asked his bodyguard to be mine.

"What have you done with Charles? Is this a ransom call? What are your demands for his safe return?" His joke is cute but I don't laugh.

"Why do you have Chucky Doll watching me?"

"Mostly because I assumed he was skilled enough to not be seen. Apparently I was wrong. He may have to dust off his résumé. I think he'd make a great clown for kids' parties. The shoes would fit."

"Is this all a joke to you? You're not funny."

"Have you been talking to my mother?"

"What?"

"Give Charles back his phone. I'll call him off."

"But why is he here in the first place?"

"I wanted to make sure you were staying somewhere safe."

"I told you I was."

"Our definitions of what is safe are not in tune." Without missing a beat, he asked, "How did your meeting go?"

I huff out my annoyance. "Better than expected. She's still willing to work with me." I stop there. I've already said too much, at least according to the very strict nondisclosure paperwork Jana already sent over.

She won't like anything I'm doing. My life makeover probably shouldn't involve whatever Brice and I are doing. What are we doing? I didn't expect to see him again. According to Jana, I'm supposed to close the door on him. To forget his dimple. His large hands. The bulge in his pants I traced with my eyes that first night on the elevator.

"I understand why you might be concerned for me. I didn't give you a great first impression. But everything is right back on track for me now. So, although I appreciate you watching out for me, it's not necessary."

I hand the phone back to Charles and tip my head up proudly. I march into the building but have to stop abruptly to hold open the door for a woman with a double-wide stroller and very pregnant belly.

She ruins my sassy exit.

I draw in a deep breath and put the thought of Brice out

of my mind. Sure, it's nice to think that someone in the city cares about me, but he and I are not meant to happen. He sees the old me. Any thoughts of him, any energy spent bantering back risks slowing me down from where I'm supposed to be.

But damn . . . those dimples.

I wave my key to the doorman as I walk past him.

"Still no bags?" he asks, looking me over nervously as though I don't belong.

"No."

"Where are the little ones?"

He looks behind me as though I'm a mother duck and my ducklings should be coming closely behind me in a row.

"No kids."

"No bags. No kids. Nice." He shrugs and seems to count himself lucky.

The lobby of the building is bustling with people coming and going. Mothers and children mostly. It isn't the crowd I hoped to rub elbows with, but they seem nice enough. What is an apartment but a place to rest your head?

"You need anything else tonight, miss?"

"No, I think I'll be all right. Where is a good place to eat dinner around here?"

The excitement of going out for a fancy meal in the city sweeps me up.

"Uh, they all like the"—he snaps his fingers as the tries to think about it—"the place with the play gym for the kids. Menu?" He reaches behind the counter and digs for the paper.

"No, thank you."

Brice would know a good place to eat. A quick call and he might even take me to dinner. Because he can't resist me?

Or because he sees me as some kind of charity case?

I sigh.

What is the chance that a man like him will be in his office thinking about a woman like me? He probably has a hot date with a model.

I google the apartment building across from his—Bachelor Tower. It is an uber elite, all-male building with a bar on the first floor that whole blogs are dedicated to describing escapades from.

Yeah, sounds like he's alone and wishing I'll call.

"You okay, ma'am?"

"I'm fine. Just thinking." I sigh. "Do you have a list of places that deliver?"

"Sure." He hands me a stack of menus.

I read them over as I walk toward the elevator. Mexican. I wonder if Brice likes Mexican or if he's too conservative for a little spice.

I hug the menus to my chest as the elevator door closes.

Someday soon I'll have a little heat in my life and it won't be from jalapenos.

I remember how good Brice's arm felt beneath my hand. It's too easy to use him in every fantasy I have of what I'll soon be doing. A woman and man enter. She gives me a look and places herself between me and her man.

I smile at her because I'm genuinely happy she has someone so good she doesn't want to share him. I look the guy over. He seems like a nice enough man. Good for her. She's glaring at me. I keep smiling. Don't worry, lady, before you know it you'll see me in the elevator with my own guy and you'll realize there are enough to go around.

I look at the menus.

Tonight, take out on my own.

Tomorrow—who knows?

CHAPTER THIRTEEN

Brice

"BEING CLANDESTINE IS literally a core function of your job," I snap. Charles calls with an apology but I know him too well. "You wanted her to see you."

"That would be insubordination," Charles counters as though that isn't exactly what this is.

"Yes, it would be."

"However, I am your Royal Guard. I would take a bullet for you, but hide in shrubbery and follow some woman you say you're not interested in? No, I don't believe that is a skill I have."

"You agreed it was important to make sure she was staying somewhere safe."

"I did that, and now we know she is. Her apartment building is in a nice location and is one I could imagine my own family living in."

"But?"

"But this feels like a game, and I don't like games."

That much has always been true about him. "You like her."

Charles clears his throat. "I have seen you with many

women over the years, Bricelion. You were young and they were willing, so I always looked the other way, but this woman is looking for more than you'd offer her."

I stand and pace my office while digesting his words. "I have no interest in dating this woman, Charles. If Mathias were here and he'd met her, he would have also wanted to ensure she was okay." Without giving him a chance to respond, I add, "Before you say I'm not my brother, I am well aware of that, but that doesn't mean I don't understand the concept of duty."

After a moment, Charles says, "You're not Mathias, but the country only needs one of him. I have a pretty good idea what we're doing in Boston, and I admire you for it. However, when it comes to this woman, I believe your judgement is clouded. You've helped her. She's in a good place. Perhaps it's time to end this and finish your work here."

It is strange to see Charles acting protective of someone besides me. It's a testament to the impression Savannah made on him. "I can't walk away until I hear from Simon again. He also has a bad feeling about this Monroe woman. If you know why I'm here, you know I'm close to my objective. I need to stay focused. This isn't a royal order, it's a personal request. Keep an eye on her tonight. I only want what you want for her . . . to make sure she's okay."

He makes a curt sound of agreement. I hang up the phone and grind my teeth. I need to eat. Sleep. Start over. I call down to the kitchen and order a meal along with an old Scotch that should clear my head. A man rolls a cart of food into my apartment and trips over my computer bag, sending crumbs flying over the dark wood floor. He hastens to clean it up.

The Pop-Tart.

Once alone I fill a glass of Scotch and walk over to my bag. The floor around my bag is clean, but I imagine how the interior is now caked with crumbs. Charles is right. Savannah Barre is nothing like the women I've chosen to be with over the years.

She's a tiny tornado of chaos. Messy.

Complicated.

Impossible to ignore.

And a virgin.

Irrelevant since I have no intention of seeing her again. Once I confirm she's not about to be sold into some kind of sex ring, I'll walk away.

I'm halfway through my meal when my phone rings. "What is it, Charles?"

"So I stayed."

"Yes."

"She went to the store."

"Okay."

"When we returned to her building there were several men outside. They seemed to be looking for her."

"A group of men?" I was instantly on my feet.

"Yes. All different ages. A tough looking crew."

"Where is she? Tell me you whisked her out of there."

"She appeared to know them."

"She said she doesn't know anyone in the city. Are they still there?"

"No, she invited them inside."

"You let that happen?" I growl the question in a tone that surprises even me.

"You did suggest that I remain less visible. If I intervened, there would be questions. Questions that might reveal who I am and then who you are. If you prefer—"

"I prefer you not let a group of men follow Savannah into her apartment. I shouldn't have to spell that out for you."

"What would you have me do, Your Highness?"

Tossing my title out is a response to me sounding like someone who requires it. I shake my head. I can circle back to that later. "I want to know who those men are to her."

"Then may I suggest you find out?"

"Me?"

"Unless you are asking me to set up a different type of surveillance on her. I can arrange for her phone calls to be routed to you or a listening device to be delivered to her apartment. Or you could ask her who they are."

He's being ridiculous. Or I am. It's too hard to tell these days. "I'll call her."

"Yes, sir."

"Stay put. If I don't like what I hear you're pulling her out of there."

"Your Highness, if you sense anything is amiss, I can easily handle and dispose of her visitors."

Now that's the Charles I know. "Let's hope that's not necessary."

I dial Savannah's number and listen as the phone goes to

voice mail. My heart thuds with adrenaline. Is this what Jana does? Sends groups of men over? I'm boiling with anger as my hands crumple into fists.

When she doesn't answer, I grab my keys and head out the door. This is none of my business. Not the serious business that brought me to Boston. This is tornado Savannah, tearing through my sanity.

On my drive to her apartment I consider a wide range of reasons why several men would be visiting Savannah, none of them I like. If I get there and any one of those men have laid a hand on her, there will be no safe haven for them. I've never utilized my political immunity, but I've also never felt such protective rage.

CHAPTER FOURTEEN

Savannah

IN THE LOBBY of my apartment building, I ask, "What are you guys doing here? Who's at the bar?"

My chest feels like a mug being slowly filled with warm cocoa. My nerves settle. My sweaty palms dry. A little bit of home just showed up on my doorstep. My guys.

"We closed the bar for the night. It won't kill everyone in town to have to drink their own booze for one night." Jimmy is wearing his best shirt with a pair of khaki pants. It's the outfit he wears to the bank to discuss his loan. And apparently the outfit he wears to the city. His hair is combed and set with gel. That's his church look. All this for me? I'm touched.

"Why would you close the bar?" My eyes are damp with tears. I've known him for most of my life. Jimmy and Murray were good friends with my father, which explains why they hired me at the bar even though I had zero experience.

For years, when I wasn't munching on grilled cheese by my grandmother's bed, I was eating a basket of chicken wings from the kitchen in the bar with these men. They are as close to family as I have left.

I still can't believe it: Jimmy, Lance, Jay, and Murray came to the city. Cleaned up. Grinning. Reminding me that, although I'm alone in Boston, I'm not alone in the world.

Jimmy reaches out a hand and pats my cheek. His rough fingers remind me of my father's. The result of a lifetime of labor. "You gave me this address before you left so I could send your last paycheck. When we talked last night something didn't sit right with me. That man who answered the phone, the way you sounded. I didn't like it. I told the guys, and we decided to take a little road trip."

"You didn't have to do that," I say with a relieved sigh. They're minimizing how much they had to do and give up to be here. Jimmy closed the bar for a day. In my lifetime, I've only seen him do it once, and that was when his wife died. He closed for a week that time. The others will miss money from the shifts they aren't working. This is big. "I shouldn't have called you. I didn't mean to worry you."

Murray holds up a round metal tin. Even in his late fifties, he intimidates people before they know him. Closer to seven than six feet and thick from head to toe, he could break up a bar fight by grabbing the offenders by the scruff of their necks and pulling them apart. He isn't in his Sunday best. The joke in Coppertop is that when he dies he wants to be buried in those jean overalls so he'll have them when he reaches the other side. What kind of heaven would it be without them? "We brought cookies from Mrs. Warren. She sends her love." His eyes sparkle as he hands them to me.

Murray's rounded center is a direct result of his belief

that Mrs. Warren's cookies can cure almost any ailment. Feeling sad? Chocolate chip. Hung over? Oatmeal. Unable to get pregnant? Macadamia. Don't ask why; some things require a leap of faith.

Mrs. Warren is a widow with a soft spot for a man who's handy with tools. We all know she and Murry are more than friends, but they still sneak around like teenagers. No one dares bring it up for fear of being cut off from what is arguably the best cookie connection on the East Coast.

I rip the top of the container off. White sugar cookies cut in the shape of shamrocks with green frosting. "For luck," was all Mrs. Warren wrote. I replace the cover and hug the container. As always, she sent exactly what I need.

It's only been a couple days but home feels so far away. I haven't let myself admit I miss any of it. Admitting that would be like suggesting I made the wrong choice to come. But the cookies cannot be denied. I'm a little homesick.

Jay crosses and then uncrosses his arms like he's not sure he belongs in this nice building. He's the youngest of the group and washes dishes at the bar. We went to school together though he was a couple grades ahead of me. He left Coppertop for a few years, but won't talk about where he went. A wool hat covers his mop of hair, and although he's self-conscious about the scar that cuts through his bottom lip to his chin, he wouldn't have trouble finding a date if he looked people in the eye. Like me, his life has become smaller and smaller. He works at the bar, the fishery, and odd jobs on his rare days off. Jimmy lets him stay in a back room of the bar. Murray told me Jimmy found him and brought him back to Coppertop.

I didn't ask why. We have an unspoken rule of not prying into each other's lives. Jay and I get along because I can
tell a filthy joke without blushing or cracking a smile. For
some reason Jay finds that hilarious. When no one else can, I
can make him laugh. If we work the same shift and I see his
ass dragging, I scour the Internet for a new joke then deliver
the material as if I've known it all along. The rest of the
night, I catch him glancing over and chuckling. I decide to
start sending dirty jokes to Murray to say to him, although I
don't know if it'll have the same effect. Wait, he could have
Mrs. Warren write them on a cookie. Now that might work.

Jay raises his eyes from the floor. "So who was the guy on
the phone?"

"If you have a boyfriend, we're not here to judge. We
just want him to know who will come for him if he fucks
up." Lance's chest puffs as he chimes in. He's my age and
about half the size of Murray, but that has never stopped
him from talking shit. He's Jimmy's nephew so he's never
had anyone question if he can live up to his own hype. We
all think he'll take over the bar from Jimmy one day. For
now he covers for his uncle and takes courses at the commu-
nity college. I'm surprised he came as well.

"No boyfriend. Just a friend." Calling Brice a friend is a
stretch that nears being a flat-out lie. For some reason, saying
Brice is just some stranger doesn't feel right. "I wish you'd
called before coming. I'm fine."

Jimmy sighs and tucks his hands into his pockets. "I
don't buy it. You call from some strange number that

belongs to a guy. Then you sound all weird on the phone. I didn't like it. What are you not telling us?"

I realize we have a growing audience so I usher them into the elevator. "Come see my apartment."

"Apartment?" Murray echoes. "That sounds like you plan on staying."

"It's a short-term lease," I assure them. As we ride to my floor I soak in their presence. Earthy colognes. The hint of cigar smoke. The scent of fish from Jay's threadbare coat.

A moment later, they're standing in the living room of my apartment looking out of place and at a loss for what to say. Murray whistles. "Nice place."

"You sure you can afford this?" Jimmy asks in a paternal tone that makes me want to hug him.

I nod. "My grandmother left me her insurance money. I'm using that first." I open the tin in my hand, take a cookie and bite into it. "With a little luck I'll be working soon."

Murray walks deeper into the room to peer down the hallway. "You live here alone?"

"Just me." I hold out the tin for Jay to take a treat. He does with a nod. "Did you guys eat?"

"No," Lance says, puffing up again like a rooster. "We wanted to get here as quick as we could. Make sure you're okay. Knock in some heads if we needed to."

I meet Jay's eyes and we both kindly hold our mirth in. Someday I might punch Lance just to see if he can actually take one. The image of him not handling it well pulls my lips into a smile I fight. Jay smiles and looks away.

"You look different," Lance says as he inspects me closely. "Why?"

I shrug. "New clothes?" Although my slacks and shirt are simple, I doubt any of them have ever seen me in anything but jeans.

"You buy them?" Jimmy asks and Murray frowns.

"None of our business, Jimmy," he says.

I grab his shoulder and squeeze. He sounds so much like I imagine my father would have that it's hard not to throw my arms around him and cry a little. "You're just going to have to trust that I know what I'm doing, Jimmy."

"What happened to your phone?" He's not sold yet. He'll get the truth out of me eventually so I just give in.

I drop my hand and look around. To buy myself some time, I place the tin of cookies on the end table beside the couch. When I turn around all four of the guys are looking at me. Waiting. "To be honest I screwed up yesterday. My purse was stolen. I couldn't get in touch with the woman I was trying to meet up with. It got really complicated. But today was different. I went to my meeting. Got to the bank. Moved into my apartment here. Everything is fine now."

Lance cocks his head thoughtfully. "You're really not telling us what all this is about? Why are you here in the first place?"

"She's moving on," Jay says in a low tone, looking me right in the eye for once. "She took care of her grandmother for all those years and then the lady dies. Do you think Savannah belongs in a bar in Coppertop?"

Jimmy frowned. "Are you okay, Savannah? I know it's been a rough time for you, but running away never solved anything."

Murray shook his head. "She needs this, Jimmy."

"I do," I say with relief. I need them to return to the place where we all accept each other's crazy without asking for explanations.

"Don't worry, Jimmy. In a few months, when the money runs out, she'll be back," Lance says.

My face warms. I wish they had more faith in me, but I haven't given them much reason to believe I'd want the life I'm stepping into. They don't know how important this is to me, so how could they understand that I won't fail because it's not an option for me?

"Shut the fuck up," Jay growls.

Lance glances at his uncle, but Jimmy doesn't step in. Murray doesn't either. If Lance isn't careful, Jay might be the first one to test if he's a crier.

Murray steps closer to me. "You can talk to us."

Can I? Okay, guys, here's the deal. I'm in Boston because I want to reinvent myself and part of becoming a confident, independent woman is shedding my virginity. I've hired someone to guide me not only into this new life, but also toward a man I won't regret fucking. Yeah, that would go over well. I boil the truth down to: "It's a woman thing."

"Oh," they say in unison and shuffle around. Want to clear a room of men like this? Ask them for a tampon. I don't play the female card often but I'm desperate.

Jimmy clears his throat nervously. "Something wrong with your lady parts? My friend's sister had some kind of lump in her stuff." He gestures at his chest. "And she's completely better now. There are good doctors in Boston."

"My lady parts are fine."

Just underutilized.

Forget about Jay, now not one of them will look me in the eye. Lance groans. "If you run short of money, I have some set aside. Not much, but it's yours if you need it."

Jimmy looks on in approval. "We're all only a phone call away."

"I'm not here to see a doctor." The lump in my throat makes it hard to swallow. Now they're worried I'm dying. "I'm fine. Really, I appreciate you all coming this far just to check on me. Closing the bar for the night. It means so much to me. But there is nothing to worry about."

Lance reaches for a cookie. Murray smacks his hand. "Those are for her."

"I'm starving," Lance whines, and Jay meets my gaze again. It's hard not to mock Lance, but we respect Jimmy too much to ever do it.

"You'll live," Murray says.

Lance pats Murray's rounded stomach. "You say that because you've got padding to go through."

Murray grabs his hand.

Lance winces.

Jimmy chuckles.

I smile. These are my guys, and although they're all showered, being in Boston hasn't changed them a bit. "I don't have any food in the house yet, but we could go somewhere to eat."

Jimmy waves me off, as the other guys get excited about

the plan. "You look tired. We can bring something back here."

"I ate, but I don't mind going with you." I am tired. It's been a long, emotional day. I yawn and rub my eyes. Still, they've come all this way to see me. I can't not show them around. "Are there any sites you want to see?"

"We're here to see you," Jimmy says with a shrug.

Which begs the question. "Do you want to stay over tonight? I only have a pullout couch, but I can get some blankets and pillows."

The guys exchange a look.

Lance says, "It was a long ride down to just turn around and head home without seeing anything."

Murray shakes his head. "The trip wasn't supposed to be fun."

"Savannah looks done in," Jimmy says. "If we head back now, we'll make it back by midnight. The last thing Savannah wants in her nice apartment is four uninvited guests."

Done in? Thanks, and here I thought I was already looking better. Guess I still have a bit to go. "First, you guys never require an invitation." I yawn again. "I am tired, but I'd love the company. Go out. Have fun. I'll set up the living room for you to crash in. We can all have breakfast together tomorrow morning before you head back."

Murray nods. "I haven't been to Boston in years. It'd be nice to walk around. Check out if some of my old haunts are still open."

Lance is smiling. Jay isn't, and I wonder if he's ever been in the city.

Jimmy says his favorite bar is on the other side of town.

I'm almost tempted to say I'll go with them. Almost.

I walk them back to the door. Jimmy pulls me in for a hug. "I'm glad you're okay, kid. I was worried. Hang in there. We'll be back tonight, and we can talk more in the morning."

As they make their way to the door, the intercom buzzes.

"Expecting someone?" Murray asks, and I blush even though I'm not.

Jimmy's eyes narrow.

"Miss Savannah," the doorman calls through the speaker.

"Yes?" I say, pressing the button on the intercom.

"You have another guest. Should I send him up?"

"Another guest?" I look around at the guys. "Is someone else from Coppertop here?"

They each shrug in turn.

"Who is it?" I ask the doorman. All the people I know who'd be willing to jump in their car and come to the city already have.

"A Mr. Hastings."

"Brice?"

Lance leans in and presses the button. "Send him up. We'd love to meet him." I push his hand away, but the doorman already agreed to.

"Anything you want to tell us about this friend of yours?" Jimmy asks in a way that makes me feel about five years old and guilty as hell.

"He's not my—he's a guy who helped me yesterday. I used his phone."

"Which is he? A friend or a guy you met yesterday?" Jimmy pins me down with a look.

I'm nervous sweaty. This is ridiculous. Murray steps next to the door like he's working as a bouncer at the bar. I go with him, ready to intervene. "Both? He met me after I lost my purse and while I was figuring out what to do. He let me crash in his office until the bank opened then lent me his driver this morning so I could get there."

"So you invited him over to thank him?"

"No," I say, my temper rising. "No, I didn't invite him over, and I'm grateful to him but not that grateful."

Jimmy nods to Jay who moves to the other side of the door. Lance comes to stand beside me. In a brawl, I'd probably be saving his ass, but it's sweet that he thinks he can protect me. Still, this is getting out of hand. "We'll just stick around to make sure that point is clear to him."

Jana's lecture comes back to me. I've hidden behind these men for too long. They're protecting me, but they're also holding me back. With my hand on the doorknob, I turn back and issue a blanket order. "Be nice to him. He's been nothing but good to me."

Jimmy's expression darkens. "Kid, don't confuse having money with being trustworthy. Creeps come in all income brackets."

"He's not a creep."

Murray raises and lowers his shoulders. "You've known him one day, Savannah."

I look across at Jay. His eyes are glued to the floor again, but his arms are flexed like he's ready to punch someone.

There's a knock on the door. "Savannah." Brice's voice is crisp. "Open the door."

"Let him in." Jimmy nods toward the door.

Before I do, I say, "Everyone take a deep breath. You guys need to trust my judgement." Jana's words echo in my head. The past will stand in my way. *Only if I let it*, I vow. "Just chill out."

"Savannah, are you okay?" Brice's tone is urgent.

Drawing a deep breath, I swing the door open and Brice, with his wide shoulders and dark eyes, stares down at me. My breath catches at the sight of him. It hasn't been a full day since I've seen him yet I feel a pull toward him as though it's been ages. As though I had time to miss him. Yearn for him.

His muscles flex under his button-down shirt. Heat charges through my body. His cologne climbs toward me, and my nipples tingle in response. My mind may not know how I feel about him showing up here but my body certainly does.

When his eyes rove over my body, his face settles from concern to relief, and it's cute to watch. I don't know what he thought was happening here but clearly seeing me safe puts his mind at ease. It's short-lived, dying away when he gets a glimpse of the guys behind me.

"Who are these men?" Brice asks in a rough voice, sizing each of them up. I'm impressed that he doesn't even blink at mammoth Murray. "Does this have to do with Jana Monroe? Did she send them here?"

I roll my eyes. This is actually getting comical. Send

them? Everything about this scene is the polar opposite of what Jana says I need in my life. Brice also falls right into the category of what I'm supposed to avoid. Still, he's here. He's gorgeous. I'm not throwing him out. The day is already a wash. "These are my friends from Maine. They were worried about me so they got in the car to come make sure I'm all right."

He narrows his sexy eyes and looks them over again. His nostrils flare, and I wonder if Jay's coat reminds him of how I smelled when we first met. "Friends from Maine?"

"I have friends. Don't look so surprised."

Jimmy folds his arms across his chest. "Savannah told us you helped her out last night. That was real nice of you."

Brice mirrors his stance. "Jimmy, I presume. Or Murray?"

"Jimmy. Murray is on your left."

Brice nods a greeting then turns back to face Jimmy. "Where are you all staying?"

"Right here," Lance interjects.

Brice's head snaps back, and he looks like he's about to say something that'll get his ass kicked. I say, "I invited them to stay over."

Lance steps forward. Blustering like a peacock. "See, we were invited. What are you doing here?"

Brice tenses. His phone beeps with a message that he responds to before pocketing his phone again. "I told Charles you're fine. He was also concerned."

"Who's Charles?" Murray asks.

"His driver." I sigh. "Your twin in a suit."

Murray smiles. He likes that idea. "You should invite him up."

Lance smirks. "I don't care how big the guy is, Murray could still kick his ass."

"No. No. No." I wave a finger at each of them. "No ass kicking in my new place. I'll lose my deposit if blood gets on the carpet." I meant it as a joke, but none of them laugh.

Brice takes another step into the apartment. He looks around as he does. "This building appears suitable for you to stay in."

Had I asked his permission? "I told you there was no reason for you to worry about me."

"Yeah, so it's time for you to go," Lance challenges.

Brice simply stares him down. Lance blinks first and looks to Jimmy.

It's a testosterone powder keg.

That's it. I'm not watching this thing blow. "Brice, these guys are my oldest friends. They're here because they care. Guys, I would have been on the street last night if Brice hadn't helped me out. Stop it. All of you."

Silence overtakes the room as they shift around uneasily. Jay leans in. "I've been to prison, and I have no fear of going back in."

This is when Jay chooses to open up and share where he was when he left Coppertop?

Brice's eyebrows arch, but he doesn't look afraid. "Good to know."

"Didn't you say you were hungry, Lance?" I ask cheerfully.

"I'm starving," Lance responds as he continues to glare at Brice. "But I can wait."

Murray steps away from the door. "I'm going to punch someone just because I'm hangry. My blood sugar is dropping down to my socks. Come on, Jimmy."

I let out a breath of relief. "I'll set up the living room while you're out. Just behave yourselves."

Brice steps closer to my side.

Lance gestures with his chin toward Brice. "We're not leaving him here, are we?"

Brice smiles. It's cocky, entitled, and I should hate it, but I don't.

"Good night, Brice," I say, planting a hand on his chest and pushing him gently back. "I had a terrible night's sleep in a chair last night and a long day being followed around. I'm going to bed." His eyes flicker with something. Desire? It licks through me too, but I don't give in to it.

He takes a long look at me, his eyes tracing down my body. Oh, hell, I'm ready to announce he can stay.

"You heard her," Jimmy says, waving them all toward the door. "We're heading out—all of us." My friends make their way into the hall with rumblings of unease.

Brice doesn't budge. "They're not staying the night at your place."

Seriously? Who died and made him king of the world? "They're my friends and where they sleep is my decision."

"Not going to happen."

Okay, bossy is not always sexy. "Goodbye."

"It's not safe."

"It is, but even if it wasn't, it's still none of your business."

He does not look happy about that. *Too bad.* "Good night, Brice."

We stand there glaring at each other, and for just a second I feel like I've stepped into a scene that ends with steamy sex. There's a sizzle in the air and I feel delicious warmth spreading through me.

Oh, yeah, this is where the hero sweeps his woman up in his arms, kicks the door shut, and ravishes her.

Or in my life, he nods once and turns to leave with her friends.

Damn.

As the men exit my house they take all that testosterone and manly smells and loud banter with them. I close the door and it's quiet. Just me in the space I'm trying to create and the silence that comes with it.

I'm a hot mess—excited by a man I shouldn't be and ready to cry because the life I walked away from just walked away from me.

Jana said to close the door on my past. To shut out the chaos and the things I've been insulating myself with. What she didn't say was how badly I might miss it all. I can't imagine walking away from that. But I also can't imagine going home to Coppertop and stepping back into my old life. I always thought when I finally got out, I'd never look back. But it's not that easy. Not now that my new apartment smells like my old friends.

CHAPTER FIFTEEN

Brice

DOWN IN THE lobby, I'm sizing them up again. Two of them are older . . . late fifties, early sixties. The other two are much younger but just as rough around the edges. These are Savannah's friends?

Depending on where they are from in Maine, it is at least a four-hour drive. That they drove all that way implies they care about her. Dressed as she was when I first met her she would blend right in with them.

I question the motives of the two younger men. One is quick with the threats but doesn't look like he's been in a fight in his life. I should know, my nose is still crooked from a punch I took a few years back when some drunk sucker punched one of my Royal Guards. Hey, they put their lives on the line every day for my family. I'm not about to let one of my men get a beating simply because he was told not to engage unless I'm in danger. So I stepped in, took that punch, and released him from any need to go easy on the man.

Mathias doesn't understand my popularity with the Royal Guard, but it stems from their knowledge that I would just as soon take a bullet for them as they would for me. Like mine, their lives are often considered nothing more than an insurance policy. Expendables have to watch out for each other.

Savannah's friend with the scar looks up from the floor, and I don't doubt his prison claim for a minute. He's damaged, and it goes a lot deeper than his scar. I don't know what he did to get himself in the first time, but he's a man who feels he has little to lose. Those can be the most dangerous.

"How did you know we were here?" he asks.

I could deny knowing they were, but I have a feeling he'd know. Even though he spends most of his time looking at the floor, my guess is he doesn't miss much. "I asked my driver to hang around to make sure she settled in okay tonight."

"So you have someone following her?" Jimmy accuses.

The lobby is mostly deserted. Just us and an uneasy doorman. "Ensuring she's safe."

"Lighten up, Jimmy. I like this guy." Murray gives my back a pat that almost sends me forward onto my face. "Brice, Savannah means a lot to us. Lance here has had a crush on her since grade school . . . and Jay. Well, she's the only one who knows how to make him smile."

I don't know how I feel about either announcement. I can't see Savannah with man-child Lance, and my comfort with her being around someone like Jay is still up for debate.

I text Charles to bring a limo around and text me when he's in the area.

Jimmy flexes his shoulders. "Don't know about the rest of you, but I could use a drink."

It would be easy enough to part ways with them here. As soon as they're out of my sight, though, I'd lose control of the situation. Keep your friends close, your enemies closer, and random men you're unsure of at least where you can see them.

Besides, nothing gets a person to open up and divulge their secrets better than a few drinks. Jimmy suggests I join them for a drink, and I look the man over with growing respect. He's no fool; he's not letting me out of his sight, either.

A message from Charles announces he is only a moment or two away. Fast, but not surprising. Money opens doors and makes the seemingly impossible almost tediously routine. I would have been shocked if he'd told me he couldn't fulfill my request.

I rub a hand across my chin thoughtfully as though I'm mulling over Jimmy's invitation. "My driver is on his way to pick me up. It'd be my pleasure to show you some of Boston."

"Get a load of this guy," Lance says with sarcasm. "He thinks all he has to do is throw his money around, and we'll be impressed."

Jimmy gives me a hard stare. "Money don't make a man."

Murray throws his opinion into the mix. "Nor does it mean we can't share a drink with him. I'm in."

"Me too," Jay says quietly.

"I suggest we start with a restaurant."

"Nothing fancy," Jimmy warns. "We don't do fancy."

I could have said I'd already discerned that from Murray's jean overalls, but I simply nod and say, "So tell me, does your palate lean more toward hamburgers or Wagyu rib eye?" When they don't appear to know what the second is, I add, "Steak so tender it literally melts in one's mouth."

"Steak sounds good," Murray says with confidence.

"Steak," Jay concurs.

Jimmy nods and Lance folds with, "I'm starving, so I don't care."

We walk out of the lobby onto the sidewalk. I text Charles about where we are but also where I want to take the men to eat. Not all the connections I've made in Boston are related to business. Tom Ray, the owner of my favorite steakhouse, understands that the menu is important, but discretion is what keeps his highest paying clientele returning.

I expect to be escorted through a side door, away from prying eyes. I expect impeccable service in a separate section of the restaurant that allows business to be conducted while overlooking the tables below. Incognito as I am, doors don't automatically open for me. Tom Ray is a connection I cultivated. Our goals are similar, to impress the fuck out of the movers and shakers in Boston. To do that, privilege and access must appear seamless. By bringing potential business partners to his restaurant, I showcase how well one of influence might be treated here. It lends me an air of importance and his restaurant a growing patronage willing to pay to be treated . . . well, as royalty.

I could have chosen a less flashy venue, but I want to bring this mutual interrogation onto my turf. Charles pulls up with a stretch SUV limo. He's out of the vehicle and holding a door open for us a moment later.

The men hesitate.

I question if my plan was a miscalculation. My intention is to maintain my advantage, not to make them feel uncomfortable. Boston is full of less expensive places to eat that might have put them more at ease.

Murray walks over to Charles. They're similar in stature and build. "So," Murray says, "that's how I'd look in a suit." He puts out his hand. "Murray. Savannah said you helped her out this morning. Any friend of Savannah is a friend of mine."

Charles removes his dark glasses then shakes Murray's hand. "That's a point we agree on. Charles."

"How long have you been a driver?" Murray asks.

He and Charles fall into a conversation, one so entertaining that Charles forgets one of his duties is to close the door after the rest of us have climbed in.

Jimmy calls out, "Murray, you getting in?"

"Nah," Murray answers. "I'll ride up front with Charles."

I close the door myself.

"A limo," Lance says, looking around the slick leather interior and opening up every small compartment within his reach. "What do you do?"

"I'm an investor."

"That's pretty vague," Jimmy says, unimpressed. "What

kinds of things do you invest in?"

There was no reason to not share some of what I was doing. "Technology companies. It's the way of the future."

Jimmy nodded. "Lance wants me to do everything on the computer now. Our accounting. Taxes. Purchases. In my day deals were made with a handshake over a beer. What happens if this whole Internet thing crashes? What will people do then?"

"I'm pretty sure the Internet is here to stay," Lance chimes in.

"People," Jimmy stresses. "Loyal customers. That's how you grow a business. Not with ads to lure strangers in."

Lance shakes his head. "You think small, Jimmy. You could have a chain of bars—coast to coast."

"Why? If you ask me . . . more money, more trouble. I like my life just the way it is."

I have to admit, Jimmy is growing on me.

Jay pulls at the neck of his T-shirt. "This place we're going to . . . are we dressed for it? I didn't bring any nice clothes."

"The owner is a friend of mine. Jimmy, you'll like Tom Ray. He says he'd rather do one restaurant right than a hundred half-assed."

As the limo pulls up to the curb, both Charles and Murray open the back doors.

"May I assist any of you out?" Murray jokes. He reaches for Jimmy's arm as if assisting an elderly person.

"Keep your damn hands to yourself," Jimmy snaps.

Lance teases, "The old are so sensitive."

I smile and exchange a look with Jay. There is laughter in his eyes. Savannah isn't the only one who can amuse him, he just keeps his sense of humor locked away from the others.

"This way please." A man with a thick French accent waves from an open door on the side of the building.

Charles and Murray are still talking. I hang back for a moment and ask, "Would you like to join us, Charles?"

He shakes his head.

Murray cocks his head in question. "What do you do while you wait? Now that I've seen the place I'm not so sure it's my scene."

Charles nods toward a place across the street. "There is a pizza place across the street. I believe they serve beer."

"Sounds perfect," Murray says, clapping a hand on his back. "Jimmy, I'll be next door."

Rather than argue the point, I trot over to my remaining guests. "Looks like we'll be four, Julienne."

"Yes, sir."

As we enter the restaurant, Jimmy, who's been mostly quiet, looks around like his head is on a swivel. "This place has more shiny shit than the fancy bank in our nearest town. Hot damn."

We're ushered up a staircase to a room that overlooks the main part of the dining room. There's a fireplace and some dim lighting. The bottom half of the wall is a specially designed frosted glass. We can see without being seen.

"Interesting place," Jimmy says as he takes a seat. "You a member of the mafia or something?"

Jay sits across the table from him. "If he is, he's not allowed to say."

"In the movies, they tell everyone," Jimmy insists.

Lance takes a seat next to Jimmy. "That's movie crap, Jimmy."

I sit and the waiter appears beside me. "What shall we start with? Drinks?"

They all order beers, so I do as well. None use the glass that is delivered along with the bottles so I don't either.

I considered getting them tipsy before jumping into my line of questioning, but I realize as they chug their beers they aren't lightweights. That plan could take a while. I don't have that kind of time.

"Why is Savannah in Boston?" I cock a brow and take a long drag off my beer.

Jimmy grunts. "I hoped you would know. We have no clue. She wouldn't say."

Lance takes a mouthful of the expensive cheese off the charcuterie board that suddenly appears. "At least it's nothing medical." When Jimmy gives him a dark look, he adds, "Not because I'm thinking about what you all thought was wrong."

Jay rolls his eyes.

I don't bother to ask. I'm sure I don't want to know. "She's been meeting with a woman named Jana Monroe. Has Savannah ever spoken about her?"

"Nope." Jimmy downs the rest of his beer and looks around. "Where are the menus?"

"No need for them," I assure him. "The best of whatever is in the kitchen tonight is the only thing they'll serve this table."

Lance waves his fingers in the air and mimics me. I don't react. He doesn't matter. I want answers. "Savannah seems to think this woman will help her get settled into the city. She's relying heavily on someone none of you know. Doesn't that strike you as odd?"

Food begins to arrive on little plates. Jimmy studies the thinly sliced meat layered on a cracker. "The portions here sure are small."

"They'll bring as many as you request."

Jimmy raises his hand and calls the waiter over. "You seem like an intelligent young man," he says.

The waiter looks to me for direction. I motion for him to defer to Jimmy's instructions.

Jimmy continues, "Look around this table. These are men who work hard and eat real portions. Now unless you want to make a hundred trips back to the kitchen, you might want to keep that in mind as you fill these plates."

"Yes, sir," the waiter says as if it's a perfectly appropriate request. Lance looks embarrassed by his uncle. He shouldn't be. Jimmy is by far not the most demanding person I've brought to Tom Ray's and his request made more sense than any of theirs.

Jimmy bites into his small appetizer then smiles. "Small, but dang, that's good."

"I'll tell the owner you approve," I add.

After a pause, Jimmy says, "I don't know who this Monroe woman is, and yes, I don't like it. One day we're at Savannah's grandmother's funeral. The next she's telling me

I need to find someone at the bar to cover her shifts. I thought she wanted some time off to mourn. Then she up and leaves for Boston."

"So she was close to her grandmother."

Jimmy nods. "She raised Savannah. Her mother died in childbirth. Her father moved back home with Savannah. Then he died too. He was a good friend of mine." He pauses, and his eyes dart away. "That little girl has not had it easy. Her grandmother was a good woman when she was younger, but you know how age can change a person. She wasn't all there. She gave Savannah a place to live, but no guidance. Savannah was always underfoot in town. Then, I don't know, maybe seven years ago her grandmother started to decline. Dementia. Her leg was amputated because of diabetes. It was bad. Savannah had to grow up quick and take care of her. I gave her a job at sixteen at the bar, busing tables. I thought I was doing her a favor, on account of knowing her dad and all. I'm the one who made out good. Never had anyone work as hard as she did."

More plates of appetizers arrived, this time overflowing.

I charge forward with my line of questioning. "What happened to her father?"

"Killed in prison," Lance announces, his eyes wide at the arrival of more food. He doesn't notice everyone giving him the evil eye for divulging too much.

My attention swings to Jay. Two prison stories. Were they somehow related?

Without raising his eyes from his plate, Jay mumbles, "He was a good man. He didn't deserve what happened to him."

I had to ask. "What didn't he deserve?"

Lance shrugged. "Sure, he killed someone, but Murray says it was self-defense. Some out-of-towner started trouble. They say he wasn't the first to throw a punch, but he was the last. The other guy went down and didn't get back up."

Jimmy made a disgusted sound. "We get people who come to town now and then who try to bring in drugs. Niles was determined to keep that element out. I spoke to Niles earlier that day. I told him to let the police handle it, but Niles lost it when he heard the guy was hanging around the school. He didn't mean to kill him."

"Sounds like self-defense. That doesn't make sense."

Lance sat back after clearing his plate. "It does once you know the guy he killed was a cousin of the chief of police back then. Niles didn't stand a chance."

Jimmy's face tightens. "Niles was a good man. All he wanted was to get out and get back to Savannah."

Jay raises his eyes to mine. "Prison is a dangerous place—especially if a person has any good left in them."

I don't expect to be moved by what I learn from these men, but I am. The picture they present is one I wish I had some ability to alter.

Jimmy added, "Niles was a big guy. Like Murray. Some people get a kick out of taking on a man like that just to see if they can. Or to prove something to the others. He died in a prison fight. We don't know what happened, but his death shook the whole town. We booted the police chief and did some housecleaning that was long overdue. Too little too late, though."

"Does Savannah have any other family?"

Jimmy clears his throat to shut Lance up, but it doesn't work.

"None that want her." When Jay shoots a glare at Lance, he puts his hands up in mock surrender. "Sorry, but it's true. I heard her grandmother tell her that more than once."

Real nice.

"We don't talk ill of the dead," Jimmy scolds. He makes the sign of the cross and mutters some kind of apology.

Lance rolls his eyes. "Jimmy believes in ghosts. Do you think Old Lady Barre followed us to Boston and is listening right now? Ooooh, I'm scared."

Jimmy's eyes narrow. "I'll give you something to be afraid of."

Jay coughs, and I catch him hiding another smile.

I sit back and mull over what I learned. For a good number of people, the more I learn about them the less I like them. Savannah is the opposite. Some people would be crushed by the situations her friends described. Not her.

I know what it's like to feel trapped by circumstance. No one asks a prince what he wants to do when he grows up. I'm not allowed the luxury of choice.

It doesn't sound as if Savannah was born with much of a choice either. How trapped she must feel. How alone.

She said she isn't poor, which meant either her grandmother left her money or she saved some for herself. Either way, she has enough to buy a ticket out of her old life. But what is her plan, and what role does Jana Monroe play in it?

The steak arrives with another round of beer. The mood of the group changes as soon as the men take their first taste.

"Holy shit," Jimmy says, cutting a second piece and stuffing it into his mouth as if his taste buds required proof of more before believing what they register. "What did you call this? Ragu?"

I smile. "Wagyu. Japanese beef."

"No shit. Next road trip we take is to Japan." Lance grins as he also goes back for a second bite. Before anyone corrects him, he waves a hand. "You know what I mean. God, this is good."

Only then I realize Jay hasn't eaten anything yet. He's not drinking either. I put my own bottle down. Maintaining an advantage in such a situation requires remaining the most clear-headed. I should have paid more attention.

I reference his untouched plate. "You don't like steak?"

He gives me a long, measured look. "Why are you doing all this?"

"I thought this was an experience you might enjoy."

His head shake is nearly imperceptible. "No one does something for nothing. They always want something."

Smart kid. "You're right. This is about appeasing my curiosity. I wanted answers."

The waiter clears Jimmy's plate.

"You paying for all this, Brice?" Jimmy asks.

"Happily," I answer.

"I'll have another then. This time medium. The first one was good, but it was still mooing. Hell, pack up a few to go. Murray will want to taste this. He'll eat two if Charles doesn't want his. We should take one back to Savannah too."

All the waiter required from me was one nod, and he was off to fulfill Jimmy's expensive request. I meet Jimmy's gaze and see that he's not oblivious. Getting those answers was going to cost me.

I send a text with instructions to Charles. Round two of the steak arrives. Jay is watching me intently. If I knew how to put the kid at ease, I would.

"You like Savannah?" His question takes me by surprise. I choke on the water I'm taking a sip of.

"I don't know her well enough to have feelings for her one way or another." That's true of how I feel above the belt. "When I met her, she was in a state of distress. It doesn't feel right to walk away until I'm sure she's okay."

"Sure," Lance spoke with his mouth full of steak. "You're just a nice guy trying to do the right thing. You think any of us believe that?"

Jimmy puts his utensils down, wipes a napkin across his face, and sits back. "Don't worry, Lance, Brice is going to think real carefully about how he proceeds with Savannah. He understands there is nowhere he could hide from us if he hurt her. Isn't that right, Brice?"

I'm not afraid of these men, but their message is loud and clear. I like them a lot for it. "I have no intention of hurting her."

"Then we don't have a problem," Jimmy says.

My phone chirps with the indication of an urgent email. My mother would swat at me for pulling out my phone, but she'd probably have a lot to say about my dinner company too. It's from Simon, and I scan his message quickly. The words that stick out are enough to set me on edge. *Jana Monroe is a fake identity. Created five years ago. She has no prior digital footprint. No banking, DMV, or passport history prior to that. The business was incorporated shortly after her identification was created.*

My blood boils. Jana Monroe is a scam—but with what aim? To fleece Savannah financially? Or worse?

"Bad news?" Lance asks.

I shake my head and pocket my phone. The only thing that telling these men will do is likely land one of them in jail. Situations like these are better handled more strategically.

Dinner plates are removed. The dessert tray is brought around. They pack it in. Even Jay breaks down and indulges in two pieces of dark chocolate cake. I've never seen any group of people put away so much food in my life. Even the waiter looks begrudgingly impressed. He announces that our takeout is ready.

"Do you have something else for me?" I ask him.

He hands me a plastic card. I hold it out to Jimmy. "The building right across the street is a hotel. I rented out the presidential suite for the four of you. No need to bunk up at Savannah's. You're only one short elevator ride from king-sized beds and a seventy-five-inch flat-screen television." I wave the key at them.

Jimmy doesn't accept the key. He stands. "No thanks."

I rise to my feet as well. "You'd rather spend the night on the floor of Savannah's apartment."

Jay moves to stand beside Jimmy as if a line is being

drawn in the sand, and he is proclaiming his side.

Jimmy gives me a hard stare that might intimidate some, but my father has a similar look he issues in place of a long lecture. It's effective. I know exactly what Jimmy is warning me not to do. The problem is—I've never been good at following the rules. So, I stand there, holding the card out to him, letting my steady gaze be an answer of its own.

"Wait," Lance takes a last swig of his beer then stands as well. "We're taking the hotel room though, right?"

"Yeah," Jimmy says with a grunt and takes the card from my hand. "Savannah asked us to trust her judgement, and he'll be here tomorrow after we go back home. We'll see her in the morning. Jay run next door and tell Murray we're staying so he should collect the car. Lance, get the takeout."

While Jimmy and I walk toward the side exit of the restaurant, he slaps a hand on my shoulder and lowers his voice. "You've got money and that there fancy suit, my friends and I have something that might be of interest to you."

I can't tell if he's about to ask me to invest in his bar or sucker punch me. I step out of the restaurant with him, face him, and ask, "And what is that?"

"A combined sixty-three years of experience hunting. Murray and I served in the Army. We know how to lie in wait. Hit our target."

It sounds familiar, similar to a threat I already received that evening.

Another measured look I don't react to.

"Nothing to say?" he pushes.

"I've issued similar cautions to young men interested in

my sister. I respect your position."

"I sure hope you're nothing more than you appear," Jimmy says in a tone that hints he might be starting to like me.

I understand this man. When it comes to keeping the people I care about safe, I'll do whatever needs to be done—even hiding out in Boston, courting business deals under an alias.

"My primary interest in seeing Savannah again is only to ensure she isn't getting mixed up with an unsavory element in Boston. There are people here who might take advantage of someone new to the city."

Lance joins us with several bags of food. Murray and Jay cross the street to us. A moment later Charles pulls up with the limo.

Murray says he'll pick up the car in the morning. Charles asks if he requires anything out of it. Murray looks to his friends and asks, "You all got your makeup bags with you?"

Jimmy bats his eyelashes—a sign that all that beer might have affected him just a little.

Laughter erupts.

"We're good," Murray announces then leans in to say something to me.

In a low tone, I say, "I know. You've served in the Army and still love to hunt. Got it."

He laughs. "Charles shared some pretty good stories about you."

"He did?" My attention snaps to Charles. I don't believe he would disclose who I really am, but I also wouldn't have guessed he would have gotten along so well with Murray.

Charles gives me a look that assures me he's neither compromised nor tipsy. Whatever he shared hasn't blown my cover.

"Good night, gentlemen," I say with a wave before sliding into the back seat of the limo.

I check my watch. It's late. Unless she's waiting up for her friends, she's probably asleep. I should go back to my office and see how the foreign markets are faring. "Stop at Savannah's."

Charles turns in his seat to get a good look at me. "Is that a good idea?"

"I should tell her that her friends are not returning."

"Oh," he laughs. "Because they won't text her with that revelation?" He turns back to face forward and pulls out into traffic. "I'll admit I'm impressed. Four men at her apartment with plans to return, and you convince them not to. Smooth."

I frown. I don't like what he's implying. "It's not like that. I need to talk to her. I received an email from Simon while we were at dinner. Nothing good. Jana Monroe is an alias."

"Poor Savannah seems to attract people who can't remember their real names."

I cross my arms over my chest and sink deeper into my seat. "So glad you find the situation amusing."

He glances at me through the rearview mirror. "Amusing? No. Complicated, yes. I would love to tell you it's a mistake to continue to have any involvement with Savannah."

"But?"

"I've spent the last few hours learning about her, and I think your instincts are correct. She's too innocent to understand the danger she might be putting herself in. A woman like her, with no family to watch out for her . . ."

"I don't want to think about the possibilities. I've told her I don't agree with her having further involvement with this Monroe, but she doesn't listen to me."

Now Charles did look amused. "If only she knew who she's dealing with."

"Exactly," I say with shared humor. I am too accustomed to women falling over themselves to catch and keep my attention. Even the expendable prince is a catch with a title many find too tempting not to vie for. Not Savannah.

We drive in silence the rest of the way. As we pull up to the front of the building, I say, "Charles, it's late. I can catch a cab home."

"I'll wait here."

"It may be a while."

"I don't think so."

I have no reason to explain anything to Charles, but when he opens the back door of the limo for me, I add, "I'm only going to talk to her."

He closes the door and leans against it. "I'll be here when you're ready."

Fine.

The doorman gives me a disapproving look when I ask him to ring her apartment. I slide him a large bill. Suddenly he's very helpful.

"Hello?" her voice comes through the speaker, sounding sleepy and sexy.

"Mr. Hastings is here. Shall I send him up?"

"Uh, yeah, I guess."

The doorman gestures to the elevator and makes himself busy with some paperwork. I use the ride up to organize my thoughts. This time, she will listen to me.

"The guys just called and said they're staying at a hotel for the night." Savannah wipes the sleep out of her eyes as she lets me in. Her pajamas are a pair of shorts and a T-shirt. She probably thinks they cover her adequately, but someone needs to tell her they are both sinfully tight. Her bare legs go on forever and the stretched material of her T-shirt accentuates how excited she is to see me.

I raise my eyes to hers. Everything below her neck is too dangerous.

I wish her lips weren't as tempting.

"I just finished dinner with your friends," I say as she closes the door behind me. Part of me wants to tell her to throw me out. Anything I have to say could be said tomorrow when I'm not sporting a boner and can think clearly again.

She moves to sit on a single chair rather than the couch, pulls her legs up in front of her and yawns. I stay rooted where I am . . . aching for her.

"Lance said they're in the presidential suite. Did you do that?"

"Yes." I can barely breathe. God, she's so beautiful.

"Why?"

Her question hangs in the air.

I've never been shy about what I am. If she weren't a virgin, I'd tell her. This is different, though. I can't tell her what I want because I'm still trying to figure out what the hell it is.

I shouldn't be here.

CHAPTER SIXTEEN

Savannah

IT'S MY FIRST night with my own place in Boston, and I already have a gorgeous man in my apartment looking like he wants to spend the night. Everywhere his gaze caresses me, my body warms. I don't know what to do about my nipples waving at him like two take-me-now beacons, so I hug my legs to my front.

Having sex is one of my goals, but the intensity of my attraction to Brice scares me. It feels dangerously impulsive. I cling to the conversation I had with Jana. If sex was all I wanted, I would have had it already. What I want is a better life for myself. Jumping into bed with the first beautiful man who pays attention to me feels like a recipe for failure.

"You really have issues." What do they call laying your crazy at someone else's door? Transference? Whatever, I need to be angry with him, or I'm going to be on my knees begging him to initiate me.

But then what? Where would we go from there? I'm not saying I may never have a one-night stand . . . but my legs are still hairy for God's sake. It's too early in my transformation to think I can handle someone like Brice.

And how would I look Jana in the eye? I told her I'd follow her plan. I paid her all that money. I don't care how amazing his lips might feel on my skin.

They'd catch on stubble. Remember that.

"*I* have issues?" The look on his face is shocked—like I'm the first to accuse him of not being perfect. It bolsters my conviction.

"You love to orchestrate things. Make them turn out the way you want."

"That's not so much an issue as a talent."

His grin is all sex, and heat surges through me. I bet he knows exactly what he's doing. How many women have fallen for that look? Have felt the same urges that are filling me and have given in to them? His grin says too many.

Time to address the elephant in the room. "I've spent the last few hours thinking about you." That didn't come out the way I meant it to.

"Really?" His eyebrows arch, and he looks pretty pleased with himself.

I rush to add, "And Lance, Murray, Jay, and Jimmy."

That removes some of the cockiness from him.

I continue, "I'm surrounding myself with the wrong men. Scaring off anyone who might actually make me happy. I need to stop hiding from life by continuing to open the door to you guys." I shrug. "Jana says this is a journey I need to take on my own, and I think she's right."

"Jana?" He huffs. "I've looked into this woman. She didn't exist five years ago. She's a liar, a scammer. Possibly worse."

I shake my head. It makes sense that Jana would be working under an assumed name. The very nature of her business is covert. "I'm sorry you have no faith in me."

He steps closer. "It's not you I have no faith in. You're a nice person, Savannah. Cities are full of people ready to take advantage of your inexperience. How long did it take you to get mugged?"

I glare at him. "Next time you bring my purse up I may have to kick your ass. I have a lot to learn. I get it. That's why I hired Jana."

Another step closer. My body is literally humming for him. I tell it to chill the fuck out.

"What did you hire her to do?" His tone is warm honey, and I can't refuse him anything in this moment.

"Fix me," I say in a raw whisper. Stop me from stopping myself from succeeding.

"You don't look broken to me." I've fantasized what it would be like to have a man look at me the way he is. I imagined how it would make me feel. This is so much more. I'm turned on, scared immobile, angry with myself, angry with him, sad that I'm being offered something before I'm ready to accept it.

I want to stand up, strip, and say . . . wax me yourself, baby.

I want to turn and run, slam the bedroom door, and hide out until I'm sure he's gone.

My indecision is proof enough that this is a bad idea.

He's right in front of my chair, looming over me. I refuse to meet his eyes. My gaze falls to his prominent bulge, and I briefly close my eyes. I'm an intelligent, confident woman who is completely in control of the situation. All I have to do is think of something intelligent and confident to say.

I open my eyes.

Oh God, I just looked at his crotch again.

I lower my gaze, still trying to come up with what to say.

He crouches in front of me, placing a hand on the arms of the chair to steady himself. I raise my eyes to his. He's so close I forget why any of this shouldn't happen.

His voice is low and measured. A change for him. "Your friends told me what you've been through. I understand now."

I don't think he does. In fact, I'm sure he doesn't. Or he'd already be kissing me. I cling to the last shreds of my anger. "Great. I'm glad you guys had a long chat over your dinner. How lovely. That doesn't make any of you an expert on me. It doesn't give you the right to tell me what I should do."

"Jana isn't going to fix you. She's going to hurt you. You need to know that."

I could lose myself in his eyes . . . in the promise of those lips of his. I'm reasonably certain he'd let me touch them, but doing so would send the opposite message than it should.

He asks, "What did she promise you? That she'd show you a way to make money?"

"I don't care about money," I say, struggling to remember what I do care about beyond this moment and how he's making me feel. "Things don't matter. I don't expect you to understand, but I have to do this. My father gave me a clock when I was little. It was antique. Special. He'd given it to my mother when he married her to represent that he would love her for all time. I clung to that clock, especially after I lost my father. I thought it mattered. Then my grandmother became very ill, and no matter how much I worked, I couldn't afford the care she needed. So I sold it. And it freed me. A part of me had been waiting for someone to swoop in and save me and that clock. I thought that was how life worked . . . that there is always a happy ending like in the movies. Sure things might get tough, but then they always turn around. Only they don't. I have to save myself. There is no prince charging in on a white horse."

"White horses are notoriously difficult to keep clean."

His joke pulls me back to the moment. "I don't know why I thought you might understand."

His expression turns serious. "I'm trying."

"Listen. Nothing you say will change my mind because working with Jana is worth the risk."

He growls. "You are the most frustrating . . . most stubborn . . ."

The kiss takes me by surprise. I'm moving . . . floating to my feet. There is no slow burn. No tentative exploration. My hands race to his hair, grabbing handfuls as his arms loop around me. Lifting me. Pressing me to his hard body. I throb all over for the want of him. Everything is instinctive. I move rhythmically against his excitement. Then his hand moves down my back and cups my ass.

It's gloriously primal.

I moan. His grip tightens on my ass, and his mouth moves to explore my neck.

I'm on the verge of reaching my hand down to explore his hardness when a moment of clarity shines through. I don't know this man. This is not the plan.

Jana's way promises a good and safe man. An experience I can remember fondly. Grow from. Hold with me forever.

This is passion. Lust.

Dangerous.

I'd be just a fuck to him.

Can I handle the brush-off that will likely follow? What if I can't, and it sends me running back to Coppertop?

I've come too far to do something stupid now.

"I can't," I whisper as I pull my hand from its path toward his belt. I fold away from him and he lets me. His eyes are wild with desire. I'm sure mine are as well. I don't care if he hates me for it, though. I'm not ready. "I can't, Brice."

He steps back and nods. "I'm sorry. I told myself that wouldn't happen."

Funny, I told myself the same thing. I walk to the door, take a deep breath, and open it. "If I'd have met you in a couple of weeks. After. Maybe. I don't know. But you met me before. You met Savannah from Coppertop, Maine, in her stinky wool coat. You're part of what I need to close the door on."

"I don't understand. You wish we'd met after what? What do you mean you have to close the door on me?"

"Brice, how many chances do people get for a fresh start? Usually one. This is mine. I need to move forward."

"Jana is not a life coach. I'll find you one, if that's what you want."

"Please don't dissect this. You won't understand it unless I explain it, and I won't." I think of the contract I signed. The nondisclosure with consequences for breaking it. "Jana is helping me. That's all anyone needs to know. Good night."

Brice walks toward the door then stops beside me. "Savannah, when someone wants to control a person the first thing they do is separate them from their support system. It's a classic manipulation and abuse move. Remember that the next time Jana tells you to close a door on anyone."

Brice walks out, and I quickly shut the door, sagging against it.

His words echo in my mind.

His taste lingers on my lips.

I push off the door and walk to my bedroom. My very empty, very chaste bedroom.

I'm going to die a virgin.

CHAPTER SEVENTEEN

Savannah

WAKE UP in a better mood.

Good idea or not, I'm staying the course. If I start second-guessing myself, I might as well go home to Coppertop.

My apartment is cozy. My apartment. *Mine.* No matter how many times I say it, I still can't believe it. It's a short-term lease. I'll have to figure out a way to be able to afford it long-term. But for now this little piece of Boston is mine. I stretch across the comfortable sheets and smile as the sun cuts through the shades.

I don't know what kind of night the guys had, but I'm certain they'll be here early. Like the tides of Maine, they are reliable.

I scramble out of bed when I hear the buzzer of my intercom. I tell the doorman to send them up then hunt down a bra.

They're laughing as they come down the hallway. I open the door for them and they fill my living room. Lance tosses a plastic bag at me. "Don't say I never gave you anything. That's presidential suite shit."

I glance in the bag. It's a stockpile of freebies you get

from a hotel. Everything, right down to the extra roll of toilet paper. I roll my eyes, but actually, I'm giddy for the tiny shampoos and lotions.

"Did you have a good time? Presidential suite? That's a big splurge for you guys."

Jimmy settles himself on my couch. "Your boyfriend paid. I kept testing the limit of his generosity, figuring there would be one, but he either wanted us to have a great time"—he gives me a hard stare—"or he wanted to keep us occupied so he could come back here."

I blush, but I'm admitting nothing. "He's not my boyfriend."

Lance plops down in one of the chairs. "So he didn't come back here?"

I prop a hand up on my hip. "Not that it's any of your business, but he dropped by to check on me, then left because I hardly know him."

Murray comes to stand beside me. "Easy, Savannah. You don't owe any of us an explanation. We're only here to make sure you're okay."

I sigh. "I'm telling you the truth." My declaration is followed by an awkward silence that I break with a question, "Are you guys hungry? We can get breakfast, but I have a lot I need to get done today."

"Like what?" Jimmy asks with a frown.

"Just first day in the city stuff." It's not enough to satisfy any of them. It'll have to do, though, because I'm not about to tell them I'm heading off to get waxed, plucked, blown out, polished, and highlighted. They'd think I'm doing it for

Brice, and I'm not.

Jimmy turns on and off the light on the table beside him as if testing to ensure it works. "No need to feed us. The hotel fed us well." He rises to his feet. "We don't like leaving you here, but we've got to get back to the bar. The town can't survive without us for two nights. There's room in the truck. Want a ride back?" His face contorts and my heart swells. These are not men who do warm and fuzzy very often. Or ever.

I consider his offer longer. It would be easy to get in that truck. We'd laugh and joke the whole way home. I could step right back into my old life.

I've never been one to take the easy way out.

"Tempting, but I have an appointment." There's another long pause. I know I need to say more. "You don't know how much it means to me that you drove all the way down just to make sure I'm okay. It's something I'll never forget."

Jimmy looks around at the other guys before saying, "People are going to ask what you're doing here. About how you are."

"Because they care too," Murray adds.

Jay nods once and I find it difficult to choose my next words. How do I separate myself from them without making it seem like I don't care? Because I do. That was never the problem. "The best thing you can do for me, is tell them nothing. Right now, there's nothing to tell. When I'm ready, I'll come back for a visit and see everyone."

Lance stands. "We won't tell anyone anything. Do you swear on a jar of fish eyes?"

I snort out a laugh. There are some things that will never make sense to anyone in the city. In Coppertop, when you're trying to let someone know you can be trusted, you stick your hand in the jar of fish eyes and make a promise. It's disgusting. Foul. But about as legally binding as Jana's nondisclosure contract. You don't enter into a fish-eye promise lightly.

I don't swear to anything, because I don't know what the future holds for me. Jana told me I had to cut these men out of my life to be successful. But she doesn't know how Jimmy always made sure I did my homework, how Jay never let me walk to my car alone, or how Murray went to the store and bought me tampons the day I ran out. I love them.

Once I have my life in order, I'll figure out a way to keep them in it.

Jimmy takes a step closer and pins me down with a look. "You're a smart girl, Savannah. And pretty. People in the city aren't like back home. You need to be careful."

"You sound like Brice," I say and instantly wish I hadn't brought up his name.

"Be careful with him too. Just because a man says all the right things doesn't mean you should trust him. Men will say anything to get what they want."

I place a hand on his tense arm. "I'm not a child, Jimmy. I know how to take care of myself."

His eyes blink fast a few times. "You're the closest I have to a daughter. I couldn't live with knowing I didn't do enough to keep you safe."

I force a confident smile. "If you all keep acting like you

don't think I can survive a day without you, I'm going to have to kick your asses to prove I can."

Murray chuckles. "She'll be fine, Jimmy."

Placing his hand over mine, Jimmy says, "She'd better be." Then he steps back.

Jay walks over and stands in front of me without speaking. He doesn't have to. I know what he can't say.

"I'll miss you too," I whisper in his ear when I hug him.

He has a sad smile on his face when he steps back.

Murry pulls me in for a hug that lifts me off my feet. I laugh through it.

I'm still smiling when Lance walks over, shaking his head. "If you take too long in Boston, Savannah, I may not be single when you come back."

"I'm willing to take that risk," I say then wink. Lance has always been a little sweet on me, but it never has and never could go anywhere. There's no spark . . . at least not on my side. If that is ever unclear to me, all I have to do is remember how simply being in the same room with Brice feels.

He shrugs and struts off. He's not a bad guy. One day he'll meet someone who'll make him forget all about me. Who knows, she might show him that we'd all like him a lot more if he didn't try so hard.

Jimmy lingers in the doorway when the others head to the elevator. No one could ever replace my father, but he's been the closest thing to it over the years. My lashes grow heavy with a dusting of tears as he kicks his head to the side and looks at me sympathetically. Is this what it's like when your parents drop you off to the bus for summer camp?

When they leave you at your new dorm for the first time? Things I never experienced but always imagined.

Jimmy seems to pluck up the courage to speak all at once and starts blurting out his fatherly advice. "You might find yourself with some fancy friends in the city, but don't you ever let any of them make you feel like you're not already wonderful. Make sure any changes you make are on the outside."

I nod and blink the blurry tears out of my eyes. He shuffles away, and I watch him turn the corner of the hallway. I want to call out. Ask him to wait. But there isn't anything else to say.

This is a solo mission.

There isn't room in a cocoon for a caterpillar and a bunch of her friends. Later, when I emerge, this butterfly can take a trip back to Coppertop.

A short time later, I'm frustrated and more than a little disappointed I didn't think to set up everything earlier. Every spa I called was booked. I could ask Jana, but I hoped to appear more capable the next time we spoke.

I could go for a run to clear my head, but I haven't had time to buy workout clothing yet. After a quick shower, I put on my slacks and blouse again, deciding to remedy that.

I'm a block from my apartment when I catch sight of a familiar face before it ducks behind a sign. On one hand it's irritating that Brice is still having his driver follow me. I'm perfectly capable of getting along on my own. On the other hand, Charles might know something about booking spa time that I don't. I wave to him. "Hey, Chucky."

He waves back.

I cross the street to join him.

"Have your friends already gone?" he asks.

"I'm surprised you don't know. Does that mean your surveillance isn't twenty-four/seven?" I counter.

The corner of his mouth twitches like he's fighting a smile. "I'm merely passing through the neighborhood."

I nod and fall into step beside him. "A coincidence. Sure. Listen, I have a question."

"If I can answer, I will."

I sigh. "I'm supposed to go dress shopping tomorrow morning. I wanted to have a little makeover before I do that, but I can't find a place that takes walk-ins for the kind of overhaul I need."

He lifts his dark glasses. "Are you asking me to book beauty services for you?"

I laugh at the horror in his eyes. "Hell no. I was hoping you'd know of a place that might have openings." The more I think my question through the less likely it seems he would. "Why would you? I'm sorry. I just hate the idea of trying on dresses with hairy legs." His eyebrows shoot up. "Normally I'd shave, but you're supposed to let your hair grow out a little if you want a wax . . ." My voice trails away. "I'm oversharing."

He clears his throat and replaces his glasses.

I stop walking, feeling like an idiot. Really, what did I think he'd do? Wave a wand over my head like a fairy godmother? When will I learn I have to do this on my own?

Charles stops as well and takes out his phone. He sends

my phone the address of a spa just a few blocks away. I'm grateful, but disappointed. "Thanks, but I already tried them. They're booked."

"They won't be by the time you get there."

I fight the giddiness welling within me. "You can do that?"

He tilts his head as if my question is ridiculous. "When you arrive simply give them a list of what you'd like done."

My smile is so wide it almost hurts. He really is Murray's twin. I hug him briefly, an act that takes him completely by surprise and has him stepping away. Too soon? "Thanks, Chucky. I owe you one."

He nods. "You're welcome, Savannah. Let's keep this favor between the two of us, shall we?"

Shall we? See that's why I can't be creeped out by him following me. Killers and kidnappers aren't that formal.

And they definitely don't make spa appointments for you.

He walks away, leaving me looking at the address on my phone and smiling.

CHAPTER EIGHTEEN

Savannah

LOOK AT ME go.

The next morning I'm strutting down a busy street. I may not yet feel like I belong in Boston, but I'm beginning to look like I do. My hair is two inches shorter, lightened in a natural fashion. Every inch of me has been buffed so smooth I'm surprised my clothing doesn't slide right off me. My slacks and shirt are new, along with my flats. I'm toasty in the camel wrap coat the sales clerk assured me will never go out of style.

I almost bought high heels, but without a car, my feet are my best mode of transportation. No wonder everyone in the city is slim. I've never walked so much in my life.

Jana sent me my first task, and I feel completely up to it. I step into a department store with confidence. She challenged me to buy a sophisticated dress . . . something to wear to a charity event she wants me to attend.

Classic.

Expensive looking.

I can do this. The mantra stays in my head right up until I realize I'm wrong. It's like a reverse *little engine that could.* I was chugging my way up that mountain and just slid all the way back down in the most embarrassing way possible.

I knew some parts of this journey would be difficult. I prepared for hard work. I just didn't know I'd break a sweat and be on the verge of tears in the changing room of a department store. No one warned me about this.

The poor clerk, Martha, has brought everything in my size. Some are too loose. Some too tight. One looked beautiful on the hanger. Top to bottom silver sequins and tiny hand-strung beads. Strapless. Meant to fall just above the knee. I'm too curvy for it, and it's too short for my comfort. A solid addition to the maybe pile.

I try the zipper.

It won't budge.

My chest tightens with anxiety. What do people do when this happens?

I want to literally rip the dress off me, but it's expensive and I don't want to not be able to afford the perfect dress because I have to also buy a shredded one.

Do I call for Martha and have her pry me out? Would someone else buy the dress and ask to wear it out of the store? Like they'd been called to some emergency cocktail party?

If I wait long enough the nervous sweat dripping down my back might act as a lubricant, and I can slide right out of it. Okay, stay calm. I can't be the first woman this has happened to. I read the sign on the inside of the changing room. Do you know what they don't list a procedure for? For this.

Even if Chucky is lurking around, I can't ask for help with this one.

I take out my phone.

911?

I groan as I imagine how my friends back home would laugh if they saw my face plastered on the news with that story. Sadly, it would not shock them.

I consider calling Jana then smack the phone on my forehead as I realize how stupid of a choice that would be. Hi, Jana. Remember how you doubted I was someone you should work with? Let me prove to you that I'm not.

No way.

My phone starts ringing—butt dialing someone.

Wait. What?

I look down at it. It's not calling Jana, it's calling Brice. I end the call and drop my phone to the cushioned bench with the vigor of someone swatting a swarm of killer bees away.

Maybe he didn't hear it.

Maybe he won't notice the missed call.

I try the zipper again. My fingers slip off because they're shaking. "I'm fucked."

"Everything okay?" Martha asks through the dressing room door. I thought I was alone. Someone needs to put a bell on her.

"I'm in luck," I shoot back quickly. "I really like this dress."

"Oh good. Should I take it and ring it up?"

"I'm not ready to take it off. I like to spend some time in dresses before I make my final choice."

There's a very understandably long pause before Martha replies cautiously, "How much time?"

"It depends."

"I'll be back in a few minutes."

Martha steps away as my phone starts to ring.

It's Brice.

I grab my phone and send the call to voice mail. It's probably not how Jana would have handled the situation, but I'm a work in progress. The phone begins ringing again. I panic and send it to voice mail again.

"Unzip," I demand of the dress as I wrestle with the zipper again. My phone rings again. This time I answer and sit down on the bench behind me. "Sorry. I called by accident."

"What's wrong?" His tone is concerned.

"Nothing. I didn't mean to dial you. Okay? I need to go."

"Why are you out of breath?"

I'd love to blame the dress, but it's mostly because he has a voice that finally explains how phone sex is possible. I've always thought there was no way a voice could turn me on, but I was wrong. He's hardly said a word and I feel all flushed and confused.

Nope, not going to say that out loud. "I'm dealing with a little situation, but nothing I can't handle."

"A situation? Look around, do you see Charles?"

"He's not here." I peek under the door for his shoes and relax when I don't see them. I'm getting used to having Charles around, but that would have been a bit much. "You really do need to stop asking him to check on me; I'm fine."

"Are you? Then tell me where you are. What kind of *situation* have you gotten yourself into?"

Nothing like his tone implies. Oh, what the hell. "I'm stuck . . ." I finish in a mumble that was likely unintelligible "…in a dress."

"You're stuck where?" The urgency in his voice makes it impossible for me to not explain. I can't let him believe I've been sold into some underground sex ring.

"In a dress," I say clearly. "I'm at a clothing store. I thought dress shopping would be fun but none of them fit right and this last one is apparently a carnivore. The zipper won't budge."

He chuckles. "You're stuck in a dress?"

"Wedged. Jammed. Crushed."

"Maybe put the thesaurus down to start and take a deep breath."

"I can't take a deep breath because this dress is ridiculously tight."

"What's your plan?" I hear his smile and it makes me want to smack him.

"My plan? Do I sound like I have one? Outside of possibly hiding in this dressing room until closing time. Or climbing up into the duct work and escaping that way."

"Unlikely you'd make it far in a tight dress."

"Thanks. You're a real help."

"What color is the dress? I'm trying to imagine the scene."

"I'm hanging up now."

"Don't. This is too amusing."

"Brice." His name is all I can muster before my voice cracks. It's enough. He suddenly stops joking.

"Hang on." He mutes our call and I almost end it. In the silence, embarrassment floods in. I'm making a big deal out of nothing. Really, I should just ask Martha to set me free. She won't care. I'm the problem here—me and my damn pride. "Do you have lip balm?"

"I do."

"My sister says if you put some on your finger and then run it along the zipper it should release."

"Your sister?" The idea that Brice is a brother, part of a family, surprises me. I pictured him as some kind of island. An autonomous man who doesn't need anything. But somewhere there's a sister.

I put the phone down beside me and try it. Like magic, it works. The zipper comes free and slides down the side of the dress all the way to my hip. "Oh thank God," I sigh as I break free from the dress and catch my breath again. "I thought I would never get out of there."

"You good now?" Grumpy Brice is sexy, amused Brice is infuriating but still hot, sweet Brice is nearly irresistible.

That thought is quickly followed by the realization that I still need to find a dress. I've lost all enthusiasm for shopping though. One task. Jana gave me one task, and I've already proven incapable. "Yeah. I am. Thank your sister for me."

"I will. There's still something wrong. What is it?"

"Nothing. What could be? I'm free to go forth and try on another hundred dresses." I make a face at myself in the mirror. *Suck it up, buttercup.* "I'll find something. I just should have left myself more time. I need it by tonight. I've got this, though."

"Why do you need a dress by tonight?"

I open my mouth to reply then remember I'm not supposed to say anything. Even if I could, he wouldn't approve of what I'm doing anyway. Thankfully, my life and my choices don't require his approval.

When I don't answer, he says, "No one is better at picking out the perfect dress for a woman than a man."

"Really?" There might be a lot I have to learn about Boston and shopping, but I recognize bullshit a mile away.

"If you don't agree, you've never been with the right man."

I don't answer and his comment hangs in the air as if he just remembered I haven't been. When he speaks again, his voice is a purr. "I'd love to show you how good . . . dress shopping can be. And if you get stuck in another, I promise I'll assist you."

I huff at that. "I bet you're an expert at undressing women."

"No. Not an expert." He chuckles. "More of an enthusiast."

I can't help but smile. I want to see him again. I know I shouldn't. There's still time to hit a few other stores on my own. The idea of laughing with him is infinitely more appealing than spending the rest of the day shopping alone.

He's right. Men know what looks good.

Sure it seems a little crazy. A little impulsive. But isn't that all relative? Compared to everything else, agreeing to go shopping with him hardly seems odd at all.

Plus, I could really get stuck in another dress. Then what would I do?

"There's another store on this block. Do you want the address?"

"No, I have a certain place in mind. They'll have exactly what you need."

Looks like it's time to either figure out how to use the T or Uber. Or hail another cab. Lance said a lot of stupid things, but his comment about what would happen if I ran out of money woke me up to how careful I need to be. I'll go back to Coppertop to visit, but not for forever and definitely not because it's my only option. "Send me the address."

"I just texted Charles. He'll take you."

"Good ole Chucky."

"He smiles when you call him that. Not many could get away with calling him a nickname."

"That's sweet." It is, but I never had a problem being one of the guys. I want more.

"Find Charles out front, and I'll meet you at the store."

I pull my bag over my shoulder and hang the woman-eating dress back on the hanger. It would be easy to start doubting myself, doubting Jana. Do I really think having my hair done and putting on a dress will make me into a woman who turns heads?

What's the alternative? Go back to being the woman who smells a little like engine oil and chicken wings? Some-one who works every night so she won't sit home alone? I want to start each day excited about the possibilities the day might hold. I want to claim my space, find my dreams again.

The real wakeup call for me was when my grandmother's nurse asked me what I would do now that she was gone . . . would I go back to school? Would I travel? What were my dreams? It wasn't until that moment I realized I don't have dreams. No goals. Nothing to strive for.

Somehow I died along with my grandmother. Slowly, a little bit more every day . . . until there was nothing left of me.

Only that doesn't have to be my story. I don't have to accept that fate.

I've only been in Boston a couple of days, and I already feel more alive than I've felt in years. I don't care if what I'm doing makes sense to anyone else—I'm not going back to how I was.

I'm still lost in that thought as I see Charles standing beside a sedan. He holds open the front passenger door and I smile because he knows me. He doesn't bother trying to get me to ride in the back anymore. We're making progress.

"Savannah. It's good to see you again."

Before getting in, I do a little spin for him. "What do you think of the hair? Nice, right? The place you sent me to was amazing. I can't thank you enough for convincing them to squeeze me in."

He smiles. "You look lovely. I'm happy I was able to help."

I climb in. He walks around and gets into the car. "We are dress shopping, I hear."

"That's the goal." I fiddle with my seat belt as he pulls

into traffic.

"Come now, it can't be all that bad. Shopping always puts my wife in a good mood."

"You're married?"

"Thirty years."

"Brice isn't, is he?" The question bursts out of me.

Charles glances at me before answering. "No, he is not married."

I sigh with relief. "Not that it really matters. We're just friends. But I wouldn't want to meet up with him if he was."

"No, that wouldn't be prudent."

Prudent. I'm not entirely sure what that means. Prudish. Like a prude? Or not like a prude? Like a whore? I take out my phone and look the word up. Oh, acting with care for the future. I like that. "Yes, and I do want to be . . . prudent.

He gives me another look. "Remember my daughters? One is twenty-two and the other is twenty-five."

I relax. "That's so nice."

"I would not allow either of them to date Brice."

A chill settles over me. What the hell? "Is he a criminal?"

"No, but nor is he who he appears. Be careful, Savannah. I wouldn't like to see you get hurt."

My eyes round. "I wouldn't like to see that either."

We pull up to the front of a small shop. I step out of the car and look back at him curiously. "This is the place?" It doesn't look like a store that would sell dresses. It's a tailor shop and an older one at that. The wooden door is thick with many layers of paint and the stone at the base of the doorway is cracked. Nope, I'm not going in.

Charles is beside me, taking note of my concern. "I shouldn't have said anything earlier. I merely meant that you're an innocent, and Brice hasn't shown an affinity to remaining with one woman."

Although his explanation makes me feel a little better, I'm still not keen to go in. "This was a bad idea. I'm just going to go—"

The door of the shop opens and a woman waves for us to enter.

I look from Charles to her and back. I can run. I'm fast, so I can probably outrun him. The woman waves again, with less patience. I've never been a coward. I allowed someone I'd never met before to lather a good portion of my nether regions with wax yesterday. That required a good amount of trust.

I survived it and outside of a slight residual discomfort, I'm pleased with the results. Brice did nothing to make me think I can't trust him. Sure, his driver has more or less shadowed me since I met him, but that is because he is worried for me.

And hearing that Brice isn't one for monogamy? Since all we are doing is dress shopping, isn't that irrelevant?

I take a step toward the door. It is silly to be worried. Brice met my friends—heard my life story. He knows there's no one to pay a ransom if his goal is kidnapping.

I shake my head. Everything he said about Jana and her possible motives is starting to make me paranoid. Totally creepy, hole-in-the-wall shops could contain an extensive collection of dresses.

Right?

CHAPTER NINETEEN

Brice

THE TURN-OF-THE-CENTURY FURNITURE reminds me of our oceanside palace. Maybe that's why I keep returning to this shop.

I heard about the place when I moved into Bachelor Tower. Boston has an elite sub-culture, places one can only access via a recommendation from another client. I glean a certain amount of satisfaction from the knowledge that I gained access on the merit of my business dealings, not on my family name. Through me, the owner Miguel has gained several prominent clients, and his gratitude is my currency today.

His specialty is not women's clothing, but his connections are far reaching. I asked him to have the best of the season available, and it's already being delivered via the back of the store.

Miguel is a round-faced man with thick glasses and only a ring of wispy hair that runs around the back of his head from ear to ear. His thin lips never smile, and he does more talking to himself than to his clients.

He's a perfectionist with a keen eye for fashion. He

knows his trade on a cellular level. Every detail. Every nuance of the industry. I respect that.

"Who is this woman you want me to dress?" he demands as he sorts through the latest delivery.

"Does it matter?"

"Of course it does. Some of these dresses are straight from the runway, others vintage. People will know where they came from. I'll dress your wife, your sister, but not your mother or your mistress."

"I'm not married, my mother will be disappointed, and Savannah is a friend."

He stops and his bushy eyebrows cock up. "You're generous with your *friends*, or is she paying?"

"Regardless of the dress she chooses, you are to tell her the cost is a hundred dollars. I'll cover the rest, but she's proud and there's no need for her to know the actual price."

Miguel hums. "So she's a fool."

"Inexperienced in these matters."

A light sparks in his eyes. "Ah, I understand. Of course. Everything is on sale today."

I shift uncomfortably. "You don't understand, but your discretion is all I require."

Miguel bows. "Of course, your majesty."

My head snaps back, but then I realize he's merely mocking me, responding to a haughty tone I hadn't realized I sometimes sport until I came to the states. "One more thing. I choose the dress."

I'm not about to explain to him that although I want Savannah to look good, there is no way in hell I'm going to send her out to God knows where looking too good. Not if where she's going might have something to do with the Monroe woman.

He shrugs and busies himself with a fresh rack of dresses that one of his workers just wheeled in. One of his assistants walks in and announces the arrival of Savannah. When she steps inside my jaw drops and all my blood heads south.

Her clothing is similar to what I saw her in the night before, but her face has a glow to it, like a woman who is fresh from being loved. Her hair is a shade or two lighter and shines in the light of the shop. My heart is thudding loudly in my chest. My cock is straining to come out and see her for himself.

She shoots me a tentative smile, and I doubt I can remember my own name in this moment.

"You found the place," I say because it's all I can think to say.

Her smile widens. "Technically, Charles did." She looks around. "Wow, there really are dresses." She steps closer, so close I catch the scent of her. It's fresh, unique, and addictive.

"Did you doubt me?" I ask.

"I did." Her lips part slightly as she speaks. Her eyes darken in response to the pulse of sexual tension between us. Miguel and his staff fade away until there is only Savannah and how much I want her.

"You're a constant surprise to me as well."

"Enough of that." Miguel makes a tsking sound. "Turn around for me. I need to know what I'm working with."

Savannah spins.

"Slower," he orders impatiently. "This is not a dance recital."

Our eyes meet as she begins to turn slowly, breaking contact only briefly. It feels intimate and sexual, even though I'm not the one she's displaying herself to.

There's a fire in her eyes that makes me rethink that.

Miguel marches off to pull dresses from a rack. He hangs them beside a closet-sized changing area blocked off by only a small curtain. That little curtain will be the only thing between Savannah's half-naked body and me.

Miguel claps his hands, snapping our attention back to him. "You need something that comes in at the waist. Your hips are full. Your waist is small. These dresses will work for that." Miguel pushes his glasses up on his nose and waits impatiently for Savannah to move.

Savannah's hands slide to her hips as her brows furrow. I want to tell her I've felt her hips, and they're perfect. Memorable. Great to grip. Instead I move to the dresses and feign interest in them.

"Cocktail party? Formal attire?" Miguel grumbles.

I glance back at Savannah. "Good question. Where are you going tonight?"

If my question surprised Miguel, he is hiding it well.

"It's a charity event," Savannah says through pursed lips. "Formal."

Miguel circles her like a vulture, eyeing her closely. "What is your date wearing?"

"I don't have one." Her eyes meet mine and then flutter

away like a butterfly. "I don't want one."

"This black one." Miguel hands her a tiny cocktail dress. She carries it into the changing area. He snaps the curtain closed between us. My view of her beneath the curtain is nothing that would be featured in a porn, but it's enough to kill my ability to think.

She steps out of her flats, kicking them aside.

Next her slacks pool at her feet before she steps out of them as well.

Two bare feet should not be enough to hold me there, mesmerized. But they are.

She lowers her voice and leans her head out of the curtain toward me. I'm rock-hard, but she looks oblivious to what she's doing to me. "Big hips? This guy better really know his stuff because otherwise he's just an ass. Hopefully I can get my fat hips through this dressing room opening to get out."

"Maybe turn sideways." The wink I offer only solicits a growl from her. It's from annoyance, but I don't mind. No man in my present state cares about much at all. "Just put the dress on." So, maybe I can think again.

The curtain drops between us again.

"It doesn't have a size tag on it. I hope it fits." The end of the dress rests on the floor while she steps into it. I hear it sliding up over her skin and drive myself nearly mad, imagining my lips following that same trail. "I cannot get away with wearing something like this. It's too—" She pushes the curtain back.

Her words are cut off by my loud whistle of approval as

she steps out. "Sexy as hell." The dress falls well above her knee, dangerously short. Easy to slide a hand up her thigh, push her lace panties to the side and tease her clit until her legs shake. The neckline plunges low enough to leave nothing to the imagination. Her perky breasts are barely covered. Holding up the dress is a crisscross style thin strap that would be easy to rip away. This dress is a *fuck-me* dress. The kind I like. It's designed to set the imagination on fire with possibilities.

No way in hell is the fuck-me message going out to any man but me.

"I don't know about that one," I say, furrowing my brows as though I'm considering it. The only thing I'm actually considering is bending her over and parting her legs. Pulling that dress up and plunging my cock deep inside her. "It's too . . ."

"That's what I thought. This dress is for someone with more—" She makes some weird gesture toward her body.

"You have plenty of everything needed for that dress. It's just not *the* dress for you."

Miguel reads my expression and rolls his eyes. I'll bring him a hundred wealthy clients if he keeps his mouth shut. "Try the off-the-shoulder red one. The dress is a heavy silk and satin. Strapless with a corset. It has a fishtail silhouette. Beautiful and appropriate for a charity event."

I jut my chin out in the direction of the small changing room and hand her the second dress. "He knows his stuff." There's more fabric in this one.

Out of the black dress. Into the red. "This one doesn't

have a size on it either. And neither have price tags. I hope I can afford them."

"The right dress is worth the expense."

"Says a rich man. The rest of us like to continue to eat as well."

She makes a less than pleased sound.

"How's the dress?"

"I don't want to say."

If Miguel weren't hovering, this would be playing out very differently, but I tell myself it's a good thing it isn't. Didn't I tell myself that my continued association with her was only to ensure her safety?

She's an innocent.

Even if I weren't in the States for business, I wouldn't be a good choice for her. I like women—as in plural. Variety is all that keeps things interesting. Sure, she has me drooling today, but a week from now? I'd be moving on to the next woman and she'd hate me.

So, I ask myself—what the hell am I doing here?

"I can't zip it," she says in a low tone.

"It won't go over your hips?"

Audible gasp. "Say it again, and I'll beat you with one of these hangers."

I laugh.

She huffs and slides the curtain to the side, stepping out backward. The smooth skin of her back fully exposed right down to the lace top of her thong. "Shut up and zip me."

I hesitate for a moment, drinking her in. She is holding her hair tucked over one shoulder.

"Don't tell me you don't know how. Just think about what you normally do . . . this is the reverse." The look she gives me over her shoulder starts off teasing then heats up.

This is already the opposite of what I do. The push and pull of us is a new experience for me. So is my restraint.

I step closer and zip her up. She spins and drops her hair. "Thanks."

Miguel is back. He adjusts the waist of the dress. "A beaded clutch. High heels. No necklace. Hair up." He ticks the list off on his fingers.

She turns toward the mirror, then meets my eyes in it. "You agree? This is the one? Does it look all right?" She's looking at me as though she's standing on the edge of a cliff and my answer will either pull her back or shove her off.

I open my mouth to answer, but nothing comes out. I imagine her, on my arm at a royal function. The visual spooks me.

That's not where this is going.

Miguel answers flatly. "It seems that we've found your dress."

"You're sure?" Savannah gestures at the rack of dresses and raises her brows high. "There are so many others."

"It's not about trying on every dress," Miguel says with authority. "It's about recognizing when you find the one that fits." He gives me a pointed look.

"He's right. This is the dress. Look." I take her hand and guide her toward a full-length, three-sided mirror.

The only thing sexier than Savannah in this dress is the expression on her face when she gets a look in the mirror.

Like she had no idea she could look like this.

"Oh man." She runs a hand down her sides and turns a little in each direction to see the dress from every angle. "Look at my ass. It even makes my ass look good."

Miguel chokes on what might have been a laugh before adding in a serious tone, "It suits you."

"Oh, boy. Now for the big question." Her cheeks redden to match the dress. "How much is it? But before you tell me, I want you to know I appreciate you letting me try it on. I'll never forget how it made me look."

Miguel's eyes dart to me, and I give a nearly imperceptible nod of my approval. "I'm happy to give you a very fair price." He waves her back into the changing room and disappears to the back room.

Savannah steps into the changing room and closes the curtain. "Brice, I don't know if Miguel and I have the same idea of a fair price."

"What kind of charity event is it?" I move closer to the curtain that separates us. "Why are you going?"

"Dammit," she says. She parts the curtain and puts her back to me, sweeping her hair away so I can unzip the gown. My hand lingers at the top of the zipper, and I hear her draw in a sharp breath as my hand brushes over her bare skin.

The curtain closes again between us and I ache for her. "You can keep asking, but the answer is none of your business."

Miguel shuffles in with several boxes which is a good thing because I'd been about to proclaim that it damn well is my business.

But it isn't.

Savannah emerges with the red dress and hands it to one of Miguel's staff. "I may be taking that. I hope."

Miguel has her try on several pairs of shoes and shows her a small bag he says completes the outfit. "One hundred for the dress and a hundred for the accessories," Miguel says with a straight face.

"That's it? Really? For a dress like that?" Savannah bounces with excitement.

"Want me to charge you more?" Miguel asks impatiently. Oh, he's good.

"No." She fishes a credit card out of her wallet and slides it to him. Turning toward me she is all smiles. "It's a new card, but I activated it. Let's hope it works."

"Yes, let's," Miguel says as he fiddles with the credit card machine.

"Can you believe this?" Savannah's wonderment is refreshing. So many people spend their lives chronically unsatisfied. Unimpressed. But not Savannah.

Her life would have crushed a lesser person, but somehow she maintained her innocence. It was enough to make a womanizing prince wish he was a better man.

"Can I believe this? No, I can't," I say coolly. I'm annoyed with myself. I swore I wouldn't let her distract me. How did she become all I can think about?

My phone vibrates in my pocket. My brother. I wince.

Line one: your real life is calling.

If I pick up, we'll repeat the same conversation we've only just had. He wants me home. They all want me to give up this foolishness and fly back.

"What's the matter?" Savannah scans my face.

"Nothing." I slide my phone back in my pocket.

Miguel steps away.

"I'm a good listener," Savannah says. "If Coppertop had a plaque for that, I'd have a wall of them."

I shake my head, but my heart warms. I understand why she's the only one who can make Jay smile. She touches my arm, and all flirtation from earlier is gone. She simply cares, and that's just as heady.

I can't explain my situation to her. I don't have that luxury, not when the price might be my brother's freedom. "It's complicated. I have family responsibilities that are in direct opposition to what I'm trying to do."

"I know how that is."

I nod. I know she does.

"I don't know what the answer is, but I've been there. I told you I spent a long time caring for my grandmother. Working and caregiving is about all I did. And people would come up to me and say, that's so amazing. Look at all you did for her. You must feel great about that. I did and I didn't. Sometimes it was too much. I blamed her for the choices I made. I blamed her illness for killing my dreams, but I put everything important to me aside. I could have cared for her and carved out a life for myself. Don't give more than you can give happily. It's not fair to you and it's not fair to them. I finally stood up and decided to claim my space in this world."

Her words resonate with me. Being royal is a privilege,

but one that comes with a price. I played the role I was told I was born for, but now I have a choice. I can continue to bow to duty and tradition, give all of myself over to it, or I can succeed in Boston and release my brother from his arranged marriage. I can claim my space.

Miguel returns and orders his staff to take the boxes to my car.

Savannah's hand drops away. "Should I call a ride or can Charles . . ."

I give her a look that silences her. "We'll drop you off on the way to my office."

Charles is on the sidewalk with the back door to the car open. Savannah stops before getting in. "Talk about not being what something appears, that place was incredible. I found my dress. And it was cheap."

Charles nods his head once. "That is a pleasure to hear."

She slides into the car.

The look Charles gives me is not as warm. I know that look. He doesn't agree with what I'm doing. That's okay, I don't either. "We'll drop Savannah off first. Then I have to get to the office."

He closes the door.

Once we pull into traffic, I turn to Savannah. "Tell me about this charity event."

She shakes her head.

"Why is it so important to have the right dress?"

She glances out the window then meets my gaze. "I want to look good."

"For whom?"

She beams. "Me."

I raise my hand to her chin, caressing her jaw with my thumb. "Does the event have anything to do with Jana Monroe?"

She moves to pull her face away, but I don't let her. When her eyes meet mine again they are flashing with irritation. "If I wanted to discuss it with you, I would. But I don't."

"You will not go to this event on your own. It's not safe."

She takes my hand in hers and pulls it away from her face. "Wow. Last night you told me to be careful of people who might want to control me by separating me from others. Now you think I can't attend a party on my own? Pot— meet kettle. I'm going to that event, and I'm going alone."

I growl and sit back, folding my arms over my chest. "You are the most difficult woman. If someone does kidnap you, they might just drop you off at the next corner."

"Then I have nothing to worry about." She mirrors my stance and turns her face away.

We don't speak for the rest of the ride to her apartment. When we park, Charles opens the door on her side. She turns to leave, stops, and looks back at me. "Thank you for helping me find the right dress. I'm sorry I can't answer your questions. I wish I could."

"Don't go alone, Savannah."

Her response is a sad smile that says she's going to do just that. Then she's gone.

On the way to my office, I say, "Charles, I have a few hours of work, then I'm going to that charity event—

wherever the hell it is."

"Do you think that's wise, Bricelion?"

"Wise? No. Necessary? Hell yes."

Charles says nothing for a moment then clears his throat. "You've never been afraid to break a rule, and I've always looked away because it was never with the intention of harming anyone. This woman is putting her life back together after a loss. Be very careful. Don't become someone you can no longer look in the eye in the mirror."

My hands fist at my sides. "I'm trying to keep her safe."

"Then perhaps add yourself to the list of what you protect her from. She deserves more than you would offer her."

I hate that he's right.

I know I should stay away from her.

I don't think I can.

CHAPTER TWENTY

Savannah

HEAD HELD HIGH, I walk into the museum lobby. The high ceilings are sloped and arched in odd ways that make them more art than architecture. The modern color scheme and low light create an elegance perfect for a gala. Or so I've always imagined. A large glass and metal chandelier hangs from the center of the room and I can't help but gaze up. No one else seems to be taking in every detail but I don't want to miss a thing.

As I pass a floor-length mirror, I smile because I don't recognize the woman who smiles back at me. Her hair is perfectly shaped in a sophisticated updo. I slip off my jacket. The dress is tight and . . . holy hell, who knew my body could fill out a dress like that? I keep walking because it isn't vanity that has me staring at myself . . . it's shock. This is me.

Finally.

From my pale pink lipstick down to my shiny pedicure, I'm pulling this off. No one would guess I accidently kicked the person doing my pedicure when she tickled me with that stupid pumice stone. Or that it took me a full hour to blink correctly after I put on these false lashes.

I vacuumed my apartment in the high heels Miguel sold me, sprinted down the hall to catch the elevator, even took a cab all so I could walk across this lobby with confidence.

And it's fucking working.

The room is lushly decorated, but for once I don't feel out of place. There are long panels of tulle and twinkling lights so beautiful I'm giddy. My smile is wider than someone normally sports when they're alone, but I can't help it. No one on the street would hand me spare change now.

I spot Jana and make my way to her. She's a welcomed familiar face in the sea of strangers.

"You look fantastic," she says, leaning in and kissing the air just above my cheek. "That dress is stunning. Milano Sana Vons?"

"Yes." I'm surprised she knows the name of the designer. "I bought it at this really small tailoring shop for just a hundred dollars. Can you believe that?"

"I can't." She eyes it closely. "It's perfect for you. Your hair and makeup are perfection as well. How do you feel?"

"Good. Excited." I hesitate and then meet her gaze. "A little nervous."

"I'd be worried if you weren't. This is a big step for you. Don't forget why you're here."

"So you can show me how to speak to people like this." I twist the gold bracelet on my wrist nervously.

Jana gives me a long look. "I'm not staying. My only role is to provide you with an opportunity. What you do with it is up to you."

"Sink or swim on my own. I can do that." My breath is quick, and it breaks up my words. I raise my chin and take a calming breath. I've made it this far. I'll make this work.

"Nothing so final. You are here to practice. Flirt. Talk. Engage. That's all. Do not go home with one of these men. No matter what they offer, you leave alone." She gives a little wave to someone across the room.

"I'm sure that won't be a problem." I almost joke that lecturing a twenty-three-year-old virgin on chastity is about as necessary as advising a vegan to cut down on fatty meats. I've got abstinence down to an art. Before the words come out of my mouth, though, I imagine how she'd respond to the joke and bite my bottom lip instead.

Like some middle school teacher who knows where my mind has gone, her eyes narrow. "This will be a test in temptation. Looking around all starry-eyed and gorgeous in that dress, there will be plenty of offers. You're here alone. You're a complete mystery. That is an intoxicating combination for men."

So prepare to be hit on? I look around and realize there are men watching me. Holy shit. My stomach flips. This is happening, really happening.

"The trick to being considered fascinating is to listen more than you speak. Everyone's favorite topic, whether they realize it or not, is themselves."

I know that from working in a bar for years. "Okay."

"Enjoy the attention, but don't give out your number. You're practicing a skill. No one here matters. Not yet. Learn how to chat casually and move on. It's no different than learning to tie your shoes or do the latest dance step. Remember, you belong here. You're here to support the charity, just like everyone else."

"For the Shriners Hospital." I say it as much to remind myself and to prove to her I read her email.

"Yes. I could have done a breakdown on who are the doctors, the philanthropists, the politicians or the socialites, but that's also part of what you need to learn—social instincts. If you listen, people tell you who they are. Quick tip, the most influential people here won't tell you who they are. They don't have to."

"I understand."

"I can't stress enough that valuing yourself means saying no. Turn them down. Walk away. You've been telling yourself for a long time there were no opportunities for you. You lived in a way that kept that true. This place is wall-to-wall opportunity. Be the woman they remember not the one they fuck and forget."

I'm shocked to hear Jana use such strong language, but I get it. It's no different than when Jimmy would tell me to fucking watch the door because some out-of-towners were about to run out without paying their tab. Her profanity is an exclamation point. I nod and almost say I swear on a jar of fish eyes.

I choke back that comment as well.

"So, will I see any of these men again?" I still don't know how the whole process works, but I'm all in.

"You may. If you take my advice and do this right. Someone will make it a point to find you. Track you down.

That's what you're here to learn—how to be worth remembering."

"They'll track me down?" Even with my newfound confidence I can't imagine any of the successful men around me pining after I leave.

As soon as the thought hits me, I push it back.

That's what this is about, isn't it? Why can't I be a woman a man will seek out later?

"Men are persistent when they see something they want. The ones who challenge them and keep them guessing."

Not laughing. I could have promised to reduce at least of few of them to laughter. Challenge them? Keep them guessing? What the heck does that look like? "I'll do my best."

"You might surprise yourself. Now, I'm going home. Call if you need anything. You'll do great."

I gulp back my nerves and push down the thought of begging her to stay. No. Like my smelly coat, I refuse to put up protective walls between me and what I want. "I can do this."

"Good girl. *Do this.*" She points around the space. "Don't do them." She points at the men in the room. "Not yet."

A little laugh escapes my lips, and she hands me a glass of champagne.

"Have fun."

She pats my shoulder and nods to a man who is standing in the corner holding her coat. He moves toward her with intention, helps her slide her coat on and then escorts her out. Her lover? Her butler? A bodyguard? I can't tell. She's damn good at being a mystery. Expert level.

I watch her sashay out of the large hall with her head held high. Men and women watch her leave. She's living her own advice.

That could be me.

What she didn't tell me was how to start. Do I walk up to them? Do I say something clever? What is considered clever to people like this?

"Looking for the coat check?" A tall man with sideburns sidles up to me and gestures at my jacket. He's dressed in a black sweater and slacks.

I hug my coat a little closer while trying to think of something sophisticated to say. "Yes. I suppose I am."

He smiles. He's a little older than I am but not by more than a few years. "Then you're in luck, I just found it myself. Allow me to escort you that way."

Escort me? Sounds so formal. Better than pointing across the room I guess. "Thank you."

He waves a hand and we begin to walk together. "Michael Stockton."

"Savannah Barre."

He places a hand on my lower back as if ushering me along, but it's too familiar. I step aside to break the contact. "I don't think we've ever met."

Less is more. "I don't believe we have." We reach a small table where a woman takes my coat in exchange for a token I tuck in my small clutch.

"New to Boston?" He ducks his head down close to

mine.

I step back, but smile. "Why do you ask?" Nerves nip at my confidence, but I look this man in the eye. I donated a hundred dollars to the hospital. I belong here as much as he does.

"Your accent. It's . . ."

I almost say unavoidable, but refuse to apologize for who I am. "Not Bostonian?" What had Jana said . . . less me, more them? "You sound like a local. Are you?"

"Born and bred, but I only come back when I have to. I prefer a warmer climate."

Now that's something I understand. I glance up at him as we make our way into the main room that has been set up with tables on one side and a small dance floor on the other. His hair has highlights that look natural, and his skin is bronzed from time in the sun. "And the beach?"

His smile is easy and friendly. "I surf. How about you?"

Surfing wasn't big in Coppertop. "Not a surfer, but I do enjoy sailing." It isn't a lie. With thousands of miles of coast, Mainers have a natural affinity to the water.

His eyes perk up. "Really? What's your craft of choice?"

"Nothing beats the windjammers in Maine. There's a historical charm to them I don't find in modern sailboats. Which do you prefer in a board? Vintage or modern?"

"Wood all the way. The heart of surfing isn't about going hi-tech. It was always about connecting to something greater—being aware—in the moment."

Our eyes meet. There isn't a spark, but that doesn't mean I'm not enjoying myself. This is what I came to do. So far so good.

Across the room I see an older gentleman wave to him. He groans. "My father. He's afraid I'll slip out before making all the perfunctory exchanges. Normally I find these events tedious, but you may have given me a new perspective on them."

Me? I keep my surprise to myself and give him a vague smile.

He glances from me to his father and back. "Have you been to Maui?"

"No." I choke out a laugh. *I haven't been anywhere. Yet.*

He tips his head up curiously at me.

I can't explain. Too much information. Not enough mystery. Telling this man I'm from Coppertop, Maine, and that I've lived a dull life will kill the mood.

I almost say I've always wanted to go, but stop myself afraid it will sound too eager. "Until recently I worked too much to travel for pleasure."

"What do you do?" His eyes rove over my body as we talk, and I pretend not to notice. If he were one of the guys back home I would have swatted him and told him to put his eyes back in his head. Tonight, though, I dressed this way so men like him will look at me that way.

I wait to feel the same kind of warm, tingly excitement that washes over me whenever I catch Brice looking at me, but it doesn't come. Why am I thinking about him at all right now? Forward, not back. "What do I do for work?" I stall. I've never been good at lying. The challenge is to make the truth sound better. "Nothing at the moment, but I'm in

Boston working on a project that looks like it will be a real life changer."

"I'd love to hear more about it, but my father looks like he's about to head over here. Give me a few minutes, and I'll meet you back here."

I take Jana's advice. "It was nice meeting you." I step away first. I accept a glass of champagne from a passing server and try to look confident, but panic is beginning to set in. There are small groups of people standing in circles all around the room. Do I simply walk up to one of them?

"Excuse me," I say to a man with jet-black hair and a roundish face. "Have you seen Rodney Layne?" I toss out the name of my sixth-grade math teacher simply as an excuse to engage the man.

"Oh, sorry, I don't know him." He looks around the room as though it may jog his memory.

"Oh that's all right. I'm sure I'll catch him at some point. Thank you." I move aside for a group of women making their way across the room.

"I can keep you company until you find him." He gestures over to a small high-top table near the bar station.

"I'd like that," I say.

"I'm Paul. Do you need another drink?"

"I'm Savannah. No, but thank you." So far, so good. Paul isn't the most attractive man in the room, but he gives off a pleasant vibe. Working in a bar has given me good instincts on people. Some people come looking for trouble, others for company. He looks like the latter.

"I hear they're going to be serving more appetizers soon.

I'm always a sucker for a crab puff. You like them?"

I smile. Now this is a conversation I can keep up with. "Who doesn't?" The music in the background is mellow. "Everything has been very nice so far. I don't come to many of these. I'm enjoying it though. But I feel a little out of place." I see him relax as I admit my unease.

"You are out of place," Paul says, grinning at me. "You look like you belong on a runway in Paris."

"Oh, thank you." I touch his shoulder. He blushes.

I'm doing pretty damn good.

"This season's Milano Sana Vons dress. Who did you have to kill to get it?"

I frown as I realize the shop I went to didn't have a name. "I found it in a little shop run by a *Miguel*?"

His eyebrows rose and fell. "Okay, so you don't want to say. I understand. We all have our sources. Just tell me, was it a purchase or a lend?"

I know from watching the Oscars that designers dress clients for promotion. Do designers do that for charity events as well? I don't think he's suggesting I borrowed it . . . like illegally. "Purchase."

He nods. "You might want to consider donating it after the event. Tax write off for you, thousands of dollars in auction for Shriners. My ex-wife used to do it all the time."

Wait. I paid a hundred dollars for this dress. Nice as he is, Paul is confused. I'm smart enough not to correct him, though. "Thanks, I'll consider it."

I think about the small shop where I bought the dress. Brice set it up. Had he also gotten me a deal on a more expensive dress?

I need to stop thinking about Brice.

"Oh. So you know a lot about fashion?" I force my attention back onto the man I'm with.

"Only what I learned from fashion week. I'd be a much richer man if my wife hadn't liked shopping as much as she did."

I wince. "Sorry?"

His cheeks flush. "I don't know why I'm talking about my ex." We share an awkward moment, and I consider politely withdrawing. "I'm not good at meeting people."

That makes me smile. "Me either."

"I do believe in the cause, though. Childhood cancer research. It's underfunded."

"That's what I've heard." I really have no idea.

"Pediatric cancers just don't get money."

"That's terrible. It's great they have people like you."

"How about you?"

"I made a general donation." Jana is so right. Less is more.

"So tell me about this Rodney? Is he your date?"

"Just someone I heard might be here."

"So where is your date?" He looks over my shoulder expectantly. "Should I watch my back?"

"No date for me. I came on my own."

"Brave. Although I'm sure you're never alone long."

Time to put on the brakes a little. "I like meeting people. The only scary part is standing around on my own. So I'm glad for the company." There that didn't sound like a come on.

"Can I ask you something?"

"Sure."

"You came alone. Are you planning on leaving alone?"

"Excuse me?" My sip of champagne clogs in my throat.

"Savannah, sorry I took so long," a man says, leaning between us. I recognize his cologne before I see his face. *Brice.*

He places a drink in front of me as if I'd asked for it.

I glare at him, but he smiles and stands too close to me.

Paul's face glows red. "You must be Rodney."

I open my mouth to announce he isn't, but Paul's already backing away. I can't really blame him, Brice is a least a foot taller than he is and acting like we're together.

"Well, it was nice to meet you, Savannah," Paul says before bolting away.

My heart is racing. I tell myself it's from anger. In a low tone, I growl, "What the hell are you doing here?"

"It's an important cause."

"You know I don't want you here."

"You're not going to thank me from getting rid of that guy for you?"

"He was a lovely man. He gives all his money to charity."

"You weren't going home with him. Just say thank you."

I'm not grateful. I'm turned on and angry with myself for being so. Brice is not part of the plan. He's the anti-plan. "I'm not going home with anyone, but that doesn't mean I can't enjoy meeting new people."

"Is that why you're here? To meet people?"

Although I wasn't about to explain why to him, maybe

he needed to hear part of the truth. "Yes, and that isn't possible with you looming over me, so can you please go away?"

"I don't like this."

There was something in his eyes that made me wish we were on an entirely different journey. It was too easy to imagine we actually were together and that if I licked my bottom lip, he'd lean down with a kiss that would have me forgetting every other man in the room.

Lust. This wasn't my first dance with it.

So much of what Jana said was spot-on. I didn't wait because no opportunity ever presented itself. In Coppertop I was afraid to let anyone in.

Boston is about letting that fear go. It is a journey that is supposed to start first with me liking myself, then finding a man. I'm so close too.

Brice could derail that. I look him in the eye. "That's not my problem."

His expression darkens. "You think you know what's happening here. You don't."

Here? Like with me and him?

Or here at the event? I shoot him an apologetic smile. "Then that makes two of us because you're driving me crazy. I wish I could tell you exactly why I'm here, but you'll just have to trust that I know what I'm doing."

"Just as you will have to trust that I'm here because I don't want anything to happen to you." He closes his eyes for a beat, clearly trying to center himself. "I'm going to the other bar in the corner. Forget I'm here."

Sure. That sounds easy. I can't forget you when you're not here.

He moves away and I fan my face.

I can't flirt if I know he's watching me. I turn away from him, away from the disaster the event is becoming, and move quickly across the open space. Is Brice so protective because he met me at my worst? I'm half tempted to march over to the bar he planted himself at and tell him I'm not that woman anymore.

You don't need to protect me.

I belong here.

In pure rom-com-disaster style I slam into a man who was heading in the opposite direction. His drink tips out and splatters onto my shoes.

"Oh I'm so sorry," I gasp, covering my mouth. Things are unraveling quickly.

"No, I am," he replies hurriedly. "I hope they're not ruined."

"They're fine," I say.

His hazel eyes catch the light overhead as he straightens. "If you need to get them cleaned or something I can probably figure out how to have that done. Do you get shoes cleaned?" The dimple that appears when he smiles is endearing.

"I don't know," I say with an answering smile. "I usually only have the kind of shoes you throw in the washing machine when they get dirty. These would probably fall apart."

"I can take your number. Or you can take mine. Maybe

we can figure it out."

"I can't," I blurt out as I remember Jana's advice.

He looks slightly embarrassed. "Too blunt? Let me try this again. My name's Kyle."

"A little blunt." We shake hands awkwardly. "Savannah."

Kyle lowers his voice and leans in a little closer. "Sorry. My in-person skills are rusty. So much easier to swipe right."

I laugh even though I'm not sure what that means.

He tugs at the collar of his shirt. "My friend was supposed to come with me tonight but had to work late. He begged me to come anyway. His company needs to fill a certain amount of chairs and I thought hell, I'll get a free dinner. But so far it's just me eating crab puffs and making very awkward conversation with people I have nothing in common with."

"Nothing?" I tuck a loose lock of hair behind my ear. "I can relate to that. This is all new for me too. You can probably tell by the way I keep trying to put my hand in my pocket only to remember I'm in a gown. I'm sure everyone can tell I don't belong here. But you must have something in common with people here. More than I do."

"Honestly nothing. I own a sausage cart outside of Fenway. Do I smell like peppers and onions right now? That's all I can think about. That people are sniffing me and realizing I don't belong here."

I grin knowingly. "You smell fine."

"We should team up. Try to hide out in some corner until this thing is over. Eat as much free food as possible. Close enough to still get appetizers but far enough to not have to talk about the stock portfolios we don't have."

It's a fun idea. He reminds me of Lance. Harmlessly bold. "I'd like that."

"Let me get you another drink, then we can hide out." His gap-toothed smile is genuine.

"I'd love another champagne." My head is swimming a bit from the drinks, just enough to take the edge off.

He puts his arm out, and I loop mine into his as we walk toward the back corner of the large and beautifully decorated hall. "Savannah, you might just turn this whole night around for me. I'll go to the bar and get us drinks."

The bar.

Where Brice is. My eyes, no matter how much I demand they don't, turn to where I saw him last. He's there with one hand in his pocket and the other on his drink. Looking like the cover of a sexy business magazine.

He glances over at me and flashes a smile. But I see something else. There's a woman at the other end of the bar with her eyes fixed on him. I want to smack the stupid diamond studded tiara out of her hair.

"Champagne?" Kyle asks, and clearly not for the first time. I'd tuned him out.

"What?"

"That's what you said you wanted, right?"

The longer I look at Brice, the more smug his smile gets. "Let me get the drinks," I sputter out. "You stay here."

"Really? I don't mind."

"What do you want to drink?" I ask without looking at Kyle. All of my attention is focused on the smile Brice just flashed the tiara woman. She swirls her straw in her drink and batts her lashes at him. I'm about to throw up.

Kyle groans with uncertainty. "A beer, I guess? Whatever they have."

"I'll be right back." I put a finger up and try to look worth waiting for.

I march over to the bar; my high heels tapping against the marble floor. I choose to sidle up right next to him at the bar, but I don't look at him. "You think you're bothering me, but you're not."

"Glad to hear that."

I flag the bartender and order two glasses of champagne. "I'm having a perfectly nice conversation with Kyle."

"Kyle?"

"Yes. And you're not going to ruin it for me."

"Got it."

He isn't taking me seriously. I spin toward him. "Brice, you're making this impossible."

"By being here?"

"Yes." I collect the two flutes of champagne and slap down a tip.

Brice glances across the room to the man I left waiting for me. "He made you get your own drink. Come on, Kyle, be a gentleman."

"I told him I wanted to get them myself so I could come tell you to stop destroying my night."

"Good, boy, Kyle. Sit. Stay."

"You're an asshole." I give him one final glare. "Don't ruin this for me."

He lets out a burst of breath. "Again, I haven't moved. I've been right here. Talk to whomever you want."

I stomp back to Kyle. He accepts the champagne, but makes a face at it. "Thanks."

"You're welcome." I turn my back to Brice. He only has the power to get to me if I let him.

"You know that guy?" Kyle asks, gesturing with his chin over to Brice.

"No. I mean I do, but he's nobody." I take a far-too-big sip of my drink and then position myself so I can keep an eye on Brice. The woman has shifted closer to him. He says something to her, and her laugh echoes across the room.

"Oh," Kyle says, sounding confused. "Well, so tell me more about what you actually do."

The woman puts her arm on Brice's arm and bends forward like she can't hear him, but she's really trying to give him a look down her dress. "Why doesn't she just jump him? How much more obvious could she be?" I huff and look to Kyle for confirmation that he's seeing what I see.

"Who?" Kyle asks, looking around.

Oh right, I'm the only one fixated on the most infuriating man in the room. "Nothing. No one. I'm sorry what were you asking?"

"I asked what you do for a living. I've been telling everyone I export Italian products. That sounds much better than I sell sausages to drunk people in the street at midnight. I figure it's not a lie, but I won't embarrass myself."

"I told someone I'm here in Boston with a real life-changing job opportunity." I cover my mouth and my nose wrinkles as I hold in a laugh. "I didn't think he'd be interested in the fact that I work at a marina in a very small fishing town in Maine." I force myself to look at Kyle. "I usually smell like fish. That's how I met that guy over there. We were stuck in an elevator, and I still had my smelly fish coat on."

"Umm, I like seafood." He chuckles awkwardly. He pauses when I don't laugh. "Do you need to talk to that guy?"

"Which guy?" I ask, my gaze naturally darting to Brice.

"The one you're obviously interested in. The big guy at the bar."

"He's not that big. You're tall, Kyle."

"Yeah, but I'm not as interesting as whatever game you're playing with him."

The woman beside Brice wiggles closer. "Why doesn't she just jump in his lap?"

Kyle cranes his neck to see from my angle. "He doesn't seem that interested in her actually."

"How can you tell?"

Kyle sighs. "Because he's been looking over here as often as you've been looking over there."

"I haven't been—"

"I'm going to go get some fresh air. Nice to meet you, Savannah." He puts his champagne down on a nearby table and walks away.

So much for me being the one to walk away and be remembered. I shoot another glare at Brice and catch him with that big fat smile on his face again.

I pick up the hem of my dress so I don't trip on it while I charge toward him. The woman beside him is thin as a rail, gaunt but still beautiful. The kind of woman who deprives herself of the joys of life so she can squeeze into the latest fashion.

"Happy?" I snap.

He makes a show of weighing nothing with his hands. "Things have been better. Things have been worse."

"Um, hello?" the woman says, taking a step back. "Do you need something?"

I want to punch her. I don't. I wouldn't have, not even if I were still in jeans and smelling like fish oil. Violence is never the answer. But that doesn't mean I don't indulge in the fantasy of socking her one.

Brice puts his arm around my waist. "I never thought I'd put up with a jealous girlfriend, but she's amazing in the sack."

With a huff the woman pushes off the bar and charges away.

I'm a tangle of confusing emotions. Relief that Brice really isn't interested in her. Frustration with myself for caring. And God, being so close to him feels good—too good. How am I going to stay angry with him if I'm reduced down to imagining his lips on mine again?

"This evening is a flop, and it's your fault."

"Flop?"

I turn in the circle of his arm and the side of my breast warms as it brushes against his chest. My breath catches in my throat. "How can I relax and meet people when I know you're watching me?"

"Is that why you're here? To meet men? If Jana set this up, do you really need more proof that she's setting you up as some kind of escort? These people are probably clients of hers and she's dangling you in front of them like a treat."

"That's disgusting. And not true."

"Really? I'd bet my crown she told you to get dressed up and flirt with the men here."

I tip my head to the side. "Your crown?"

He looks stumped for a second, then picks up a drink from the bar. "Crown Royal."

How many drinks in is he? He doesn't know a gin and tonic from a Crown Royal? "Whatever. Today was nearly perfect, and I proved something to myself."

"What did you prove? That you can make a man want you? I could have told you that. You're beautiful, Savannah. Whatever Jana is telling you, it's not true. You don't need her."

There's a possessive look in his eyes that is as scary as it is exciting. Jana told me if I played this right I would attract a man. I remember what Charles said about Brice not having an affinity to monogamy. The way he's looking at me is probably the same way he's looked at hundreds of women before me and will look at just as many after me. I don't want that. "I'm tired, and I'm going home. I appreciate you babysitting me, but as you can see, it wasn't necessary. I'm taking a cab. It's only five blocks. Is that all right with you? I'd hate to do anything you don't approve of."

He shakes his head in response to my heavy sarcasm. I

don't know if he's annoyed with me or himself, and I honestly don't care.

"Good night." I turn my back and tip my chin up proudly.

Charles meets me at the door. I thank him for the offer, but instead ask the attendant to flag a cab for me.

I spend the short ride back to my apartment telling myself to focus on what went right. Jana now sees me as someone she can work with. I flirted with some degree of success. I didn't fall on my face in these heels. Didn't choke on a shrimp tart. I'm still tallying my points as I walk into the lobby of my apartment. *My apartment.* Brice can't take the excitement of that from me.

"You're back." A woman with two long braids over her shoulders touches my arm and smiles. "We were just talking about you."

My eyebrows raise.

She quickly adds, "All nice things. We saw you leave in that dress earlier and wished we could go with you. You're the most exciting thing that has happened in this building since it turned into this mom jungle."

"I am?"

"Yes. I'm Claire. It's nice to meet you." Her braids bounce on her shoulders as she practically skips at my side.

"Savannah."

The other woman is a brunette who is more physically fit than I'll ever be. Her name is Ronda. She shakes my hand too vigorously. "Tell us it's none of our business, but we have to know . . . are you dating any of the men we've seen visit you? My guess is you moved to the city for the man in the suit. Am I right?" She claps her hands together with excitement.

"No." I laugh nervously. "I'm not dating any of them."

"Keeping it casual," Ronda says knowingly. "That's what people do these days."

"No, they're all just friends."

"Where were you tonight?" Claire asks, looking over my dress again.

"A charity event. Very nice. I talked to a lot of interesting people."

"Please let us live vicariously through you. Claire, how long has it been since I've worn high heels?" Ronda asks as she looks across at her friend.

"Two babies ago." This is the closest thing to *girl talk* I've ever had, and I like it. "Did you go with the hottie?"

"No, but he was there."

"Of course he was. He likes you," Claire declares.

"It's not like that. I hardly know him. He's just paranoid that someone is going to snatch me or sell me off. I don't know."

Claire sighed. "I remember when my husband thought every man I met wanted me. Know what we do now when we get a babysitter? We nap. It's heaven."

Ronda gives her friend a look. "If that's true, you need to up your game, Claire. Babies or not, if you're not with your husband someone else will be."

"They won't want him, because if he ever cheats on me, I'll remove the part they'd want."

I snort. These ladies are great.

Ronda turns her attention back to me. "Enough about us. Back to Mr. Hottie. How are you not all over that?"

I have nothing to lose by sharing a little. "He's a player, and I'm not looking for that."

Claire nods. "I can see that."

Ronda taps a finger on her chin. "Sometimes you have a driver. Sometimes you take a cab. That isn't his driver by any chance?"

I blush. "It is."

"Sweetie, that man is not with you for friendship."

Warmth spreads through me even as I fight against it. "Well, that's all he's going to get from me."

Claire and Ronda exchange a look. "Would it be wrong if we took bets on that?"

Funny thing about people in the city, they aren't so different from the people in Coppertop after all. Ballbusters, all of them. "Not wrong at all. Five dollars says I never sleep with him."

Ronda shakes on that. "Five dollars says he's sleeping over by next week."

Claire put a hand on her heart. "A hundred dollars says you marry him." When Ronda rolls her eyes, Claire sputters, "Hey, I'm a romantic at heart."

We all laugh as we head toward the elevators. It's not until I'm back in my apartment that I think of a bet I wouldn't want to win. A thousand dollars says if I sleep with him, he breaks my heart, and I wish I'd never come to Boston.

I pull the dress over my head and hang it carefully in my closet. In the mix, I forgot to donate it, but if it really is worth anything, I'll offer it to the charity tomorrow.

As I let my hair down and remove my makeup, I give myself a stern talking to. No man, not even one with a voice that makes me want to strip for him, is worth risking my future. Brice will never break my heart, because I'm ending things with him now.

He wouldn't have known about the charity event if I hadn't told him. It's my fault he went. I told him just enough to make him think I don't know what I'm doing. I'm sabotaging my own path to success.

Failure here is not an option.

I'm not going back to Coppertop, brokenhearted, with my tail between my legs.

You hear me, Brice Hastings? We're done.

CHAPTER TWENTY-ONE

Brice

A WAREHOUSE. WHY in the world would she be going into some warehouse in the middle of the afternoon? The cars outside don't bring me any comfort: BMWs, Volvos, Hondas. Most look in good condition. The selection of vehicles implies the people inside are neither wealthy nor poor. Money isn't an indicator of character, though.

I told Charles I was heading to the gym because I don't want to look him in the eye and try to defend what is clearly becoming an obsession. I should be in my office concentrating on closing any one of the deals I have in progress. Instead, I'm chasing some damn woman around the city.

She clearly doesn't want me involved in whatever she's doing. That should be enough to get me to back off. I've never been the hero type. My family would have me hauled back home, duct taped if necessary, if they knew I'd made what was already a crazy mission into a solo one. Hell, my brother probably should marry soon and start popping out heirs because I don't know what I'm walking into. All I know is I'm not leaving without Savannah.

The industrial entrance opens to a carpeted hallway lined

with bland enough looking conference rooms. There's a small piece of paper taped to the door. I lean in to read it.

Barrier Breakers Conference. Empowerment through effective communication.
Presented By Trent Bixby.

A conference? That's what she's doing here?

That's the problem with using Simon as a source of information. He provides only what he's asked for. When I told him to keep me updated on her location and he said he tracked her phone to a warehouse on the edge of the city . . . all kinds of B-rated movies that involve human trafficking propelled me here.

Unarmed because . . . there's a shred of sanity left in me.

I find where the conference is being held and step through the door quietly. There's a pot of coffee and some Styrofoam cups sitting on a small table in the back of the room. Chairs are lined up facing a little podium where a man stands fiddling with the microphone, trying to get it to work. He doesn't need it though. I'm assuming this is Trent Bixby. There are only about twenty people, and I spot Savannah immediately. Her hair is in silky long locks, bouncing a little as she nods her head. She's sitting in the front row, soaking up every word Bixby says.

She's not in danger.

The audience is a mix of men and women. Some look like fresh college graduates. Others are older, but have that new penny shine to them that says they came to impress.

She hasn't seen me. It would be easy to slip out now, but

I'm fascinated. How does a conference on effective communication fit into everything I've learned about her so far?

Is it as simple as my little Savannah wanting to better herself? After losing her grandmother, she came to the city, sought out someone she hopes will help her transform into what?

Her yearning for a better life is beautiful, but it could also leave her vulnerable to being taken advantage of. Someone as shady as Jana Monroe would see that instantly.

Were the others in the crowd also Monroe's clients/targets? Bixby's slicked-back hair and oversized suit coat don't sell him as someone I'd listen to.

I take a seat in the back, six empty rows behind the others. I cross my arms over my chest as the man launches into a speech about confidence. How to *fake it till you make it.* Skepticism is my speed in general, but in a place like this I go into hyper drive.

To my surprise, the audience seems completely engaged. Leaning in. Bixby launches into a rationale for creating a vision board. Before you can achieve it or share your vision with others, you need to clarify it for yourself. Clip photos online or with scissors. Choose the people you admire. Listen to how they express themselves. Become the person you admire.

I make an audible scoffing noise I can't hold back. A few heads turn my way but not Savannah's.

Trent Bixby waves me up suddenly. "Sir, thanks for joining us. Why don't you move up here so you can engage in the dialogue?"

"No, thanks." At my curt response, Savannah spins around and her mouth drops open in a mix of surprise and annoyance. "I'm good back here."

Bixby shakes his head. "But you're not. The back of the room is where people hide. It's where we all hide. You belong up here. It's scary, but you can do it. We're here for you."

I smirk. "I'm fine where I am."

Trent takes the microphone off the podium and walks toward me with a look of empathy. "I know how you feel. Trust me I have been the guy in the back of the room. But you can do this. It's the first step. Join us."

My eyes move quickly off Savannah and focus on Bixby. "I'm not afraid to go up there."

"You should be," Savannah calls angrily.

Bixby gives her a confused look. "This needs to be a safe place for every attendee."

"What's your name?" Bixby asks with a gentle voice. He looks like he's trying not to spook a skittish woodland creature.

"Hastings." It's a lie I've told so many times it feels real.

Savannah stands, hands on hips. "This is taking it too far, Brice." She storms down the aisle toward me. "You're not ruining this for me too."

Now I feel like an ass.

I want her to find what she came to Boston looking for.

I rise to my feet. "I'm not here to ruin it, Savannah. I'm here to support you."

Her chest is heaving. "Supportive people call and ask

what you're doing. They wait to be invited. You are a controlling, smug"—she pokes a finger into my chest—"infuriating man who thinks he knows what's best for me. News flash. You don't."

From beside us, Bixby says, "Although it's good to express how you're feeling, this is probably not the appropriate space for you to do it."

Her anger intensifies and her eyes flash at me. "Do you see what you've done, Brice? Now he thinks I don't belong here." Oh, no. Her lip quivers. "But I do. You're the one who doesn't."

Bixby clears his throat. "You should both go."

I don't care about him, but he's buzzing around like a fly so I take a swat. "And you should back the fuck away from us. Did I communicate that effectively?"

He does. "Anger management is two doors down on Wednesday."

Savannah looks around the room, realizes all eyes are on us, and there is likely no way she can salvage the situation. Chin high, she marches to her seat, retrieves her purse, then walks out of the conference room.

I trot after her. It's not the first time I've done something I regret, but knowing I hurt Savannah cuts through me.

Without speaking, she escapes through the first door she finds in the hallway. I'm right there with her, searching for something to say that will make her feel better.

"Dumpsters. Of course." Her cheeks are red. Her eyes blazing with anger. It's illogical. Impulsive. But also inevitable. I pull her in for a kiss. My hand wraps up in her hair.

The other on the small of her back. The passion she's channeled toward being angry with me is replaced quickly by desire.

Her hands are just as hungry. Her body writhes against mine as she opens her mouth for me. It's a kiss that defies logic, a passion that simply is.

We are both breathing heavily when she breaks off the kiss. Her hands plant on my chest, and she shoves back. Like a cord yanked from an outlet, we jolt apart.

"This is insanity." She stares up at me with frantic eyes.

"Savannah. I just came to—"

She shakes her head. "It doesn't matter why you came. It matters why I was there. And why now I'm out here by a dumpster."

"That class is a joke. You don't need to be listening to some guy named Trent telling you about vision boards in a warehouse. What are you looking for? Tell me."

She rubs her hands over her face. "I don't need to justify my decisions to you. I don't expect you to understand what I'm doing. You were probably educated at the best schools. Surrounded by sophisticated people. Given every opportunity to succeed. Well shocker, that hasn't been my experience. But I'm trying to learn." A tear escapes and runs down her cheek. "I'm trying so hard, and I can't let you stand in my way."

"I'm not standing in your way, Savannah. I'm on your side. I just don't want to see you hurt."

"Brice, I've been hurting every day for a long time. That's the part you're missing. This is the first time in a long time I'm not hurting. Being here, on my own, working to be a better version of myself. I need this. Don't take this from me."

My gut twists painfully. "I don't want to take anything from you." If I knew what she wanted, I'd move heaven and earth to give it to her.

"This is important to me."

"I know it is."

"Do you? Then you know when something is important, it's worth the sacrifice."

Sacrifice?

She continues, "Obviously, there is something between us. I'd be a hypocrite to deny it, but I can't let it derail me."

She's stronger than I am, and it's a humbling realization.

She has dedicated herself to a course, and Charles is right—the last thing she needs is a fling with a playboy prince.

Is that still all I am? All I can offer her? I work all hours of the night, orchestrating deals that may change my family's future and sustain us financially for generations. It's quite possible I might be more than a spare-tire prince.

I want to be more.

I'm still processing the depth of my feelings for her, when she says, "You know what they have back in Coppertop? Dumpsters. Back alleys just like this one. And any night of the week behind the bar I work at I could get in an argument with a guy and end up back here if I wanted to. I'm trying to have something different. But here I am outside by a dumpster. I should be in that conference." She wipes away another tear. "I belong in that conference."

I don't have words to articulate the mix of emotions whirling within me. I've never felt so wrong, so deeply invested in how someone else feels. Her pain is ripping through me.

Without blinking, I could buy the fucking building that conference is happening in, but I can't undo what just happened in there. I could walk her back in, explain that I'm the ass, but it wouldn't return to what it was for her.

"I'm sorry, Savannah. You do belong in there. I shouldn't have come today."

She blinks a few times and nods. "I shouldn't have gotten so defensive and told you to leave."

We walk out of the alley together. "Do you need a ride back?" I ask.

She sniffs and looks around. "I don't know if I can face Chucky right now."

"I drove my own car."

She shoots me a sidelong look. "Really?"

She deserves the truth. "Charles would not have condoned my appearance here today."

She searches my face. My heart is thudding wildly in my chest. "This is about more than just keeping me safe, isn't it?"

I nod. "I can't get you out of my head."

"It's the same for me."

It should have been a moment that ended with us in each other's arms. There is too much sadness in her eyes, though, for me not to understand this is goodbye.

I raise a hand and cup her cheek. "I wish I knew how to help you, Savannah."

She places her hand over mine, steps back, and breaks the contact. "I wish I hadn't met you when I wasn't ready to." She takes out her phone, types away on it, then pockets it again. "I called for a car to pick me up. Tell Charles I said thank you for everything. I really am grateful for your help. I just can't . . ."

She turns and walks away.

I'm left with my tumultuous thoughts and a conviction to set things right for her. No matter what that takes.

CHAPTER TWENTY-TWO

Brice

I'M ON THE fifteenth floor of my office building. I'm done circling around, worrying that Jana Monroe might have nefarious intentions. She will be the resource Savannah believes she is, or she will feel my royal wrath.

I've never summoned my men for anything but late-night partying, however they'd come at my command. I haven't used my connections outside of business deals, but my associates now include some who could make her and her organization disappear. Even Charles, disapproving as he has been lately, didn't try to dissuade me when I told him where I was going. We don't know if Monroe is acting on her own or if she's part of a larger, more dangerous organization.

When one is about to go to battle, it's best to at least prepare one's army.

I made an appointment because I'm willing to give her an opportunity to resolve this in a civilized manner. As far as I know, she hasn't done anything to harm Savannah yet. God help her if I discover that's not the case.

Her secretary leads me into her office. I take a seat. Calm. Ready.

"How can I help you?" Jana sits back coolly and taps her long fingernails on her glass-top desk. "Your request to see me was a surprise."

"I'm sure it was. I'm here about Savannah Barre."

"I'm still not sure how I can help you."

"She's a client of yours. Not sure what your other clients are like. Are they also naïve women from small towns?"

She arches an eyebrow. "That's an interesting assumption. I'm intrigued. It appears we have a mutual friend who isn't representing my services well."

"Your services? And what exactly is it that you do?"

"I'm sorry, but confidentiality is essential to the success of what I do and for a positive outcome for my clients. I'm disappointed that Savannah does not appear to understand that."

I lean forward and growl. "Let's make one thing clear. Whatever you've promised Savannah, whatever plans you have for her, from this day on you clear them with me. She's under my protection."

Her laugh is an insult by itself, but she adds, "How outdated and unnecessary. *She's under your protection?*"

"Careful. You don't know who you're dealing with."

Jana rises to her feet. "Nor do you. Although it's kind of sweet . . . I guess . . . that you felt coming here and threatening me would help Savannah, but all you did is confirm that it was a mistake to take her on in the first place. I gave her an opportunity to pull herself above the life she was born into. She chose chaos and you. It's a shame, though. My way would have had long-term benefits." She looks me up and down. "You come across to me as a one weekender."

I don't care what she thinks of me. I don't even care that her assessment of me—at least as far as who I was before I came to Boston—is correct. "You speak with real conviction. Is that how you lure your victims in? Promise to help them better themselves? You miscalculated when you chose Savannah, though. She is not desperate and alone, ripe for your picking and manipulation. If I were you, I would tread carefully with how you deal with her. My guess is your business would shrivel if exposed to the spotlight of media attention. People in your business are always popular until your other clients fear you'll name them in a plea bargain."

"You think I'm a madam?" Jana's eyes go wide. Now she looks shaken. "Is that what Savannah thinks I am?"

I push out of the chair and rest my hands on her desk. "It's what I think you are. Care to correct me? I'd love to hear your version of what you do."

She shakes her head. "I can't do that."

"Then we have a problem, don't we?" I straighten. She may not be ready to confess, but we understand each other now. "You either include me in every decision you make regarding your 'plans' for Savannah, or you cut ties with her."

"You don't intimidate me."

"Then you're not nearly as intelligent as you think you are."

Jana blinks first and sways on her feet before sitting back down. I won this time, but I can't leave until I'm sure there won't be a round two.

"Let's be clear, if you hurt her, you're done. You and everyone associated with you."

"I'm not what you think I am."

I smile. "Let's hope not. Because you're on my radar now. I'll be watching. If I see you 'helping' another unsuspecting woman, there won't be a safe place for you to hide."

I leave the office without another word and slip past her young receptionist.

Charles meets me in the hallway.

"It's done," I say.

"Done?" His eyes round. "As in, the conversation went well or I need to bring the car around so we can stash a body in the trunk?"

One side of my mouth twitches. Sarcastic bastard. "Jana Monroe is no longer a problem. She's now aware of how dangerous further association with Savannah would prove to be."

We enter the elevator together, turning to face the door as it closes. "So, she's not working with Savannah anymore?"

Was I not clear on that? "Exactly. Savannah is safe now. She can find self-improvement courses on her own without being groomed for whatever that woman had in mind for her."

His silence is telling.

"It had to be done, Charles. You yourself said you were uncomfortable with the secrecy surrounding the Monroe woman."

"I did say that."

"But."

My phone beeps, ending our conversation there. It's the text I've been waiting for, confirmation that one of the tech companies I've courted will allow me to buy in as a private investor. The deal will prove lucrative for both sides, especially if the software they're developing becomes as successful as I think it will.

After a lifetime of having my every whim anticipated and fulfilled, I championed for my people and won. The partnership will bring in much needed funds and future job opportunities. My brother will soon have a second option to bring needed funds to our country.

Savannah is no longer in danger.

Two goals—both achieved.

The satisfaction I expected to feel doesn't come.

Charles and I step out onto the thirtieth floor. "Charles, have you ever done something that felt right and wrong at the same time?"

He takes a deep breath. "Yes, and that's always a sign for me to back out of the situation. It's time to go home, Bricelion."

"Not yet, Charles."

Not yet.

CHAPTER TWENTY-THREE

Savannah

POWERING THROUGH IS my nature. Do I want to see Brice again? Yes. But not everything a person wants is what they need. So instead I'm taking Jana's advice about self-care. I just ended an hour-long massage at the spa Chucky introduced me to and am feeling human again.

I can't give my energy to every mistake I've made. All I can do is try to do better from this moment on.

I'm halfway through getting dressed in the changing room when my phone rings. "Hello?"

"Savannah, we need to talk." Jana's voice is formal to the point that my stomach instantly twists into knots. I know the tone bad news takes. It has a knife's edge. Steely and cold.

"What's going on?"

"We had an agreement. Rules of engagement." Jana sighs. "I was very clear with my expectations."

"Yes, I know. I've been making it to all the appointments you've set for me. I thought the event went pretty well." My face blazes red with worry. "Is this about the conference? I can explain."

"I had a visitor today."

"A visitor?"

"A man who said you were under his protection. He insisted I should back off and leave you alone."

I sag against the wall. I'm going to kill that man. First I'm going to fix this, then he needs to die. "Jana, I'm so sorry. Brice thinks he's helping. I'll talk to him. Please. You won't see him again."

"Savannah, what I do is only possible because there is confidentiality. I do wish you luck. I'm rooting for you, really. But I can no longer work with you."

The line cuts out, and I stand in the hallway wide-eyed and gasping. What happened? It's over. Every single thing I did to get here, stay here, and grow here, is over now. My knees knock together as I lean against the wall.

I'm still in shock as I finish dressing. Maybe I paid for the massage. I don't know. I'm not even sure how I make it back to my apartment building, but that's where I am before I know it.

This has to be a dream. I must have fallen asleep on the massage table. That's all this is. A post-massage nightmare.

"Hey girl, what's going on?" Claire flips one of her long braids over her shoulder as she steps in my path to the elevator.

I look at her, completely at a loss for what to say.

"Oh, my God, did something happen?" She ushers me gently over to a padded bench in the lobby and rests a hand on my shoulder as we sit.

I'm not dreaming. This is my fucking reality. I did this. I

told Brice about Jana. "I screwed up. I screwed everything up by opening my big mouth."

"Now hang on, there's hardly anything in this world that can't be undone and fixed. Tell me what happened and we'll come up with something to make it right."

"I had a plan—a good plan. Now I have nothing."

She rubs my shoulder like one would a child. "Plans change. It would be pretty boring if everything went exactly how we expect it to."

A tear runs down my cheek. "I guess."

"My mom always said that when things get tough there are really only two choices a person has. You can lie down and give up or you can get up and keep fighting. I'm a fighter. Which are you?"

I sniff. "I'm definitely a fighter."

"Okay then. Don't let this beat you. Whatever plan you had that isn't happening, it's not your only path. Come up with a new plan."

I meet her gaze and realize she probably talks like this to her children. I never had that. I hear her, though. I choose how much power to give this. If I give up and go home now, it's not Jana's fault. It's not even Brice's. It's my future and my responsibility to fight for it. "I thought I knew what I was doing, but you're right, all I need is a new plan."

"That's right." Claire smiles. "And maybe some carbs. They always lift my spirits. Would you like to come over for dinner tonight? I guarantee it will be loud, messy, and chaotic, but I make a mean spaghetti. To balance that out, though, we'll need to put in an hour at the gym. Also good for improving your mood."

"I'd love that." I remember where I came from and say, "I just had a massage so I won't be able to lift weights."

"Walk on the treadmill then. Best way to remind yourself to keep putting one foot in front of the other."

I rise and give her an impulsive hug. "You are one wise mama."

Claire pats my back gently as she squeezes me. "Meet you in the gym in an hour?"

"You're on," I say. "I do have something I need to do first. But I'll be there."

I return to my apartment and take out one of the few possessions I brought with me. It's a small, tattered notebook I used to write in when I was a teenager. It is full of angst, but also of my dreams.

I settle onto the couch and flip through it. I had planned to open it after my transformation. A few days ago everything in it had felt out of reach to me, but this was my vision board.

What had I wanted before I lost myself?

I'd wanted a family.

Friends.

A job doing something important.

Nothing so crazy I couldn't make it happen on my own.

I'm a fighter.

I flip to the back of the book and trace a circle around a name and number I wrote there a long time ago. I do have family. My mother had a sister who had children of her own. Somewhere in western Massachusetts, I have a family I've never been brave enough to contact.

Soon after my father went to prison, my grandmother told me I'd be staying with her because no one else wanted me. Years later, she told me she reached out after my father died and my aunt hadn't changed her mind. She wanted nothing to do with me.

The answer to why I've hidden away is right here in my teenage handwriting. They didn't want me and I didn't want to be rejected again.

I lay down and accepted it . . . for too long.

What would a fighter do?

I close the book and hug it to me.

I can hear my father telling me that no one is better than anyone else. That the only way to overcome a fear is to face it.

I can do this on my own.

I don't need Jana to make friends for me.

I don't need her to show me how I can make a difference in the world.

I hug the book tighter.

I'm going to find my mother's family and see for myself how they feel about me.

That's my new plan.

CHAPTER TWENTY-FOUR

Brice

I'M BOARDING A private jet a few days later, and pause to look back across the airfield. I hate the idea of leaving without seeing Savannah again. Without apologizing one more time.

Charles is right behind me. "Are we not leaving?"

I sigh. "We're leaving."

He chuckles.

I glare at him and continue on into the jet. I settle into a seat, and he takes the one across from me. He says something to me, but my thoughts are with Savannah. I called her—she didn't answer. Not so much as a text in response.

She made her choice.

We're in the air before I pull my attention from buildings that are getting smaller and smaller the higher we go. I hope Savannah finds what she came to Boston for.

I smile as I remember the first time we met. It's hard to believe the woman who had strode away from me at the warehouse, the one who'd left me standing there with my heart in her hand, was the same one I'd first thought was a lost homeless person. Every single day with her had been full of the unexpected . . . and I hadn't meant to get so involved, but the pull of her had been irresistible.

I rub my forehead with disgust as I remember how I practically chased her around Boston. I never would, but if I ever did share the story with my friends, no one would believe me. There has always been a steady supply of willing women—and if I ever came across a woman who wasn't interested, I don't remember the experience. I certainly haven't cared enough to pursue any of them.

Was it because I felt she needed someone to protect her?

Was it her yearning to better herself that called to a part of me that wanted the same for myself? Two very different people, each trying to find their footing.

She said she wasn't ready to meet me. What does she think isn't already incredible about her, because I haven't found anything.

She's resilient.

Brave.

Funny as hell.

Does she think she isn't polished enough? I would have fucked her in that stinky coat of hers. How she tangled me up on the inside had nothing to do with if her hair was styled and highlighted.

"Coffee, Your Highness?" a member of the royal staff asked.

I decline with a shake of my head. We aren't even back in Calvadria, and my needs are already being anticipated. In Bachelor Tower, I definitely took advantage of the house-keeping and dinner service, but it was nice to put something down and not have it instantly put away.

I enjoy walking into situations where people are not pre-disposed to agree with me. It forces me to sharpen my awareness of others and what they want. In a few hours, I'll be once again surrounded by people who will tell me every idea I have is brilliant.

Not my family. They'll warn me not to bring the wild-ness of my partying home.

I glance across at Charles.

And not him. He doesn't tell me what I want to hear.

I remember bursting into tears once when I skinned my knee. I'd been walking on a stone wall while my tutor quizzed me on math facts. Charles had taken me aside and told me a prince doesn't cry in public. Never. Did I want my tutor to respect me? Did I want the staff to? Then I had to be strong.

I didn't tell my mother what he'd said. She would have told me crying was perfectly fine. My father would have fired the tutor for putting me in danger in the first place. Mathias would have promised to watch over me. My little sister, Bianca, would have cried with me.

Not Charles. He told me the truth, even when it wasn't easy to hear. Tutors often gossip, and although our people were still loyal to the royal family, they wouldn't remain so if they perceived us as weak and incapable. They trusted us to maintain our borders, our economy, even our social stability.

I've never seen Mathias cry. I wonder if someone gave him the same talk.

"Bricelion," Charles says, pulling my attention back to

him, "when you first said you wanted to spend time in the United States without anyone knowing who you are, I hoped it would be a humbling experience for you. I had no idea I'd be flying home with a beaten pup."

My shoulders flex and I sit up straighter. "I didn't lose, Charles. I won. I'm an equal partner of Nintech, and we'll be moving the headquarters to Calvadria. The financial benefits to this union outweigh what any arranged marriage could. Mathias is free."

Charles nods. I expected him to at least look surprised by the news, but he doesn't. "Mathias may honor the announcement out of a sense of duty, but at least you've provided him with an option."

"Yes."

"What you've done is truly impressive, Bricelion. It has changed the course of our country."

"Then why have I never felt worse?" I hit my thigh with a fisted hand.

"Love is a double-edged sword. It can bring joy, but it cuts deep."

"Love?" I dismiss the idea with a grunt. "Impossible. A week ago I didn't know her. I'm homesick, that's all. I'm sure I won't remember her name by the time we land."

Charles doesn't look impressed by my claim. "Did you attempt to contact her before we left?"

"I did."

"And that's it?"

Now I'm confused. "You didn't approve of my interest in her. Didn't you suggest I should protect her from myself as well? I clearly remember you saying it was time for us to go home."

"I said all that. I'm just surprised you listened to me."

I look out the window of the jet without speaking for several minutes. Outside of my family, there is no one I trust more than the man across from me. "She wasn't ready, Charles. You were right; she's putting herself back together after losing her grandmother. I thought I could help her, but I was becoming the reason she might fail. I couldn't do that to her."

I take out my laptop.

Charles closes his eyes and reclines as if he might nap. "Did you tell her you're a prince?"

His question takes me by surprise. "No. It didn't seem relevant."

Leaving without her was hard.

Having her suddenly change her mind about being with me—solely based on my title would have been tougher to swallow.

After a pause, I add, "My family doesn't know about Savannah. I'd like to keep it that way."

"Of course."

"Do we still have anyone in Boston?"

"We do. I thought it was prudent to maintain a presence since you'll likely be returning for business."

It makes sense. My next request, possibly not so much. "Have them watch over her. Nothing obvious or intrusive. Just have them available in case she gets into any trouble."

He watches me from beneath mostly closed lids. "Will

you be expecting reports?"

"Not unless she gets herself into a situation that requires assistance. Then I want to ensure it's handled appropriately."

"Appropriately?"

I'm still working out what that means as well. I take a stab at it. "She shouldn't know we're involved. I'd rather have her believe her luck has turned around."

"So let's say she gets a flat tire, our men are Good Samaritans who stop to assist?"

His question puts me on the defensive. "Just for a short time, until she's established in Boston with a network of friends."

"Okay," Charles says then closes his eyes again. "I'm proud of you, Bricelion. You've become the man I hoped you'd grow to be."

I like that he didn't say *the prince*. Boston wasn't about that.

LATER THAT EVENING, I'm standing beside the lit fireplace in the receiving room of my family's countryside castle. We've shared a formal meal over which, per norm, very little of importance had been discussed. The staff was ever-present, and one learned at an early age to hold private conversations for times that were—private.

My father is seated in his favorite chair, reading on his tablet.

My mother is similarly occupied.

Bianca sighs loudly, clearly having something she wants to say. Being the youngest in this family and the only girl is a burden she doesn't appreciate carrying. As protective as my father is of Mathias and me, it's Bianca that has been the most sheltered. Or so my parents believe.

"What is it?" I ask, as she sighs again. "What's the problem?"

"I'm just wondering if you enjoyed your trip?" Her voice has a sharp edge. She's not happy for me or curious about my travels. She's mad she's not been allowed to do the same.

"I was working," I remind her. "It wasn't the least bit exciting."

"Sure." She snaps closed the book she was reading and places it down on the table by me.

"Mother I'm going to meet up with my friends at the barn. If that's not too far for me to go."

She gets only a nod in return to her clear sarcasm.

"I did miss you," I offer, shooting her a look as she sweeps her long hair off her shoulder.

"Yeah, it was way too quiet around here without you arguing with Father." That was her version of I missed you too.

I'll take it.

Mathias is hovering. I told him I have an announcement but refused to give him a clue as to what it pertains to.

Now I'm gathering my thoughts, choosing my words carefully. Suggesting a break in tradition might meet with resistance. I don't want my father to make the marriage a matter of honor, or Mathias won't consider not going forward with the engagement.

"Did I mention I ran into one of Princess Kalisa's friends

while I was in Spain?" I direct the question to Mathias but ask in a voice loud enough for our parents to hear.

"No, you didn't," Mathias answers. "You sped off to the States before saying much of anything about Spain."

"She told me the princess is heartbroken. She's been dating someone she met at university before her parents informed her of the arranged marriage."

"And that's why women don't belong at university," my father says without looking up from his tablet.

Mathias and I both groan.

Our mother throws a pillow at him.

He catches the pillow and places it on the floor beside his chair. "I'm merely saying the old ways are difficult for those who are exposed to other cultures."

"Perhaps because some of our traditions are outdated?" I counter gently. It's a delicate subject of too much importance to rush.

"Perhaps," our father concedes. He sighs and lowers his tablet. "The world is much different than when your mother and I wed. I understand the choices we made are less palatable today, but the prosperity of Calvadria depends on alliances with our neighbors. Mathias understands that. Princess Kalisa does as well. With time, they may grow to love each other as your mother and I have."

Our mother purses her lips before saying, "I would not trade my life or my family. Your father is right, love came to us. But it took time, and we were lucky. Not all unions have been as blessed."

"It's a shame there isn't a viable alternative," I muse

aloud.

Mathias squares his shoulders. "I accept my role without complaint, and Princess Kalisa and I have been friends since childhood. I will do my best to make it a happy union for her."

I move to sit in a chair beside my father. "There are whispers that their family and their country is not as stable and wealthy as it once was. Kalisa's father has not moved forward with the times and in his stubbornness has squandered much of their wealth. Mathias's freedom is a high price to pay for what might prove to be very little gain. If only there was another way to boost our economy. Something more sustainable."

My father waves a hand skyward. "From your mouth to God's ears. Our population is double what it was when I was a child. When Mathias takes the throne, he will be challenged with addressing that concern as well as many others. Too many of our citizens cling to farming and producing exports that can be made cheaper elsewhere. It might be time, Mathias, to court the technology industry. Sadly, it's the future for all of us."

"Funny that you say that Father, because I didn't go to the United States to party . . ."

CHAPTER TWENTY-FIVE

Savannah

THE NOISE OF the city doesn't bother me anymore. I hardly hear the grinding engines of buses or the honking of angry horns. The buildings feel smaller every day. I turn a corner and rather than being lost, I join up with the herd of people as naturally as if I'd always been a part of them. I navigate the T with ease. Tuck high heels into my purse so I can slip into them seamlessly when I reach my destination. The corner deli knows my order and gets it ready when they see me get in line.

I have friends. Female friends. Go figure.

I used to think I wanted to be the kind of woman who went from man to man without care or shame. I'm still a virgin, but I no longer mind. The more time I spend with women who have husbands and children, the more I realize I want that.

At first, I judged myself for that desire. Did it mean I didn't want to be more? Claire and Ronda have helped me see there is no right or wrong. I'm not living my life to impress anyone else. I'm living for me.

It's okay to live on my terms. It's not a crime to want to

be loved.

That doesn't mean I'm not happy. I am. I'm carving out my place in this world.

I've extended the lease on my apartment. Started classes at BU. And I'm the lead phone agent at a child services hotline. I love clothes, but my closet has balance now. Yes, I have nice dresses, but I also have jeans and workout clothes. I'm finally comfortable in my own skin.

Brice still lingers in my thoughts. Often at the oddest times. I took a shortcut through a park one evening. The sun went down earlier than I thought it would. I'm never nervous about being out at night, but I watch the news enough to know Boston isn't as safe as Coppertop. I was walking at a brisk pace when I felt like someone else was there. When I turned, no one was. Ridiculous as it sounds, I feel like Brice is still watching over me.

And it's nice. In my imagination, I have my own guardian angel.

My phone fell out of my pocket one day. I thought it happened while I was jogging, but the doorman said someone found it right outside the door and turned it in. In jest, I said, "Thanks, Brice."

Ronda says I need to forget him. She has a list of men she says she can set me up with. I might take her up on that offer one day, but for now I'm concentrating on me.

Claire still thinks there's a chance I'll hear from Brice again. I'm not holding my breath. Turning him down wasn't easy, but it still feels like the right decision. My head was spinning back then. I didn't know what I wanted, and I needed time to figure that out.

I don't blame him for not waiting around.

I still smile every time I remember how he popped up everywhere and how crazy it made me. I wanted to strangle him for going to Jana. It took me a while to forgive him for that, but now I see that he did me a favor.

I didn't need her.

I did this on my own and that feels pretty damn good.

Good enough that I reached out to my family—an act that brings me here. I settle into a booth in an Italian restaurant.

A man approaches the table. "Savannah?" Dark hair. Dark eyes. He looks like the photos he sent me.

"Joel?" I ask, scanning his face as he takes a seat across from me. "It's nice to finally meet you." I connected with him online a few weeks ago.

"You look so much like my mom." Joel's eyes go wide as he takes in my features. "I didn't know our grandmother, but you lived with her?"

"I did. You and I met, but you were probably too small to remember. Your mother came to my father's funeral. I bet you were only four."

He shrugs apologetically. "Yeah, I don't remember. Sorry."

"It's all right. She was coming to meet me. Or that was the plan. I was supposed to go back to Connecticut with you and your family."

"Really? What happened?"

"She must not have liked what she saw." I sniffle back

the emotion. It's not Joel's fault; he was a child.

He drops his head down. "My mother was crazy protective. She said your father was a violent man."

"He wasn't," I defended. "He was a good man who did something terrible while trying to do something good. To me, he was a hero."

He nods. It's not an easy conversation to have. "My mother died a few years ago. Cancer. She mentioned you once at the end. I think she felt guilty she wasn't there when you were born. She wanted to take you then, but your father wanted to raise you. When she met you, she thought you were too old . . . too . . ."

"Damaged," I say the word in a whisper.

He doesn't deny it. "Her opinion of your father was jaded. She didn't know anyone who'd ever been arrested, never mind gone to jail. It wasn't part of our life. I guess she was afraid that you might—"

I snort. "Infect you?"

He shrugs, and I remind myself he isn't the one who rejected me. He's being honest with me, and I'm grateful for that, even if it hurts.

"How do you feel?" I ask.

His smile reassures me. "I like the idea of having a cousin."

Now I'm smiling. "Me too."

"Let's not make this just a one-time thing, okay? I'm like an hour and a half from here. I'd like to hear about our grandmother. My mother wasn't big on mingling with family, but I reconnected with some of them after she died.

They'd love to meet you."

"I'd love that."

Joel and I spend a long lunch chatting about things we have in common. Little quirks that solidify us as cousins. The way our thumbs bend in a funny way. Our similar freckles.

After we part, I go over what he said. There was a time when I saw myself the way his mother saw me.

Damaged.

Unlovable.

That's not me.

I'm a survivor, and a kick-ass one at that.

My story is not defined by others. I'm writing it for myself. I want to meet the family Joel mentioned. They'll love me or they won't. Either way, it won't change how I see myself.

I stop at a store on the way back. Both Claire's and Ronda's husbands are working late, so I promised to cook for all of us. We'll fill Ronda's kitchen with screaming kids, lively conversation, and laughter.

I have the weekend off from classes and no shifts at the kids' advocacy center for a few days. The possibilities to fill the time are exciting. I can explore some of Boston's history. Hit one of the museums I've wanted to see. Eat at that new restaurant in the North End with only four tables. Alone or with friends. Either way is okay.

I haven't been back to Coppertop yet, but I FaceTime with them every couple days. I called them when I signed up for my college courses. I called them when I got a job. Jimmy says the updates always make Jay smile. Murray holds up the phone so I watch karaoke. Lance swears he's dating someone, but so far no one has seen her.

And I'd be a whole lot thinner if Mrs. Warren stopped sending care packages of cookies. I'll never ask her to, though. They're too good.

CHAPTER TWENTY-SIX

Brice

THE SEA CRASHES loudly against the shore as I stand on the balcony of our seaside estate. There's a storm coming, and the staff is scurrying around making sure the castle is ready for impact. The antiques, like the royal family, must be protected.

"Is it the storm that has you scowling?" Mathias claps a hand on my back before taking a spot beside me.

I turn, resting my back on the railing. "No. Just going over the proposed building plans in my head. We break ground next week."

Mathias cocks an eyebrow. "You never used to lie to me, Brother."

I grin. "I believe there were years when seventy-five percent of what I told you was a fabrication. None of the Royal Guards helped me study. We were playing poker and drinking."

"Shocking, and so unlike you." He's smiling.

I shrug. "I might have been a little wild back then."

"Indeed. And Charles always covered for you. I've always envied the relationship you have with the guards. They are loyal to you, and not because it's their duty to be."

My head snaps around. That doesn't sound like Mathias. He didn't envy anyone. "I was afforded freedoms you weren't. Father would never have tolerated his first son behaving as I did."

He grips the railing of the balcony. "That's my achievement—being born first. It doesn't measure up somehow to bringing Nintech here."

Wait. Who is this humble man? And where is my brother? "Has something happened, Mathias?"

"Yes. You freed me from a role I had resigned myself to. You brought real promise of prosperity back to Calvadria. You deserve the crown."

I spin on my heel toward him. "Oh, hell no. I don't enjoy performing the first waltz at a ball. I am not interested in being the face of the family. Tourists recognize you, they don't recognize me, and I prefer it that way." He looks like he might argue, so I add, "Besides, you've got that pretty-boy face the media loves. I'd rather work behind the scenes."

He gives me a long look. "Now that there is no impending engagement announcement, women follow me everywhere. I feel—hunted."

I chuckle but stop when I realize he's serious. "It's a problem few men would complain about."

He sighs. "What was it like to be Brice Hastings? To have no one know you were a royal?"

"It was . . . humbling at first. Then invigorating. I didn't know what I was capable of, but even my failures felt good. They made my eventual success that much sweeter."

"And yet, you hardly smile anymore. Charles won't say why. Was there something you found in the States that was hard to leave? Someone, perhaps?"

I weigh his question. It doesn't feel like he's asking out of curiosity. We've had years when we were close and years when we lived our lives so differently that there was no common ground on which to connect. Never once, though, has Mathias disappointed me. If I need him, he is there. Simple as that.

This time he seems to need me, his brother. So, I tell him about Savannah. Every crazy detail. I conclude with the admission that I still have a Royal Guard watching over her.

"You need to go to her," he says.

"I believe you missed the point where she told me to leave her alone."

"You said she wasn't ready. How do you know she's not ready now?"

I laugh. "It's not that simple."

"Not long ago I thought there was only one path for me. You changed that. It woke me up. You had the courage to challenge hundreds of years of tradition. Are you saying you're afraid to contact a woman? Did you leave your balls in the US?"

I cough a laugh. My brother is never vulgar. Never. I doubt he ever let out an undignified cry as an infant. Still, that doesn't mean I agree with him. "She doesn't know I'm a prince."

"Men have been forgiven for more serious transgressions."

Neither of us say anything for a while.

Mathias speaks first. "You didn't tell her?"

"I did not."

"If you do not seek out this woman again, I will. Perhaps her taste is more for a king."

I tense. He's pushing me. It's obvious. It shouldn't be working, but it is. My temper rises. Dark clouds roll toward shore and lightning dances in the sky. "I wonder if I still become king if I'm the one who murders my brother."

His eyes widen, then he throws back his head and laughs. "So, tell me, are you going to seek her out on your own, or must I race you to her side?"

Two months. All reports of how she is doing have been positive. I want to see her again, but not the way I did before. This time, I want my intentions to be clear from the start. "I can't kill you since I really don't have any desire to be king. So it seems, I shall have to arrange to see Savannah again."

Mathias and I exchange a grin. He wins this round. Although he challenges me, it has been out of kindness, and that is what he will bring to the throne. Mathias promises to explain my absence to our parents. Dignity, yes, but also loyalty and kindness. I can think of no better traits for a king.

As soon as the storm passes, I have Charles ready one of our jets.

"Where to?" he asks.

"Coppertop, Maine."

"As of our last report, Savannah is still in Boston."

The storm passes. The sky is as clear as my thoughts. "I understand that, but there's something there I want to retrieve before I see her again."

IT'S DARK BY the time I reach Coppertop. I can practically picture Savannah walking these streets with that big smile and smelly jacket.

The bar is tucked away down a narrow road, and I can hear the crowd cheering from the street. There is a boxing match on the large television as I walk in.

Jimmy is behind the bar. He gives me a funny look and then nudges Murray with his elbow. It's not long before all four men are huddled around me in the only relatively quiet corner of the bar. I take a swig of the beer they hand me.

"What are you doing here?" Jimmy asks, looking unsure if he's supposed to be mad or friendly. Waiting to decide.

"I need your help."

"Help from us?" Jay asks skeptically.

"Is it about Savannah?" Murray asks.

"Did something happen to her?" Jay asks.

"Nah, he's probably stalking her again," Lance says with a roll of his eyes.

"Wait," Jimmy says, snapping his fingers. "Are you the one who just landed on the air strip with that fancy jet?"

"News travels fast in this town," I joke.

"Bet your ass," Jimmy says.

"You have a jet?" Jay leans back. Their banter is quick and pointed. "I guess you *are* rich."

"It's my family's jet."

Lance wobbles his head in disgust. "Look at me, Mr. I Have My Own Jet. Next you'll tell us you're fucking royalty."

"Hey, where's Charles?" Murray asks.

"He's outside with our car."

"Well, his ass belongs in here. I'll be right back." Murray walks across the bar and out the door.

"I'm here because I care about Savannah. Would it matter if I actually were a prince?"

Jimmy shrugs. "It'd make the stalking less creepy."

Creepy? Me?

Never one to miss a topic, Lance jumps in. "Princes get away with a lot of shit regular guys can't. They can kiss unconscious women, and everyone calls it true love. If one of us tried that we'd be behind bars."

Jay's eyes squint. "Because we're not in a fucking fairy tale. Sometimes I don't know what the fuck you're thinking."

Lance's mouth drops open.

Jimmy laughs.

I do my best to not openly laugh along.

The boxing match has gotten intense, and it's hard to hear them over the crowd. "I need your help. Savannah mentioned a clock her mother once owned. It was very special, but she had to sell it. Do you know who bought it?"

Jimmy gives me a long look. "You really do care about her."

"I do."

"Then I'll just give you the clock." Jimmy beams proudly.

"You have it?" Jay asks, clearly as surprised as I am.

"I sent a friend to buy it. I knew it meant a lot to her. I was waiting for the right time to give it back to her. She's a proud little thing. I didn't want to return it until she was ready to take it."

The sentiment makes perfect sense to me.

Jimmy leaves for a moment and returns with a small wooden clock, about a foot tall and about half that in width. Cherry wood. Gold-plated face. Not expensive—but still priceless. "I've kept it locked in my bottom desk drawer all this time."

Charles enters the bar with Murray, and they join us after stopping by the bar and getting their own beers. He looks at the clock and says, "So, you found it."

"Jimmy had it," I answer. "He knew it was too important for her to lose it."

Charles shakes Jimmy's hand and smiles.

Jimmy is grinning from ear to ear.

Even Jay looks unusually happy.

Lance throws up a hand and walks away.

"He'll get over it," Jimmy says. "He has some growing up to do before he'll be ready for a woman like Savannah."

"There is no other woman like Savannah," I say and raise my glass to her.

The others raise theirs as well. "To Savannah," Murray says.

"To Savannah," we all repeat and take a swig.

It's late so I relax and nurse a second beer. I have what I came for.

Next stop—Boston.

Jimmy leans over, puts a hand on my shoulder, and says, "Look me in the eye, son, and tell me what your intentions are with our Savannah."

That's easy enough. "I love her. If she'll have me, I'll make her my princess."

With a laugh, Jimmy sits back. "Oh, I wouldn't choose that nickname. I don't see Savannah ever liking to be called that."

Charles and I exchange a look. With a straight face, I say, "I believe I can sell her on the merit of it."

EARLY THE NEXT day, with the boxed clock tucked beneath my arm, I take the elevator to the fifteenth floor of my office building. I didn't make an appointment. I walk right past Jana Monroe's secretary and let myself into her office.

She stands as I enter. "Well, I wish I could say this is a pleasant surprise."

I take a seat, propping the box on my knee. "You're in luck. I haven't found a single person who has anything negative to say about you. They won't talk about what they did with you, but I can't find one who seems harmed from their association with you."

Tone heavy with sarcasm, she says, "You can't imagine my relief."

I continue on as if she hadn't spoken. "Which is why I'm here for a favor."

She slowly takes her seat behind her desk, tense and watchful. "Just what do you think I might be able to do for you?"

"I have a present for Savannah, something I believe she thinks was lost to her. I want you to arrange for her to meet with me."

Jana's eyes narrow. "Is there a reason you can't call her yourself?"

"No, but you will help me do this in a way that fulfills what she thought she would get from you."

"I don't think you understand what I do."

I put the clock aside and lean forward. "I don't think you understand I'm not asking."

"Just who do you think you are?" she snarls.

I mull the question for a moment. There was a time when I would have defined myself by my birth order. I might have also boasted of my prowess with women or my popularity with the Royal Guards. Those are all things that felt important before I came to Boston and met Savannah.

I can threaten Jana into helping me. She's already shown she'd back down under threat of being exposed. Yes, that path is open to me.

I look at the box at my feet and ask myself why I am here. Why haven't I simply taken the clock to Savannah myself?

I want to return something I took from her. Will the truth move a woman like Jana Monroe? If it doesn't, I'm not above threatening her again.

But I'll give her a chance.

"I'd like to tell you a story about a woman who came to Boston to find herself and ended up winning the heart of a prince . . ."

CHAPTER TWENTY-SEVEN

Savannah

THEY CALL OUT my order at the coffee shop when my phone starts to ring. It's Jana. Did she butt dial me? No, impossible. She's flawless. No way she makes that kind of mistake.

"Hello?"

"Savannah, how are you?"

"Good?" I say, dragging the word out slowly. Fully confused.

"You've been on my mind since the last time we talked a couple months ago. You didn't go back to Maine?"

I take time to fill her in on all I've been doing. All I've accomplished.

"That's so incredible, Savannah. You've really made the most of your situation. A few of the men from the charity event asked me about you. They saw us talking, and I hope you don't mind that I passed along your information."

"I did hear from a couple."

"No one you were interested in?"

"Not really. No spark."

"I'm sorry to hear that. But it might be for the best. I

263

had the most interesting conversation with a man today, and all I could think of was how perfect he'd be for you."

"For me?"

"Yes. I know we're not technically working together right now, but I felt compelled to call you. I think you should meet him."

"Really?"

"Yes," she laughs. "Savannah, you deserve happiness. In my line of work I have rules for a reason. I'm sorry it didn't work out the way you thought it would, but I might have been too hasty when I told you I couldn't work with you. I sent the man down to the gazebo at The Commons Park. Do you know the one by the fountain?"

"Yes." I take a little pride in how well I know the city now.

"I believe this man would be a good match for you."

I can barely breathe. I stopped looking, stopped hoping. I decided to let things happen naturally. Her offer confuses me. "I don't know."

"Life tosses us opportunities. This is one I wouldn't pass on if I were you, but you're the only one who can say if you're ready for it."

I swallow hard. Am I ready?

I still see Brice in the face of other men.

Isn't that sign enough that I should at least see who she thinks I would like? "How will I know it's him?"

"He's gorgeous. You can't miss him. Dark hair. Dark eyes. If you don't stop in your tracks when you see him, I misjudged what you want. Listen, I have to go. Fill me in on how it goes. Good luck." The line cuts off, and I'm left with a million questions. The first: what the hell is his name?

I think of the best pair of dark eyes I've ever stared into and a pang of hurt floods me. I'm not ready to let go of the idea of him yet. How can he still be so vivid in my mind after two months? I didn't know him that long. All we did was kiss.

He probably forgot all about me. I can't cling to a memory. I can't have a family with a fantasy. Brice Hastings, I'm sorry, I have to let you go.

Jana has a reputation for knowing what people need. If she thinks this guy will be perfect for me, maybe he will be.

I throw a lid on my coffee and take off in a fast walk toward the park. This time I don't have to wonder what I'll talk about. I have a lot of choices now. Classes. A life. Friends here and back in Maine. I don't need to pretend to be someone else. I'm good enough as I am.

My chin rises.

Better than good enough. The man I end up with will see that.

Still, my feet drag a little as I near the gazebo. I duck behind a tree and catch my breath. Meeting someone doesn't mean I'll sleep with him. I talk to people who ride next to me on the bus. I can talk to anyone.

This is a park meeting. We didn't commit to coffee. If there's no spark, I don't have to say more than hello.

"Are you going to climb that thing so you can get a better look?"

I jump and turn to see Brice standing there, his hands

casually tucked in his pockets, his smile so warm and sexy.

"Brice, what are you doing here?" My hand flies to my heart to keep it from thudding out of my chest.

"Waiting for you."

My head is spinning. Tears are filling my eyes. Is it possible? "You're the man Jana sent me to meet?"

I wanted it to be him more than I will ever admit.

He steps closer. "Depends, did she mention how good-looking he'd be?"

I sniff and decide to give him a little shit. "She told me to look beyond his flaws because he has a good *personality*."

He steps closer still. "You've always been good at keeping me humble."

We stand for a long moment, simply looking into each other's eyes. God, it's good to see him again. It has to be said, so I do. "Sorry I didn't call you back. I had things I needed to work through."

"I know. I understood."

In my fantasy version of this meeting, I fly into his arms, pull his mouth to mine, and everything else fades away—unimportant in the face of our passion. Instead, I simply stand here, trying to think of what else to say. Although our lives temporarily overlapped, we haven't exactly been friends. What were we? What are we now?

He searches my face. Is he asking himself the same questions?

I clasp my hands in front of me. "How did you convince Jana to set up this meeting? She was anti both of us the last time I spoke to her."

"I told her why I wanted to see you. She's a sucker for a romantic story."

My breath catches in my throat. Exciting as it sounds, if Brice is back for sex, for the chance of being my first, I'll have to say no again. If the last few months have shown me anything, it's that I want more, and he is already too difficult to forget.

He offers me his hand. "Walk with me?"

I take his hand and we begin to walk side by side. That simple touch is all it takes for my body to warm to him. I have to be careful. I don't need Jana to remind me that settling for less than what I need will not get me the life I want. I know I can captain my own ship. He needs to know that as well. "I have a job, Brice."

"You do?" He doesn't sound surprised.

"It's a small child advocacy center. Nonprofit. I answer the phones. It doesn't pay much, but I feel good helping people."

He smiles down at me, and I bask in the open approval in his eyes. "I can see you in that job. You're a natural at knowing what people need."

I scoff at the praise. "I don't know about that, but I'm learning. I'm taking classes at BU, just general ones for now, but I'd like to get a degree in child psychology. Children don't choose the situations they end up in. And it makes them angry, rough on the outside. Some people dismiss them as damaged. Like being a victim of something somehow makes them less worthy of being loved. I've been there. I know the pain, but I also know a path out of it. I'm a survivor, Brice. I can say that proudly now. I'm not ashamed of my journey, and I understand I'm just as deserving of love as anyone else. That's what I want to learn how to show children."

He stops, and his hand tightens on mine. "You are easily the most amazing person I've ever known."

I look away and blush. "You're just saying that because you know why I went to Jana. I should tell you, I've come up with a better plan."

He tips my chin up so my eyes once again meet his. "She didn't tell me what you went to her for or what your first plan was. Isn't it time you tell me?"

I could lie, but that would mean I'm embarrassed by my journey, and I am not. If I hadn't sought out Jana, I wouldn't have come to Boston. If I hadn't come to Boston, I wouldn't have rediscovered my dreams. So, regardless of how it turned out, I don't regret a penny of what I paid Jana. I take a deep breath before speaking. "Jana specializes in helping women improve their situations. No two plans are the same, but mine included removing the barriers that were standing between me and happiness."

His jaw tightens. "Did one of those barriers happen to be your virginity?"

I refuse to be ashamed of my inexperience or my desire to shed it. Refuse. I hold his gaze. "That was part of it. She's not a matchmaker. I wasn't looking for a relationship. I wanted the confidence that would follow that step. What she promised was a selection of safe men I could choose to make that happen with."

His eyes burn down into mine. "And did you? Did you take that step?"

What will he do if I say yes? There is a temptation to see what will happen. I don't want him to be here to be with a virgin. I want him to want *me*.

He takes my silence as my answer. "I hate the idea of you with another man. Hate it. I've had partners before you." He caresses my cheek. "Just none since. It changes nothing beyond that I need to know if he was kind to you."

I believe him, and it brings tears to my eyes. I don't know why Brice is back, but I can no longer deny that—crazy as it sounds—I love this man. "I didn't go through with it, Brice. Not via Jana. Not on my own. I thought virginity was holding me back, and that sex would liberate me, but I freed myself. I want my first time to be with someone I love." This is where it gets tricky. "And who loves me."

He places his hands on my hips and pulls me a little closer. "I have a gift for you."

Is he referring to himself? My mouth goes dry. I just told him I'm no longer interested in losing my virginity to a man. I want more. I should pull away, but I melt against him. I can't function when I'm this close to him. Eventually, I say, "I haven't seen you in two months."

He rests his forehead on mine. Our breaths mingle. "I had business that required my attention. And I knew you needed time."

"I did."

"Do you trust me, Savannah?"

A delightful fire spreads through me. I shudder against him. Right now I'm not sure I trust me, but there's no way I'm saying that. "I think so." He frowns. "I'm like sixty-five percent sure I do."

"Looks like I have some work to do." His mouth lowers to mine.

Nothing ever felt more like coming home. My body flows into his. My arms wind around his neck. Our tongues circle each other like lovers reuniting.

When he raises his head, he says, "I want to introduce you to my parents."

I freeze. "Your parents."

"And my brother and my sister."

I sway a little. I thought he might ask me to lunch. Possibly a romantic date. I must be hearing him wrong.

"Call your job and tell them you need time off to travel."

"Travel? Wait, where are your parents?"

"They're in Calvadria. I'm not a US citizen. Is that a deal breaker?"

"Stop the bus. I can't fly anywhere. I don't have a passport."

"I'll have one for you by the time we take off. Just say you'll come."

A battle wages in me. Things like this don't happen to me. Men don't swoop in and offer to fly me home to meet their families.

Brice isn't like any man I've ever known.

And I want this to be real so badly I ache.

But can it be?

I love this crazy, impulsive man. If I were writing my own story, this is exactly how it would go. The problem is, life very rarely works out the way I think it should. To say yes, I need to believe something like this is possible.

For me.

"You'll want to tell Claire and Ronda you'll be out of town."

Of course he knows about them. I would be scared if being in his arms didn't feel so damn delicious. "Have you had someone watching me?"

He kisses his way up my jaw and growls into my ear, "I protect what's mine."

A hot shiver passes through me. My sex is wet and eager. I'm a tangle of a modern woman's protest that I belong to no one and a primal need. I want to be his. I want this. We can talk about how he words it later.

I push out of his arms and rub my hands over my face. I need to think, and that's not possible while my body is practically hyperventilating with desire. Stop. Breathe. "Why? Why do you want me to meet your family?"

His eyes fill with amusement. "Isn't it obvious? I love you, Savannah. I think I fell for you the night you camped out in my office. I knew then I'd never be the same."

I sway on my feet. "Say it again."

He pulls me slowly back into his arms, resting me against his bulging cock. "Which part?"

"All of it."

He laughs. "I love you, Savannah Barre. Every side of you. I love your brave spirit, your strength. I love your loyalty, your humor, even the way you call me on my shit. I left because I didn't want to hold you back, but I've missed you every damn day. I know we'll have things to sort out, but we'll do it—together. Just say yes."

I search his face. All I see is love. I throw my arms around his neck and say, "I love you too. It doesn't make sense. It wasn't part of Jana's plan. It isn't part of mine, but I missed you every damn day too. I wasn't ready for you when we met, but I'm ready now."

I go up onto my tiptoes. His head lowers. Our mouths meet in the middle. I whisper, "Yes" between our kisses. Yes, yes, holy fuck, yes.

After we reluctantly end the kiss, we walk—or float, I'm not sure—out of the park. Charles is standing beside a car. I can't look him in the eye. I'm sure I look just as sex-crazed as I feel. Thankfully after greeting me, he doesn't say more.

I don't know where we're going, and I should care, but all that matters is Brice is back. I run my hand up his muscular thigh and love how his nostrils flare and he inhales sharply. Is it possible that I affect him the way he does me?

He puts his hand over mine and stills it. "Easy, Savannah. I want to do this right."

Me too. Oh, God, me too.

I want to do it right now.

"Remember that present?" he asks in a husky voice.

My eyes fall to his crotch. His present is bulging against the front of his pants. I'm okay with calling his cock a present. We do need to lose Chucky, though.

He laughs. "Eyes up here, princess."

I lift my eyes to his. He's laughing, but in a way that makes it feel like we're sharing a sexy joke. He lifts a box off the floor and hands it to me.

I take it onto my lap. It's heavy and not at all where I thought this was going. "You really brought me a gift? You didn't have to."

"Open it, Savannah."

I tear back the paper. The box gives no hint at what it contains. I pull back the flap and begin to remove the packing.

My jaw falls open. It can't be.

I run my hands over the clock. "My clock. How did you find it?"

"Jimmy had it. He knew you'd want it back one day."

Now I'm crying. Like ugly crying. This is the most thoughtful thing anyone has ever done for me.

Brice lifts me, clock and all, onto his lap and wraps his arms around me. "I hope all those tears mean you like it."

I put the clock aside and kiss him with everything I have. I kiss him the way I wanted to that first day in the elevator, with the intensity of a woman who thought she'd lost him forever, and the love of one who realizes this just might be it.

This infuriating.

Intoxicating.

Undeniable man.

Being with him required a leap of faith I wasn't capable of a few months earlier, but he came back to me. I'm not about to lose him twice.

"We're here," Charles announces.

Brice breaks off the kiss.

I'm shattered.

Dazed.

Ready to follow him off a cliff if that's where he leads me.

He sets me down and we both catch our breath. "Before we go any further, there's something I should tell you."

My stomach twists. "Are you married?" Please don't be married.

"No." He chuckles and kisses me. "But I hope to be in the near future."

A part of me sinks. Is it too much to believe I can feel this kind of passion for a man who doesn't already have someone else?

He raises my chin. "To you, princess."

"Don't call me princess," I say absently. Wait, he wants to marry me? Holy shit. Did he just say that?

He traces the one side of my neck. "You don't like the term?"

"It's a little condescending," I say in a breathy voice. "I could get used to it, though." The man did just say he could picture marrying me. None of this might seem like a good idea later, but I'm all in.

He chuckles and caresses the skin exposed by the gaping neckline of my shirt, playing with the button holding it closed. "Glad to hear that. I feel like I have to be clear about where this is going because taking you home will be considered a declaration to my family. I want to make sure you're sure."

"About?" Does the ability to concentrate return after sex? I sure hope so.

His eyes fill with laughter again. The bastard knows exactly what he's doing to me. "The part about you and me possibly spending forever together."

I almost agree with that, since his rock-hard cock is pressing so intimately against me—how can I be expected to pay attention to anything else—but his ego doesn't need that added boost. I slide off his lap and take several gulps of air. When my eyes meet his again, I'm serious. "That's a big step. And fast."

He takes my hand in his. "Savannah, I've spent the last two months telling myself that what I feel couldn't have been real. I didn't believe in love, much less love at first sight. Or should I say smell."

I swat his thigh. "That's not nice."

He laughs. "I'm an ass. I know. But I'm an ass who can't imagine a life without you in it."

I'm trying to remain at least a little cautious. When I allow myself to believe this is real, I have to face that going forward with it will change things. "I like my job. I like helping people. I have friends now, and I'm taking classes. I won't give that up."

"We'll figure it out. I can work in Boston. We'll have to travel, but we can make it work, Savannah. I don't want to take you away from your journey, I want to go on it with you."

I look past him to the jet on the airfield and run a hand over my hair. "I can't meet your family like this."

"There's a washroom onboard as well as a change of clothing for you."

My eyes round then I put a hand on one hip. "Hang on. You were that sure I'd say yes?"

He kisses my lips gently. "That hopeful."

He's smooth.

Charles opens the car door. I have to say something to him. "Hey, Chucky."

"Hi, princess," he says and winks.

I blush down to my toes. Did he hear everything we said? Talk about embarrassing. "He's taking me home to meet his parents."

"They will adore you," Charles assures me.

We walk up the steps of the jet. Charles stays behind. "You're not coming?" I ask.

"Not this time, princess," Brice says. "But you'll see him again soon."

I'm really going to have to talk to Brice about not calling me that. "Why . . .?" I meet Brice's eyes again and the question dies on my lips. "Oh."

Forget about desk sex. I'm about seventy-five percent sure I'm about to have jet sex. Brice offers me his hand. I take it and beam a smile at him. His smile is a decadent promise.

Correction . . . I am one hundred percent sure I'm going to love flying.

CHAPTER TWENTY-EIGHT

Brice

LIVED A wild life. Before Savannah, I would say that anticipation, the kind that makes your heart thud in your chest and your senses hyper sensitive, was no longer something I was capable of.

I had threesomes.

Hell, I had foursomes.

Savannah isn't my first virgin, although it's been years. I prefer to be remembered as a woman's best rather than her first. Women with less experience tend to see sex as a more emotional experience than I ever found it.

I settle myself into a seat beside Savannah and ask her if she's okay. She shoots me a bright, brave smile and says she is.

My ability to speak fades away.

There is no staff on this flight. Just the pilots and the two of us. I ensured privacy in case—well, in case what I want ends up what she wants as well. She's given me all the signs that it is, even said she loves me.

Let that sink in for a minute. She said she loves me and instead of sending me running, it has me flying high even before the jet takes off.

Is this what's best for her, though?

I'm taking her home to meet my parents. I know how I feel and she said how she feels. This is us stepping forward together.

As easy as it would be to give in to how I feel, we need to talk first. There are things I need to know. The door to the jet closes and we begin to taxi down the runway.

Her hand clenches the arm of her chair. She's nervous. I'd rather die a slow death than rush her into something she's not ready for. She needs to know that as well. I put my hand over hers. "Savannah, nothing will happen between us until you're ready for it to. We have forever. I can wait."

Eyes wide, she turns to meet my gaze. "Sorry. I'm freaking out a little bit. I've never flown before, and I thought it would be exciting, but now I'm not so sure."

I pry her hand off the armrest and lace my fingers with hers. I know how to get her to relax. I give her my most charming smile and say, "The first time you do anything is scary. That's why it's best to fly with an experienced pilot. A very, very talented and experienced pilot with a solid track record of ensuring a quality landing for all."

Humor replaces some of her fear. "Really? And just how much experience should I look for in a pilot? And is it important that I know about how many flights he's successfully flown?"

She's good. "Simply knowing that one is qualified is sufficient."

We leave the ground and her hand tightens on mine.

I lean over and speak softly into her ear. "The trick is to enjoy every part of the experience. That feeling in your stomach as we rise up through the clouds? For me, it's a sensation that means I'm headed off somewhere wonderful. Look out the window."

She does.

I continue, "See how small everything becomes? That always reminds me the problems I feel are insurmountable really aren't that big if I step back and give myself a better perspective of them. Like life, sometimes the ride is smooth. Sometimes it's bumpy. I try to remember to savor when it is smooth so when the turbulence comes, and it always does, I know what to hold on to."

She turns toward me. "Wait are we still talking about sex?"

I throw my head back and laugh. "No, I went off on a life tangent."

Her smile is cheeky. "Good because I'm hoping for a smooth ride."

"I'll do my best." I cringe at my eager promise. Holy hell, she can turn me on and turn me inside out like no one else—ever. I try to appear less affected than I am. What I'd really like to do is stand up, strip down, and show her that a little turbulence is also enjoyable.

"Do you want to wait, Savannah?" Her mouth drops open. I'm just as surprised as she is that I asked. "I want you, Savannah, so much. But your first time will be something you always remember. If you have any doubts now, after things get heated, you just say it. We won't do a single thing you're not ready for. It's important to me that you understand that."

She releases her seat belt and turns fully in her seat. "Guess what I'm not when I'm with you."

"What are you not?"

"Guess."

I shake my head. I don't know.

She rises to her feet and stands between my legs. "I'm not afraid. I'm also not a child, Brice. I'm twenty-three, and I want you too." She leans down, a hand on either side of my chair and gives me a kiss so wanton and so trusting that any concerns I have fall away.

I'm on my feet, removing her clothing as I savor every inch of her mouth.

She pulls my shirt out of my pants and runs her hands up my back. I groan and pull her blouse up and over her head. Her bra hits the floor a second later and I cup those perfectly round tits of hers. So small. So firm. I have to taste them.

She arches back, giving me better access to them.

This, gentlemen, is where boys separate from men. Every partner is different. Sex is a dance one learns the steps to as they go. I know what turns other women on. I was guided by some to experiment and adapt as I go. Does Savannah enjoy having my tongue swirl around her nipple? She appears to. Does suckling make her beg for more? How about a gentle nipple tug with my teeth?

She grabs my shoulders and gasps.

"Tell me when you like it, princess. Tell me every fucking time it's good for you, and this will only get better."

I move to her other nipple and showcase my talents in a different order. It's the tongue nipple flick followed by a gentle tug, then swirl and repeat that has her begging me not to stop.

She reaches for my belt, but I stop her. I'm already excited beyond where I want to be. I don't want to rush, and if those delicious hands of hers wraps around my cock, I'll be a goner.

I shed my shirt and between tongue-intertwining kisses, I remove the rest of her clothing. I pick her up and carry her toward the rear of the plane where there is a small bedroom. I lay her gently down on the bed and force myself to wait before I join her.

"Are you sure?" If I sense hesitation, I need to have the control to walk away.

People say sex is different with someone you love, but I didn't believe it until just now. No amount of promised pleasure, nothing I want, is more important than confirming that Savannah feels safe and loved.

Eyes burning with desire, she holds her hand out to me. Rather than take it, I shed my trousers and move to the end of the bed. I kiss my way up the arch of one of her feet, while caressing the other. And gently I push them apart.

And move a little higher.

I kiss her calf, the inside of her leg behind her knee, then move to love the other. I run my hands up and down the sides of her legs as I do.

Spread before me, her bare sex opening like a flower for

me, I take my time. I like a bare mound. I'll thank her later. Right now I'm enjoying the view and the fact that her sex is wet and glistening, even though I have yet to touch it.

Her hands grip the sheets on either side of her. I edge her legs farther apart and kiss my way up her inner thighs. Her hips jut upward.

I blow on her exposed labia. She shivers and makes a sound that tells me this is driving her as wild as it's driving me.

There is nothing like the scent of a woman. I part her sex and lap up her taste. It's heady. Exciting. I could feast on this alone and die a happy man. Any man who feels differently isn't worth fucking.

Here, too, women differ in what they want. I've heard some men rush for the clit and rub the shit out of it. They attack it like they want a woman to attack their dick. It's not the same. A woman's engine runs just as hot if it's given time to rev.

I kiss, tease, lick, suck, rub with my jaw. When I come across what drives her wild, I do it long enough to have her writhing, then move on and circle back to it. The best orgasms are the ones that build and build until they crash like a wave over a person. I'm a connoisseur, and I'll teach Savannah to be as well. Sometimes hot and fast is good. With forever before us, there will be time to explore those as well. This time, I want her to experience the orgasm that is all consuming, undeniable.

Her hands are in my hair, fisting almost painfully.

Has she brought herself pleasure in the past? I earmark

that question for later as well. Either way, it's something she'll do for me. I want to know all the ways she orgasms—by my hand, by hers, through whatever toys she is comfortable with exploring.

I slip a finger inside her. She's wet, tight, and tense. We're not there yet.

I kiss my way up and down her legs again, returning my tongue and my fingers to her sex. Wet, nearly ready, I continue to tease her clit until she is spreading her legs wider and begging me to take her.

I pause only long enough to slip on a condom, then I'm above her, positioning myself between her legs. I draw her knees up on either side and kiss her deeply.

As she opens up to my tongue, her legs wrap around my waist. I move so the tip of my cock grazes her parted sex. Once again, experience has taught me the restraint I show now will bring both of us more pleasure.

She moves her hips to meet mine and the tip of my cock dips inside her. I kiss my way to her ear. "I love you, Savannah."

"I love you too," she says in a breathless voice.

I slowly push through her folds, gently filling her.

Our eyes meet.

"You okay?" I ask.

"Oh, yes," she says.

I pull out slowly, then fill her again. This time going balls deep. She smiles.

Once again slowly.

Her hips begin to move with mine, and I lose some control. She feels so fucking good.

I shift, raising her ass off the bed and plunge deeper. When I partially withdraw, there is a hint of pink on my condom, but her expression hasn't changed. She's ready.

I drive into her with more force. She gasps, but says, "Oh, God, that's good."

That's all I need to hear.

I thrust deeper, harder, faster. All thinking suspends. There's only me, her, and desire rocketing through me. I'm pounding into her. She's thrusting up to meet me, letting me in deeper.

She cries out as she comes. I feel the spasms pass through her, revel in how her sex clenches around me.

I keep pounding. I can't stop. She's so wet. So tight.

Then I'm coming. Grunting. Groaning. Exploding.

I collapse onto my elbows and kiss her as I come back down to earth.

I roll off her, head to the bathroom, and clean myself off. I return with a warm, wet towel and wash her. There is nothing more beautiful than the evidence of her innocence. I don't say it because I meant it when I said my feelings wouldn't have changed if she said she gave this gift to another man.

But she saved it for me.

I dispose of the towel, pull her into my arms, and wrap a blanket around both of us. She traces a design on my chest. Does she have any regrets? I tip her head up so she looks me in the eye, and I say, "So that's one flight pattern. There are many more."

She chuckles, an act that makes her bare breasts jiggle delightfully against my side. "So, we're holding to this aviation analogy?"

I try to look offended. "It's not genius?"

She goes up onto one elbow and kisses me before answering. "It's amazing. You're amazing."

I cock an eyebrow. "That's what I've been told."

She rolls her eyes and smacks me in the chest, not hard enough to hurt, just a clap of reprimand. "Since I have nothing to compare it to, I'll take your word for it."

"Oh, really?" I growl and roll her so she's beneath me again. "Just so we're clear, this airline has a strict loyalty policy."

She cups my face with both hands. "Just so we're clear, so do I."

We laugh and roll so now she's on top, gloriously sprawled across me. "I'm okay with that, princess."

Smiling, she runs a finger over my lips. "I want to tell you not to call me that, but I may be starting to like it. What does that say about me?"

That's she's meant to be a princess? I could tell her now, but we have a long flight, and I know her well enough to know her mind will start racing if I do. Yes, my family is royal, but not as stuffy as the British. I'd worry that some of my father's old-fashioned ideas might offend her, but Savannah isn't a wilting flower, and I've met her friends. They're proof she can overlook a few flaws.

Will she be upset that I didn't tell her I'm a prince?

I'm reasonably certain that's something women find easy to forgive.

CHAPTER TWENTY-NINE

Savannah

AFTER NAPPING IN Brice's arms, we showered together then changed into surprisingly formal clothing. On his suggestion, I took the time to do my hair and makeup. He said his family is meeting us at the airport, and I want to make a good impression.

I'm sitting beside Brice again, each chastely in our own seats. Every time our eyes meet I blush. In the shower we'd made love a second time, and it had been just as wonderful as I imagined shower sex would be. Soaping each other. Boldly exploring each other's bodies. Did I mention that I love his talented tongue?

And his dick.

Big. Hard. Eager for more soon after we finish. He, and it, definitely lived up to my fantasies.

Me? I could have done better than my first attempt at giving him oral sex, but he didn't complain. He says the more we do it, the better it gets. He doesn't have to convince me. It's already incredible. But I'm willing to follow his lead on this. After all, he is an expert pilot.

I chuckle.

The actual pilot announces our descent and my post-multiple-orgasm peace dissolves. I clench Brice's hand so tightly I'm leaving marks. We land with a bump.

He kisses my cheek. "My brother will be waiting for us when we get off the plane. His name is Mathias."

"Okay."

"Just breathe."

I look out the window to see flashing cameras and a crowd of people. "Is there someone famous here or something?"

"The royal family always draws a big crowd."

"Royalty? Here? Will we get a glimpse of them?"

"Yes. I'm sure you will."

"That's exciting."

As we disembark the plane a man who looks like a slightly older version of Brice stands with a straight back and serious face. He's surrounded by men in suits and most of the cameras point in his direction.

Then the cameras point at us as we walk over to him.

"Brother," Brice says with a smile as we are quickly escorted toward a waiting SUV, "this is Savannah." We stop and they turn toward the cameras as we wait by the vehicle. I stand nervously to the side, wanting to hide behind Brice.

"It's nice to meet you. I hope you had a good flight."

"Very good," I say, hoping he never hears how good. "What's going on here? Brice said something about a royal family. Are they here as well?"

"You haven't told her?" Mathias says with a laugh.

"Savannah, this is my older brother, Mathias, the future

king of Calvadria."

What? My jaw drops open. Get the fuck out.

Mathias gestures to Brice. "And this is my brother, Brice-lion. The second in line for the crown if I do something stupid and fall off a cliff or something."

I swing toward Brice and wag a finger at him. "You're a prince? The family you want to introduce me to is royalty? Like king and queen royalty?"

Brice nods.

I'm not ready to believe it yet. "Wait, you two are messing with me, right?"

Another SUV pulls up and all the photographers turn toward them. An older couple steps out. The man is in a dark suit. His white hair is combed down in a conservative style. The woman is in a flowing dress and has her hair in a loose bun. They approach with a dignified air that makes me want to curtsey or something. They're surrounded by guards who flank their way to us.

"Just be yourself," Brice says in my ear, before he kisses my cheek. "Mother, Father, this is Savannah."

Their warm smiles seem guarded, but I can hardly blame them. They're likely as gobsmacked by me showing up as I am.

His father speaks first. "It's a pleasure to meet you, Savannah Barre. You're the first woman my son has brought home."

"And I'd better be the last," I joke, then cover my mouth with my hand. "Sorry."

Brice is the first to laugh. Followed by his brother.

His father looks like he wants to.

His mother not as much. She looks me over from head to toe. There was a time when I would have cowered before such an appraisal, but I raise my chin and return her gaze. No one is better than anyone else. I am here because Brice asked me to be. That's all that matters.

"Please excuse that Brice's sister, Bianca, isn't here. Teenagers are impossible sometimes. Even royal ones."

"No worries. I'm sure she's as lovely as all of you. I'll meet her when she's ready."

Her expression softens. "I've heard you work with children."

I relax. "Not yet. I'm taking classes to learn how to help children who have experienced trauma. I've only just started, but it's what I feel called to do."

Her smile returns. "That's an admirable goal."

"Thanks," I say. "I'm sure as a queen you help a lot of people as well. I'm still processing the news that Brice is a prince. The cameras really gave it away."

She cocks her head to one side and looks from me to Brice and back. "Did my son tell you he was a prince before you came here?"

"Not one damn word about it."

I see the laughter in her eyes before she lets out a delightful, cultured laugh. "My son always has been a bit of a rascal."

Brice puts his arm around my waist. "That is undeniable." He smiles down at me. "Are you still willing to take me on?"

"Yes." I look around. The old me would have been intimidated, but I can do this. "I swear on a jar of fish eyes."

When his family gives me an odd look, he says, "I never know what she'll say, but that's part of what I love about her."

EPILOGUE

"ARE YOU UPSET?" Brice's arm drapes over my shoulder as we move down one of the long corridors of the palace. The biggest surprise of this castle, besides the fact that it belongs to Brice's family, is how welcoming it is. Somehow, in spite of the size, there is a sense of home around every corner.

"Upset?" I look out the large arched window at the grounds of the property and wonder how anyone could be upset here. Perfectly sculpted landscaping and vibrantly blooming flowers. Pathways leading down to the sea, all lined with intricately carved wood lanterns.

"I had my reasons for not telling you I was a prince. But I wouldn't blame you for being upset."

"Yes." I say flatly. "I'm insulted by your secret giant castle and wonderful royal family. How could you? You monster."

He chuckles, a rumble from his chest. "I just thought our situation was complex enough. We didn't need to throw me being a prince into the mix."

"I will admit I'm slightly intimidated. Your parents are lovely, but they seem like very serious people."

"They are."

"I don't know if you've noticed, but I'm a bit—"

"Quirky?"

He could have blown it there. Quirky will do. "Yes. That works. I'm not sure I'll be what your parents want for you. It's been two days and I feel like maybe they're questioning your decision to bring me here."

"My parents are worried about Bianca who is acting as though rebelling against the monarchy is her job. They're still processing the fact that Mathias won't need to marry someone he doesn't want to. You, they like. They will grow to love you as I do."

"How can you tell?"

"My father hasn't said a single foolish outdated thing in front of you. My mother hasn't made a comment about my royal duties. They're enjoying your company and more than that, they can see how happy you make me."

"Is that enough? I don't know the rules for a royal family. I'm sure I'm breaking them left and right." I run my hand along the textured stonework of the wall and realize suddenly maybe this is a misstep too.

"Nothing makes us more compatible than the rules we'll break together. I'll prove it to you. Are you ready for your next surprise? Something that might put you more at ease about how serious it is around here?"

"Are we off to some old timey horse race where we chase foxes? Do you wear a top hat?"

"I'm worried you're basing all your ideas about royalty on what you've seen on television."

"Yes I do, Your Highness." I curtsy awkwardly to prove

my point.

After rolling his eyes, he looks both ways and quiets his voice as we approach a wall. "Are you ready?"

"Am I ready to look at this wall? Is it a royal wall?"

He taps lightly on it twice and suddenly the wall opens. Now this is straight out of a movie.

"Holy hell," I say as he tugs me inside and the wall closes behind us. Around a large table sit a few familiar faces. Some of the guards and staff I've met over the last couple of days grin at me.

Charles, who would normally stand dutifully, doesn't get up. I'm glad to see that. "You play poker, Miss Savannah?"

"I win at poker," I counter quickly. This draws a laugh from the group, and I'm relieved. Up until this point the staff has been mostly stoic each time I've been introduced. But here, with just Brice and me, there seems to be a sense of familiarity. I pull out a chair and join them. "This better not be strip poker though. Then I wouldn't know if winning or losing would be better with this crew."

Any of the men who looked tentative upon my arrival suddenly relax. "Don't worry guys, she's one of us." Brice winks at me and I wonder what that might mean. He's a prince. These men are meant to serve him, yet here, they look like peers. I'm glad for that.

"But she hasn't been initiated into the group yet." Torrey is the tallest of the men around the table and with a build exactly how you'd want your bodyguard. His smile is gap-toothed, but handsome. His face marked with tiny scars that must have very interesting original stories. Right now, as he challenges me with something I don't yet know about, there is a mischievous twinkle in his eyes.

"Should I be worried?"

Torrey nods. "Especially if you're squeamish. No woman I know would be up for this challenge."

"Good. I'm betting you don't know any women like me." I prop my elbows up on the table and wait. I'll admit my stomach tightens with apprehension, but how bad could it be? "Does it involve fish eyes? Eating them? Really, it can't be worse than anything we do in Coppertop. I've been scaling and gutting fish since I could reach the knives."

Torrey roars out a laugh. "If that's not enough to make her one of us, I don't know what is. Tell me, little American, do you know how to play five-card stud?"

I try to look as if I might not for a moment. I full on bite my lip, scratch my head, put real time into considering it then I say, "I think so. Is that the game where I repeatedly kick all of your asses, leave you broke, and I go home smiling with all your money? I might know that game."

Brice hugs me and jokes, "We keep our bets small. Never the family jewels."

My eyes round and I realize he's serious. I nearly bust a gut trying to hold back a laugh. I lower my voice so only he can hear. "Right. Never bet like a tiara and diamond necklace. Family jewels mean something very different in my hometown."

He gives me a curious look.

I glance down at his package then meet his eyes again.

With a mock serious expression he says, "Never bet those

either."

We share a laugh. The guards look confused. Torrey asks, "Does she know how to play or not?"

Brice holds my gaze. All I see in his eyes is love and forever. He says, "Oh, she knows." Then he clears his throat. "Who is ready to see if my little lady knows how to kick butt?"

I don't want to brag, but there are a lot of sad faces when I walk away from the table that night. No one likes to lose, and considering I didn't know them well, I could have gone easier on them—but I wanted to show them what I was made of.

As much as I've grown over these months I occasionally let the voice of doubt creep back in. A brand-new set of circumstances lies before me and the challenge rattles me. "I kicked ass."

"I knew you would."

"You want me to be your princess, join this royal family. I want you, but I don't want to hold you back or embarrass you. Are you sure you want to do this?"

"I want you to join my family, my life, precisely because of all the wonderful ways you're different. Those moments when you stand up and shine—strong, proud of your history—make me love you even more. I'm glad you didn't leave that piece of yourself behind. You could have easily changed in all the wrong ways and sliced away the parts that make you unique. I don't want someone who is a pretty decoration. I want someone by my side if I have to take the fight to the backroom. No, that sounds wrong. I don't want you to ever fight."

I place my hand over his. "I know what you mean. I want the same from my partner." I take a breath and plow forward. "I have classes back in Boston in a couple days." Imagining forever and sorting out the practical side of making it work are two different things. One is fun, the other intimidating—even for an ass-kicking, fish-gutting, poker player. We've avoided these questions for days. We can't avoid them forever.

"I know. We have some decisions to make. We shouldn't put it off any longer. I know how much going to Boston means to you."

"After seeing Calvadria, Boston won't look quite as magical."

"There is no utopia, but this is my home." He makes a hum-like sound as he mulls. "It took me leaving to appreciate all it has to offer. Being here with you makes me want to stay and work here with you, but . . ."

"You want to stay?" I try not to sound alarmed or desperate. I know if Brice and I had to be apart for a little while, we could make that work. I also know that's the last thing I want.

"But we're in this together. I told you on the plane, I'm not ever going to stand in the way of your dreams. You want to help people. We'll make compromises . . . figure this out together."

Compromises? What did that look like? Wasn't a prince's place in his country? I couldn't expect him to follow me back to the US. "What about all the changes here? They need you. What would you do? Live in my tiny apartment and work while I went to school?"

"Yes."

"Instead of living in this castle?"

"Well, so you know, if we stayed here there is no way in hell we'd live in this castle. My family has a property on the sea, a safe distance from here. It would be ours."

"A house or a castle?"

"Which would you prefer?"

I consider the question. "So it's not like you can't raise a family in one."

"Kids?"

"Am I scaring you off?"

"You're making me very happy. I'm second in line. I can go where I please. Live where I please. Work for the betterment of Calvadria from anywhere in the world." He pushes a lock of my hair back behind my ears. "The property is a house, not a castle. A big house. Room for your friends to visit. Room to raise a family. There's a small farm area out back. A beautiful garden."

"That sounds lovely. I've always wanted a garden."

His brow creases as he leans down to see me full-on. "But what about Boston?"

"Are there people here who need help?" My lips curve into a smile as I wait for the obvious answer.

"There are people here, and all over the world, who would be lucky to have you around. We could travel. Do good in all different places. There have been many in our family who have dedicated their lives to worthy causes. It would be part of my family's legacy. Part of ours."

"Really? That would be possible?"

"Anything is possible. Especially when we're together. We can see the world and work on behalf of this country and my family to help people. If you'd feel fulfilled in that."

"I would." The words come out like a childish squeal. Like I've been promised a pony if I'm a good girl.

We begin walking again, this time with a hurried pace. Desperate to be alone, in private together again. The room we have is breathtaking and elegant. Views of the ocean only add to the serenity of it all. Last night he threw open the doors to the balcony and we made love to the rhythm of the crashing waves. I wonder with a fluttering feeling in my stomach, what tonight will hold for us.

"Notice anything different?" he asks, gesturing toward the fireplace. My clock sits atop the mantel looking smaller than ever in the massive room with its high ceilings. It still brings me immense joy to know that Brice knew enough to bring it back into my life.

"The interior decorator of this castle will not like that addition."

"I don't care. I love it."

"Thank you again for finding it." This man knows how to ruin my makeup. I wipe happy tears away. "I thought it was lost forever."

"I did make one small adjustment to it. I hope you don't mind."

"Adjustment?"

"Addition really." He waves me over to the clock and I

lean in, trying to see what might be different. On the front under the face is an inscription. *Time is free, but every minute with you is priceless.*

"That's beautiful," I coo as I clutch his arm. He points again to the clock and finally I see it. A ring, tied with ribbon dangling over the side.

"Savannah, I don't want a single second to pass between us that isn't filled with the love I feel right now. Marry me. Become my princess. Spend the rest of your life reminding me what really matters."

My eyes well with tears as he slips the ring off the ribbon, drops to a knee, and takes my hand.

"You're like the prince and I'm the kitchen maid," I gasp out. It could go down in history as the stupidest reaction to a proposal ever. He probably doesn't even remember the book I was reading the first night we met. "Sorry. I don't know what I'm saying."

"You never told me how that book ended." He offers a sweet and understanding smile. He gets me. Which is really saying something.

"Err." My face contorts with apology. "Basically everyone died or lived a tortured life of regret."

"Oh."

"Maybe just ask me again. Do over."

He nods. "Savannah Barre, will you marry me?"

"Yes." I purse my lips to make sure I don't say anything else that's completely dumb. Brice stands and I loop my arms around his neck. Lifting me off my feet, he spins me in his arms.

A light knock on the door has us freezing like a couple of high school kids who've been caught necking.

"How in the world did my mother find out about the engagement already? She's got magic level skills."

"I hope she's got magic level love for a kitchen maid."

Brice opens the door and Mathias is standing there looking uneasy. "Can we talk?" His voice is low as he nods a hello to me. I busy myself with closing the windows.

"Come in." Brice gestures to the table in the corner of the room and I wonder if I should go. Maybe I could sit on the balcony and give them privacy.

"Should I step out?"

"No," Mathias says pulling a chair out for me. "This concerns both of you." He looks at the ring on my finger. I'm suddenly self-conscious. It's a beautifully cut diamond in an antique looking setting.

"You gave her grandmother's ring. That means she said yes?"

"She said some other things first but then we got to the yes." Brice flashes a smile at me as I sit.

"I'm thrilled for you both. And for what it means for our family. That's why I'm here. Savannah, I've been paying close attention to you these last couple of days."

"Is this about the fork I dropped at dinner last night? I had butter on my hands and it was really slippery."

Mathias laughs. Not something I've seen him do much of. "No. That's not what this is about. I've been watching how you carry yourself. How you listen when people speak. Your empathy. The staff adores you already. My parents are over the moon about you."

"Really?"

"Yes. We spoke about you tonight after dinner. It's really quite impressive to win over so many different kinds of people so quickly. It's easy to see why my brother loves you so much."

"Thank you." My throat goes dry as I try to take the compliments instead of dismissing them as I normally would.

"I've always known my brother was a good man. What he's done for my future and the future of this country was enough for me to consider him a fit for the crown. But now that he has you by his side, it's even more clear to me."

"Mathias." Brice puts a firm hand on the table. "You are the first in line for the crown. You've spent your entire life working toward that."

"Exactly. I've been dutiful. Measured. Readying to be king in a textbook way."

"What's wrong with that?" I ask, looking between the two men. They are locked in a conversation I can't begin to understand.

"You cannot abdicate your crown to me." Brice shakes his head vehemently. "Why are you even considering this?"

"Envy."

"What?"

"You left. You forged a path all your own. You fell in love. You moved to a place where no one knew your lineage. I've never had that."

Brice's eyes drop to his hand on the table. "I'm the spare

heir. I have the luxury of taking those risks."

"As would I if you stepped into my role. You're engaged. Settled. You've brought the possibility of a strong future to us. Father would be lucky to have you here. That is if you've considered staying. I suppose maybe you plan to return to Boston."

"We don't," I chime in quickly. "We've decided to stay here."

Mathias grins. His eyes light with possibility. "That's promising news. It means I can leave."

Brice stands and paces the room. "No. I don't accept this. Where would you go? What would you do?"

"Bianca has plans to visit colleges in the United States. I could escort her. Father would certainly feel better knowing I'm there."

"You think you can keep Bianca out of trouble? Not likely."

"I'd certainly try. And maybe in the process I could breathe."

"Breathe?" I ask, watching the lines in his forehead crease. He and Brice look similar but he lacks the light jovial demeanor his brother flashes from time to time. I imagine it's under all the formality and duty he's been saddled with.

Mathias squares his shoulders. "Bricelion, I need this. There will never be a better time than now. The stars have aligned."

Brice turns toward me and raises a questioning brow. I panic. "Don't look at me. I have exactly forty-eight hours of experience around a royal family. I don't have anything to offer in the way of advice."

"I know you have an opinion. Lord knows you've never had a problem sharing it before."

He's got me there. And I love him more for wanting to hear it. "Your brother is asking for a chance to live for a time free from the burden of his role. He's clearly dedicated his entire life to it."

"He has."

"And judging by your parents' good health and spunky spirits they're not going anywhere any time soon. It's not like either of you will be king tomorrow."

Brice nods. "You're right. We don't have to decide today. Mathias you deserve a chance to find your way home—the way I did. Don't make a decision now. Things are good here now, Brother." He clutches his brother's shoulder and squeezes. "Be free, Brother. Go and experience what life is like without the weight of the crown. Then, and only then, come home and make your decision."

THE LONG EVENING stretches before us as Mathias leaves our room with a skip in his step. I don't know exactly what we've agreed to, but I know why we've agreed to it. For now that's enough. I pull the soft silk robe tight on my body as I join Brice on the balcony. He's staring out into the darkness of the night.

"What is it?" I plant a hand on the tense muscles of his back.

"You can't see the ocean." I follow his gaze out to the darkness. The moon is covered by thick clouds, snuffing out any light it might have offered.

"Not tonight."

"But you know it's there?"

"Of course," I offer a little laugh. "Where would it go?"

"I'm asking the world of you. Asking you to walk out into something you can't see clearly yet. Something completely foreign to you. My brother is considering abdicating. If that happens, I'll one day be king and you'll be Calvadria's queen. It's an enormous undertaking."

Holy shit. "I certainly never pictured myself as a queen. I don't think I'm remotely qualified. But with you by my side, I know I could do anything. We could do anything."

"My brave Savannah. I didn't doubt your response for a second. I want my brother to have a chance at even a fraction of the happiness I feel with you. Here or wherever his heart takes him. A crown should never be a shackle." Brice takes my hands in his and kisses my knuckles gently. "I've asked you to be my wife. The rules of the game have changed since then. So, tell me, will you still marry me? We might end up more tied to my country than I promised you."

"On one condition." He looks worried enough that I say it quickly, "I want my friends back home to attend the wedding."

"We'll fly them out for the royal wedding. Do you think they would wear tuxedos with tails?"

"For me they would." I smile because I'd do just about anything for them as well.

"If you get homesick, we have fish here. You can put some in the pockets of your gowns. Try to replicate that old smell." *Oh, now he's giving me shit?* He runs his fingers up my side and I squirm with laughter, instantly forgiving him.

"I'll be Savannah Morgan Hastina, Princess of Calvadria, keeper of the smelly fish."

"It has a nice ring to it. But I predict you'll be referred to as compassionate. Free spirited. A breath of fresh air. They'll write about you for generations to come."

"You've given me more than I could have ever imagined. I've traded in a smelly coat for a crown. What could I possibly give you in return?"

"Your heart. Your love." He pulls me into his arms and slides his hands down my back. "This perfect ass."

With a compliment like that, how could I refuse?

"Every bit of me belongs to you. Forever."

Our lips crush together as the sound of the waves crash loudly against the shore. I don't know what lies ahead, but I'm not afraid as Brice's arms wrap tightly around me. Princess. Queen. Keeper of the fish. I don't care as long as we're together.

THE END

Sign up for my newsletter to hear about upcoming releases and sales:
forms.aweber.com/form/58/1378607658.htm

Love my alpha men? Dive into my billionaire world with The Legacy Collection

The wild ride started with Dominic Corisi. . .

FREE in Kindle Unlimited

So many yummy billionaire romances all set in the same world.

The Legacy Collection

The Andrades

The Barringtons

The Westerlys

Corisi Billionaires

For an entire reading list of my books visit my website at www.ruthcardello.com

About the Author

Ruth Cardello was born the youngest of 11 children in a small city in southern Massachusetts. She spent her young adult years moving as far away as she could from her large extended family. She lived in Boston, Paris, Orlando, New York—then came full circle and moved back to New England. She now happily lives one town over from the one she was born in. For her, family trumped the warmer weather and international scene.

She was an educator for 20 years, the last 11 as a kindergarten teacher. When her school district began cutting jobs, Ruth turned a serious eye toward her second love– writing and has never been happier. When she's not writing, you can find her chasing her children around her small farm, riding her horses, or connecting with her readers online.

Contact Ruth:

Website: RuthCardello.com

Email: ruthcardello@gmail.com

FaceBook: Author Ruth Cardello

Twitter: @RuthieCardello

Made in the USA
Coppell, TX
04 June 2021